# The Flinch
# Factor

**Books by Michael A. Kahn**

The Rachel Gold Mysteries
*Grave Designs*
*Death Benefits*
*Firm Ambitions*
*Due Diligence*
*Sheer Gall*
*Bearing Witness*
*Trophy Widow*
*The Flinch Factor*

Writing as Michael Baron
*The Mourning Sexton*

# The Flinch Factor

A Rachel Gold Mystery

## Michael A. Kahn

Poisoned Pen Press

Copyright © 2013 by Michael A. Kahn

First Edition 2013

10 9 8 7 6 5 4 3 2 1

Library of Congress Catalog Card Number: 2012920261

ISBN: 9781464201400     Hardcover
         9781464201424     Trade Paperback

Poisoned Pen Press
6962 E. First Ave., Ste. 103
Scottsdale, AZ 85251
www.poisonedpenpress.com
info@poisonedpenpress.com

Printed in the United States of America

*To my mother-in-law Ann Lenga,*
*with love and admiration*

*The best laid schemes of mice and men oft go awry,*
*And leave us nothing but grief and pain for promised joy.*
—Robert Burns, *To a Mouse* (1785)

*"Vanity of vanities,"* says the Preacher. *"All is vanity."*
—Ecclesiastes

# Chapter One

The year *People* magazine selected George Clooney as its Sexiest Man in the World, women in that part of the world known as St. Louis shook their heads. Their first choice was Nick Moran. Hands down. Although Nick could have passed for George Clooney's bearded, blue-eyed, younger brother, his appeal went beyond his good looks. He was, after all, the Moran of Moran Renovations. George Clooney's credits might include *Out of Sight* and *Michael Clayton*, but Nick Moran's included exquisitely remodeled kitchens and bathrooms in upscale neighborhoods throughout St. Louis. For the women of those households, the star of Moran Renovations was way hotter than the star of *Ocean's Eleven*.

Although the men of those households might write out the checks to Moran Renovations, the women were the real clients. Few of those husbands shared their wives' passions for the particulars of countertops and cabinet styles and lighting. Nick, though, would listen to the women for hours. He'd sit with them at the kitchen table leafing through stacks of *Architectural Digest* and *House Beautiful* and spend afternoons shopping with them for the perfect light fixtures or the ideal countertops. Granite, ceramic tile, or Cambria Quartz? These were profound questions, and Nick treated them as such.

There were rumors, of course but what do you expect? Nothing gets neighbors talking more than the thought of a bored wealthy wife spending days at home with a handsome contractor in faded Levis, black T-shirt, and low-slung tool belt.

I understood. Nick had remodeled my kitchen and rehabbed the coach house out back for my mother. Barely a week into the kitchen renovations, and I was smitten—and embarrassed. Nick was too classy to flirt with his clients. He had the aura of the earnest tradesman devoted to his craft. And thus I resisted the urge—on more than one occasion—to seduce him right there on the new maple floor or atop the Corian counter.

I always recommended Nick to friends and colleagues who were thinking about redoing their kitchen or updating their bathrooms. Frankly, he was just about every woman's first choice. According to his office manager, Nick had a three-year waiting list when he died.

We, his devotees, were devastated by his death and, as the details emerged, surprised. According to the police report, the two officers came upon Nick's pickup truck shortly after nine in the morning. It was parked along an isolated lane in Forest Park known to its habitués and the vice squad as Gay Way.

The mere juxtaposition of Nick Moran and Gay Way was a shocker for us. On most evenings, the cars begin arriving at Gay Way at sunset—one man per car. They park along the right side of the lane. Some of the men remain in their cars while others saunter down the lane in search of a suitable companion. The anonymous action takes place in the front seat, and then the visitor returns to his car. Both men eventually drive off, and others take their places. On a typical night, more than a hundred cars come and go. By sunrise, the only evidence of the prior night's activities is the fresh cigarette butts, an empty beer can or two, and a scattering of used condoms.

Except on the morning in question.

Inside that lone pickup truck along Gay Way the cops found Nick's corpse. The body was slumped against the passenger door, pants unzipped, penis exposed, a coil of rubber tubing on the seat next to the body, an empty syringe on the floor. According to the medical examiner, the cause of death was a lethal overdose of heroin. Time of death: sometime the prior evening between six p.m. and midnight.

I was one of the scores of women who attended Nick's funeral. We outnumbered the men ten to one. Some of us had jobs, while others were from that rarified breed who consider themselves professional volunteers. But whether we were women who took lunch breaks or Ladies Who Lunch, we generally considered ourselves sophisticated modern women, and thus we struggled to connect the dots between the Nick Moran we thought we knew and the Nick Moran who OD'ed on Gay Way.

Being a lawyer—and, unfortunately, one who has handled several nasty divorce cases—I'd had prior encounters with secret lives that were out of sync with public images, from evangelical pedophiles and Orthodox Jewish wife beaters to Transcendental Meditating meth heads. After awhile, you just shrug your shoulders and fall back on one of those old chestnuts about looks being deceiving or never knowing what goes on behind closed doors.

Even so, Nick Moran's death made no sense to me.

That would change.

Looking back, I sometimes wish that it still made no sense to me.

They say that the truth will set you free.

Not always.

# Chapter Two

Susannah Beale was in her late twenties. She wore unstylish glasses and had curly blond hair long overdue for a cut. She had the frazzled air of a woman in her situation, which was six months into her third pregnancy with two other children under the age of four.

"Thank you for seeing me, Miss Gold."

"I am sorry for your loss, Susannah. I knew your brother. He was a wonderful man."

Her lips quivered and she lowered her head.

"Thank you," she said in a hoarse whisper.

I leaned across the desk to hand her a tissue. "Here."

She took it from me and pressed it against her nose.

I gave her a sympathetic smile.

I knew that Nick Moran had a sister. He'd mentioned her to me, and he'd shown me pictures from his wallet of her children—his niece and nephew. He'd told me his sister married her high school sweetheart, who now worked at the Chrysler assembly plant in Fenton, but I don't think he'd ever mentioned her first name or that she'd married a man named Beale. And thus when I'd called my office that morning as I left federal court, I was puzzled to learn that a woman named Susannah Beale was waiting to see me.

"Beale? Does she have an appointment, Dorian?"

"No," my assistant said. "She came in a half hour ago. She wanted to see if she could *make* an appointment."

"Just like that?"

"Not for today." My assistant paused. "I felt bad for her, Rachel. She's never been to a lawyer in her life. She didn't know whether you could just call for an appointment or had to come in to make one, so she drove all the way in from Fenton. Took her forty-five minutes. Left her kids with her mother-in-law. I checked your calendar. You didn't have anything else scheduled until your lunch meeting, so I told her if she could wait around you might be able to see her."

I was having trouble focusing. My thoughts kept drifting toward the nasty court hearing set for that afternoon in my Frankenstein case.

"What does she want to see me about?"

"Her brother. She said you knew him."

"Beale?"

"No. Moran. Nick Moran."

"Oh. You did the right thing, Dorian. Tell her I'll be at the office in ten minutes."

Susannah looked up, wiped her eyes with the tissue and gave me a smile. "Sorry."

"I understand, Susannah. I lost my husband almost four years ago but I still have trouble talking about him without crying."

"Oh, I'm so sorry for you. I'm sure he's with Jesus now."

I forced a smile, trying to imagine Jonathan's reaction to that destination point. "So tell me why you're here."

She brushed her hair from her eyes with her fingers. "They don't care."

"Who doesn't?"

"The police. I went to see them last Friday. I talked to the detective who handled Nick's case. I told him what I knew. I told him that Nick didn't do drugs. I told him Nick wasn't a…one of those homosexual-type people. Nick liked women. He had girlfriends. I told him that. I told him all of that. He didn't care."

"Who did you talk to? Do you remember his name?"

"Italian. Tomasi, I think."

"Tomaso?"

"Yes. Detective Tomaso. Do you know him?"

"I do. He seems like a good detective."

"Not this time." She sighed and shook her head. "He wasn't interested. He listened to what I said, and when I was done he told me there are lots of people who have secret lives that their families don't know about."

"Bert Tomaso is an experienced homicide detective, Susannah. When he talks about secret lives, it's not just talk. He's seen plenty of them."

"Maybe so, Miss Gold, but not with my brother. I know Nick. He wasn't like that."

I leaned back in my chair. I knew where this was headed—and I didn't know how to sidetrack it.

"That's why I came here," she said. "Nick really thought a lot of you, Miss Gold. He told me that a whole bunch of times."

"Your brother was a good man, Susannah, but Bert Tomaso is a good detective. I'm not sure if there is anything I could add. Bert has been doing police work for more than twenty years."

"Maybe he's been doing it for too long. Maybe he's so used to seeing stuff one way that he doesn't notice the little things that don't belong there."

"Like what?"

She shrugged. "I don't know. I'm not a cop, and I'm not a lawyer. But I am his sister. I've known him all my life. I may not know much, but I know what I know, and I know my brother wasn't a drug user and he wasn't a homo."

She took a deep breath and exhaled.

"He was my brother. I loved him. I can't just move on. I need someone to take another look at his death. I owe him that."

She gave me a sad smile.

"I'm a big girl," she said. "If it turns out he really did die the way they say he did—well, I'll learn to live with it. I really will. I promise. I won't have no choice. But if someone killed my brother—if someone did that, I can't just walk away. I just can't. You understand, don't you?"

Her eyes were red. She rubbed the tissue against her nose.

"I need to know the truth, Miss Gold. I just have to know. Please help me."

There are times I need a business manager—someone like Robert Di Niro in *Casino* or Marlon Brando in *Guys and Dolls*. Someone to pull me aside, lean in close, and tell me, *Listen, honey, you ain't running one of them eleemosynary organizations here. You got payrolls to meet and a mortgage to pay and a young son to raise and two stepdaughters to put through to college. Just like I told you before you got yourself stuck in that damn Frankenstein case, taking this Susannah gal on as a client just ain't gonna help move any of them pieces around the board.*

But I don't have a business manager.

# Chapter Three

At 2:30 that afternoon I was standing before the worst judge in the Circuit Court of St. Louis County—and possibly the worst judge in the State of Missouri.

All I could think was how lucky I was.

The judge in question is the aptly named Howard Flinch, whose last name describes the reaction of most attorneys at the moment they learn he has been assigned to their case. Judge Flinch is arbitrary and capricious. He is short-tempered and foul-mouthed. He has the attention span of a housefly, and his grasp of the law is comparable to my grasp of quantum mechanics.

Indeed, he is so bad that Missouri Supreme Court Rule 51.05—the rule that grants each party the right to one automatic change of judge at the outset of a case—has come to be known among practitioners in the Circuit Court of St. Louis County as the Flinch Factor. Although each new case is assigned at random to one of the twenty or so judges of the circuit, so many of the parties drawing Judge Flinch exercise their right to a change of judge that his case docket is but a fraction the size of his colleagues' dockets. Entire days can pass without anyone entering or leaving the chambers of Judge Flinch. Oh, but on the days His Honor strides into his courtroom, his unbuttoned black robe flapping behind him, it can feel like the judicial equivalent of Grendel emerging from his den.

The Flinch Factor reverberates throughout the courthouse, a few of whose chambers include judges with demeanors and abilities that could charitably be described as curtailed. In any other judicial circuit, those are the very judges who might trigger a Rule 51.05 reassignment, but the chilling possibility of drawing Judge Flinch on the rebound keeps their dockets full.

Only a betting man would dare evoke a Rule 51.05 request with the knowledge that he might be reassigned to Judge Flinch. Rob Crane and his client most certainly were betting men. Indeed, their annual high-roller junket to Vegas usually made it into the local gossip column. And thus when they were served three months ago with the court papers in *Finkelstein, et al. v. City of Cloverdale, et al.* and discovered that it had been assigned to Judge Gerber—a good jurist but one who occasionally showed sympathy for the little guy—they invoked Rule 51.05. Despite the 20-1 odds, they drew Judge Flinch.

That reassignment put the ball back in my court as counsel for the plaintiffs. I had thirty days to request a new judge. I mulled it over. The only type of case where it might help to have an arbitrary and capricious judge is a weak case. *Finkelstein* had already started morphing into *Frankenstein*. I let the time expire.

Judge Flinch stared down at Rob Crane.

"A bicycle?" he demanded.

"Yes, Your Honor."

Judge Flinch lurched back in his chair, eyes wide in either real or feigned astonishment. I could never tell which.

The judge asked, "He's a man, right?"

Crane nodded. "He is."

The judge smirked. With his bald head and bushy eyebrows and flared nostrils and black handlebar mustache, Judge Flinch is God's gift to editorial cartoonists.

"Your client's not a little light in the loafers, is he? A little sugar in the old gas tank?"

"Absolutely not, Your Honor."

I tried to keep a straight face.

Although Rob Crane and I had an unpleasant history dating (literally) back to high school, he was nevertheless an excellent trial lawyer with a powerful courtroom presence. He was tall, had thick dark hair flecked with gray, and wore expensive dark suits that accentuated his athletic build, which he'd maintained since his linebacker days at Princeton.

But all such assets were for naught inside the alternative universe of Judge Flinch's courtroom. No matter who you were or where you went to law school or how many Fortune 500 companies you represented, you were at His Honor's mercy. Depending upon the case and the mood of the judge, the courtroom experience could resemble anything from Pee Wee's Playhouse to Don Corleone's darkened study to today's version, which appeared to be Amateur Night at the Comedy Club.

The judge shook his head and snorted. "Mr. Crane, you expect me to believe that your client would rather pedal around on a bike than sit across the table from this pretty gal and answer her questions?"

The judge gave me a big wink as he twirled one end of his handlebar mustache between his thumb and finger.

"Heck," he said with a chuckle, "you can take my deposition anytime you want, Miss Gold."

I formed a polite smile. "Thank you, Your Honor."

Flinch was in his forties and single. He frequented singles' bars, according to a female friend of mine. He arrived occasionally in his judicial robe, apparently in the belief that it would improve his chances. She was in a bar once when he pulled out a gavel from under his robe and pounded it on the bar, demanding another Loch Ness Monster, a favorite drink of his that includes equal parts Bailey's Irish Cream, Jägermeister, and liqueur.

Crane said, "My client has no problem answering Miss Gold's questions. The problem is scheduling the deposition. As the Court may know, Mr. Rubenstein is an avid triathlon competitor. Moreover, he uses each triathlon as an opportunity to benefit our community by making a significant charitable pledge tied to his scores at the event. At last summer's triathlon in San Diego, his scores translated into a contribution to the Arthritis Foundation of fifty thousand dollars. Fifty thousand, Your Honor. This time he's made the pledge to the Children's Foundation. Those poor disadvantaged children need my client to stick with his training schedule."

"Triathlons, eh?" the judge said. "Reminds me of a Jewish joke. Heard it last week from Judge Bernstein. He's a Jew, so there's nothing offensive here—or if there is, take it up with him. Anyway, he told me he was heading off to the JCC for a Jewish triathlon. I ask him, 'What the heck is a Jewish triathlon?' Know what he said?"

Rob Crane stared at the judge, his expression neutral. "I do not know, Your Honor."

"A shvitz, a whirlpool, and a massage." The judge laughed, shaking his head. "That's a good one, eh? Yessiree, bob."

His smile faded. "Where were we?"

I said, "We were discussing Mr. Crane's client's purported scheduling problems, Your Honor."

"There is nothing *purported* about it," Crane snapped.

"Your Honor," I said, "I have been trying to schedule Mr. Rubenstein's deposition for more than two months. Every date I've offered has been rejected because of some alleged scheduling conflict. Two weeks ago I sent Mr. Crane a letter in which I set forth twelve different dates this month and asked him to pick the one most convenient to his client. He had one of his associates send me a reply stating that Mr. Rubenstein was unavailable on *all* twelve dates and was not available at *anytime* in the foreseeable future. Here is that correspondence."

I handed photocopies to the judge and Crane.

While the judge studied the letters, I said, "You will note that one of the days I proposed in my letter was the third of this month."

"Let me see—ah, yes, here it is. The third."

"And that was one of the days that Mr. Rubenstein was supposedly too busy to be deposed."

Judge Flinch glanced at the other letter and nodded. "Yep. Too busy."

"The third was last Monday. Here is a copy of an article that appeared in the *Post-Dispatch* four days later on Friday."

I handed copies to the judge and Crane.

"As you can see," I continued, "it's a feature story on the growing number of men who go to spas for facials and other treatments. Let me direct the Court's attention to the seventh paragraph, which I will now read into the record."

"'On Monday of this week,'" I read, "'I visited the lavish Stonewater Spa in the upscale Plaza Frontenac shopping mall in the hopes of getting some insights into this trend. Who should I find in the lounge area talking business on his cell phone? None other than high-powered real estate developer Ken Rubenstein, who was treating himself that day to the $250 Man Collection package, which features a pedicure, a manicure, a facial and a 60-minute deep tissue massage.' End quote."

I set my copy of the article down on the podium.

"In short, Your Honor," I said, "Mr. Rubenstein couldn't be deposed last Monday because he was getting his toes moisturized."

Judge Flinch leaned back in his chair, smirking at Crane. "Busted, bee-atch! What do you say to that?"

"I am quite certain that at the time we responded to Ms. Gold's letter my client was busy on that date. As we all know, appointments change, meetings get cancelled, schedules free up at the last moment. Those things happen."

"Not here, Mr. Crane. Your motion is denied."

The judge turned to me. "When do you want the deposition?"

"Next Friday. Starting at ten a.m."

"Friday it is. Draft me an order."

"Your Honor," Crane said, anger in voice, "my client has a training schedule. He needs to get his miles in that day."

"Tell him to bring his bike to the depo, Mr. Crane. He can pedal himself out of there as soon as Ms. Gold says she has no further questions." He paused, a smile forming. "By the way, does your guy wear one of those goofy outfits when he goes biking?"

Crane frowned. "Goofy outfits?"

"You know what I mean. Those little tight Spandex shorts."

"I would assume that he wears the accepted cycling attire, Your Honor, including bicycle shorts."

"Is he going to wear those things around Miss Gold?"

Crane glanced over at me, irritated. "If he has to, he will. She's a big girl."

The judge laughed. "Your client better be the big one. If he's going to be parading around in mixed company in a pair of tights, I hope for his sake he can fill them out, if you know what I mean."

Crane gazed at the judge, his jaw clenched.

"Well, Counselor?"

"I can assure the Court and Ms. Gold that Mr. Rubenstein fills his shorts most impressively."

The judge widened his eyes and looked at me. "My, my. What do you make of that claim, Miss Gold?"

"If anyone would know, Your Honor, it would be Mr. Crane."

The judge exploded into laughter. "Bull's-eye!"

He stood, still laughing, and headed toward the door to his chambers.

Pausing, he turned back to us.

"Draft me an order, Miss Gold."

He glanced at his long-suffering court reporter. "Court is in recess, Lois."

He turned back to us. "I'm starting to feel the public's need to know." He raised his eyebrows. "This one might be ready for prime time."

He made a pistol with his hand, took aim at us, and said, "See you later, alligator."

I wrote out the order and waited in the courtroom while his clerk walked it into the judge's chamber for his signature and then made copies for the lawyers. It took about ten minutes, which I devoted to an internal monologue of complaints to my mother for getting me involved in this Frankenstein case. Although fairness and decency were on my clients' side, the rule of law was not—and the rule of law is what counts, even in the courtroom of Judge Flinch.

Flinch's last comment—about the public's need to know and the case's almost-ready-for-prime-time status—raised the prospect of yet another unwelcome complication, namely, television coverage. While Oliver Wendell Holmes, Jr., Louis Brandeis, and Learned Hand might top the list of exemplars for most judges, Howard Flinch's two idols are Lance Ito and Judy "Judge Judy" Scheindlin. He has signed photos of each framed and hanging on the wall of his chambers. A framed custom-made bumper sticker above his desk reads "WWJJD?"—which stands for "What would Judge Judy do?" While others might quote Confucius or Mark Twain, Flinch preferred to preface his profundities with a reference to the presiding judge in the OJ Simpson case, as in: "Ah, yes, as Judge Ito would say,…"

About once a year over the past decade—mostly for trials but sometimes for hearings—Judge Flinch has unilaterally declared that the public's "sacred right of access" trumped local court rules and required that his courtroom be opened to all media. Each time—to the exasperation of the presiding judge—the local stations sent over film crews, confident that a Judge Flinch Extravaganza would deliver ratings worth preempting their soaps. Would my Frankenstein case provide Judge Flinch with his next television performance? The thought made me shudder.

When I stepped off the elevator on the first floor I was surprised to find Rob Crane waiting for me in the lobby. He ended his cell phone call as I approached.

"Here's your copy of the order," I said, handing it to him.

"I spoke to my client."

"Good. Be sure to tell him I want the deposition to start on time. If he tries to pull what O'Brien did, I'll come back here that day and ask the judge for sanctions."

O'Brien was the vice-president of Rubenstein's company, Ruby Productions. His deposition had been scheduled to start at one p.m. a week ago. He and his attorney (one of Crane's associates) arrived two hours late.

"Calm down, Rachel. I wasn't talking to him about the starting time of the deposition. I was discussing a more important issue in this case."

"You mean whether to show up in a business suit or bicycle shorts? Since it's a video deposition, I vote for bicycle shorts."

"I'm not joking here, Rachel."

"Rob, we've spent enough time together for one day. If you have something to say, say it. I need to get going."

"The issue I discussed with my client concerned the fate of your lawsuit. Specifically, our prior settlement offer. The deposition is next Friday. If your clients would like to settle this dispute, they have until the close of business next Wednesday. We previously offered to pay each of your clients an amount equal to ten percent above the appraised value of their homes. That is a generous offer by any measure. We are now willing to augment that offer. Until the close of business on Wednesday, my client is willing to pay each of your clients fifteen percent above the appraised value. It has to be unanimous, though. Every one of your clients has to sign on. If your clients reject that offer, my client has instructed me to ramp up this litigation. I currently have one associate and one partner assisting me on this case. If the settlement deadline passes, I will add two more associates."

"Five to one, eh?"

He gave me a cold smile. "Correct."

"Maybe I better start lifting weights."

"Maybe you better start talking some sense to your clients. This is a good settlement offer. If your clients don't take it, I can assure you they will get exactly what they deserve. As will you."

"Give it a rest, Rob. We're lawyers. Our job is to try to get our clients what they deserve. Maybe we'll both succeed. Meanwhile, I will pass along your offer—and your threat."

I turned and walked away.

# Chapter Four

Benny was seated on a stool at the kitchen island. I was at the sink, a dishtowel in my hand. We'd been discussing my Frankenstein case, including the bizarre hearing before Judge Flinch yesterday afternoon. Benny took another swig of beer and set the bottle down in front of him. I started drying a pot as he studied the bottle.

"Well?" I asked.

He looked up, the hint of a smile on his lips. "I believe Benjamin Franklin said it first and said it best."

"Is that so?" I leaned back against the sink. "And what was it that Ben said?"

"For want of a handjob the case was lost."

I started drying the colander. "Benjamin Franklin, eh?"

His grin broadened. "*Poor Richard's Almanac*, I believe."

I set down the colander. "I don't recall that one."

"That is why you are still a working stiff—albeit a gorgeous one with an All-World tush—while I have become a tenured professor of law."

He looked, of course, nothing like a professor of law, tenured or otherwise. He was unshaven, and his shaggy Jew-fro was in need of a trim. He wore a vintage green-and-white New York Jets Joe Namath jersey, baggy khakis, and red Chuck Taylor All-Star Hi Tops. Nevertheless, he was a professor, and a noteworthy one at that. He had come to my house for dinner direct from the law school, where that afternoon he had taught his Advanced Antitrust Seminar. If you want to get away with that scruffy look, especially at an ambitious law school like Washington University's, you better reside in the academic stratosphere with Professor Benjamin Goldberg.

I placed my dishtowel over my heart in feigned gratitude. "I thank you, Professor, and my tush thanks you. Now what are you talking about? Specifically, what handjob?"

"The missing one."

"Missing from what?"

"From your date with Rob Crane."

"What date with Rob Crane?"

"Back in high school. Your senior year, I believe."

"How do you know about that?"

"Your mom told me."

"My mother told you that I went on a date with Rob Crane back in high school?"

"A date. Singular. That would appear to be the key."

"The key to what?"

"To this screwed up lawsuit you're in. Am I right?"

"About what?"

"That you didn't give Rob Crane a handjob at the end of that night. Correct?"

"What does that have to do with—"

"—am I right?"

I reddened slightly. "You are."

He leaned back with a knowing grin and lifted his beer bottle. "I rest my case."

Despite his national reputation in the field of trade regulation law, Professor Benjamin Goldberg remains my beloved Benny: vulgar, fat, gluttonous and rowdy. But also ferociously loyal and wonderfully funny and my very best friend in the whole world. I love him like the brother I never had. We met as junior associates in the Chicago offices of Abbott & Windsor. A few years later, we both escaped that LaSalle Street sweatshop—Benny to teach law at De Paul, me to go solo as Rachel Gold, Attorney at Law. Different reasons brought us to St. Louis. For me, it was a yearning to live closer to my mother after my father died. For Benny, a year later, it was an offer he couldn't refuse from Washington University.

He finished off the beer in two slugs.

"Another one?" I asked.

He pondered the question as he semi-stifled a belch that rattled the china.

"Ordinarily I'd say no, but I better have one for health reasons."

I opened the fridge and took out another bottle of Sam Adams Boston Lager from the six-pack Benny had brought for dinner along with a bouquet of flowers and a kosher salami he'd ordered for me from the butcher in his New Jersey hometown and that he claimed was sufficient justification, on its own, for the laws of kashruth. I pried off the bottle cap and handed him the beer. "What health reasons?"

"Some brilliant scientist has discovered that beer contains antioxidants, whatever the hell they are. But, as the old saying goes, eternal vigilance is the price of health."

"Benjamin Franklin again?"

"You might be right."

"Can we return to Rob Crane?"

"My pleasure."

"Of what possible relevance is my date with him back then?"

"According to your Mom, Rob Crane was a big shot at St. Louis Country Day. President of the class, all-state in football senior year. Right?"

"Okay."

"I wasn't born or raised here, so I don't have that bizarre St. Louis obsession with where you went to high school and what that fact says about you, but I've been here long enough to figure out that if you're talking about a guy who went to Country Day, the odds of him being an arrogant jerk are significantly higher than a guy who went to, say, Kirkwood. You with me so far?"

"Continue."

"And if you're talking about a *Jewish* guy that went to Country Day—especially back then—the chances approach one-hundred percent. So let's return to the night in question. We have Mr. Big Man on Campus who has stooped to take out a cheerleader from a public high school. Now granted, she's smart and feisty and beautiful and possesses the aforementioned All-World *tuchus*, but she's still a *public* school girl. That means she's supposed to be in awe of Mr. Country Day Stud. She's supposed to feel like she's on a date with a goddam rock star."

He took a swig of beer.

"You with me so far?"

"Continue."

"There are certain rules of behavior that govern such a date, including the female's execution of the appropriate closing act. The only acceptable alternative to that act would be what in the vernacular of that era was known as 'bare second.' I am assuming that Mr. Wonderful did not experience the celestial delights of bare second. Correct?"

"Are you kidding? No way."

Benny chuckled. "Did you at least kiss the bastard?"

"I shook his hand."

Benny burst into laughter. "That's all?"

"That was more than enough."

"Weren't too wild about him, eh?"

"He was stuck on himself. The whole night, every time we passed by a mirror, he'd pause to check himself out. I couldn't wait to get away from him. At the end of the night, he tried to kiss me in the car. I told him no. I tried to be nice about it. I didn't want to be mean. I just wanted to get away from him. He walked me to the door. Before he could try to kiss me again, I held out my hand."

"You go, girl."

"He shook my hand."

"Did he ask you out again?"

"He did."

"Did you go out with him?"

"No."

Benny was grinning. "Trust me, Rachel, he's never forgotten that handshake. He's still pissed."

"That was more than twenty years ago."

"Doesn't matter. He remembers. That's why he's trying to get his revenge now."

"That's ridiculous, Benny."

"That's life, Rachel. He's a guy. Guys are jackasses. Haven't you figured that out by now?"

"Not all."

"Maybe not me. But the rest of us? Come on. Look at your *fakakta* Frankenstein case. You have three primo jackasses in it, including that whackjob judge."

I sighed. "It's quite a crew."

"Oy, vey. As if that wasn't bad enough, your case is a piece of shit."

"It does have some flaws," I conceded.

"Some *flaws*? That's like calling the bubonic plague a mild infection."

"They upped their offer this afternoon."

"To what?"

"They're willing to pay each homeowner a fifteen percent premium over the appraised value."

"That's pretty damn good."

"We'll see. I'm meeting with Muriel and the homeowners' committee tomorrow night."

"They'd be nuts not to settle."

I sighed. "Benny, it's not about the money. These are their homes. Their neighborhood. Their school system. For a lot of them it's a matter of principle."

"A matter of principle?" Benny sighed. "Tell them it's a matter of eminent domain. If the city wants to let Rubenstein bulldoze their homes and put up his gated community, it has the power to do so."

"They know it's an uphill battle, Benny. I'll explain the settlement and see what they want to do."

Benny gave me a sympathetic smile. "What a mess."

"What?" my mother said from around the corner. "What mess?"

I turned toward the kitchen entranceway as my mother walked in with Sam. She'd gone upstairs with him after dinner to give him a bath.

Benny said, "Awesome PJs, Schmul."

Schmul was one of Benny's many nicknames for my son.

Sam grinned. He had on his St. Louis Cardinals pajamas, which were a replica of the team's red-and-white home uniform, including the birds-on-the-bat logo. I'd bought them last month for his sixth birthday. On the back of the pajama top was the number 4—the number of his favorite player. But instead of the name Molina in red letters above the number, I'd sewn on the name Wolf. It was Sam's second favorite pair. His favorite, currently in the dirty clothes, were his train pajamas, which he liked to wear to bed with his engineer's cap.

Sam's smile brightened my day and swept away my angst over the Frankenstein case. He had his father's dark features, my curly hair and green eyes, and the gentle disposition of his namesake, my dear late father Seymour, whose Hebrew name was Samuel.

I knelt down and held out my arms. "Come here, Smooch."

He rolled his eyes. "Mommy."

"Get over here, handsome."

Despite the indignity of being hugged in public by your mom while wearing your official St. Louis Cardinals pajamas, he made the trek over to me and endured the hug and the kiss.

I stood and turned to my mother. "Put some tea on, Mom. I'm going to put Smooch to bed. Then I'll fill you guys in on some interesting information I learned today."

"Someone I know?" she said.

"Nick Moran."

She raised her eyebrows. "My, my."

# Chapter Five

The unifying theme tonight was New England. We'd started in the hills of Maine with *Blueberries for Sal*, moved down to Boston for *Make Way for Ducklings*, and were now in the fictional Yankee village of Popperville for *Mike Mulligan and His Steam Shovel*. I had been reading this book to Sam at least three times a week since he was two. He loved it so much that he had his own toy steam shovel named Mary Anne.

The three of us were snuggled together on the bed—Sam, Yadi, and me. Sam was under the covers, I was seated on the edge of his bed near his pillow, and Yadi was in his usual bedtime spot, curled up on the comforter at the foot of Sam's bed.

Yadi was our four-year-old collie-shepherd mix. We got him as a puppy at the Humane Society after my beloved golden retriever Ozzie died at the age of fifteen. Many people mistook Yadi for part wolf—a golden-haired version of a grey wolf—but his ears and personality belied that idea. He had one straight German shepherd ear, one floppy collie ear, and a sweet temperament. He jogged with me in the morning and walked with me before bedtime, but the rest of his life was devoted to Sam.

Our copy of *Mike Mulligan and His Steam Shovel*—with the raring-to-go open-mouthed Mary Anne bursting through the bright red book cover—was the same copy my mother had read to me as a little girl. I, too, had once had a toy steam shovel named Mary Anne. Though the book cover had faded and many pages were dog-eared or stained, the story had lost none of its magic for me either.

When I closed the book after that wonderful final page—which finds the two of them in the comfy basement of the Popperville Town Hall, Mike smoking a pipe in his green rocking chair next to Mary Anne, who is now the furnace—Sam smiled up at me and glanced over to where his Mary Anne sat on the carpet by the bookcase.

I turned off the light, sang him a bedtime song—tonight's was "Where Have All the Flowers Gone"—gave him a kiss and hug, told him again how much I loved him, patted Yadi on the head, and said a final goodnight to both at the door.

As I went downstairs, I could hear Benny and my mother in the kitchen discussing his appearance last Sunday on NBC's "Meet the Press." Literally, his appearance.

"It's the same suit you wore on that CNN program."

"It's my TV suit, Sarah."

"It's your only suit."

"Same difference. They make me wear a suit and tie. That's the one I wear."

"But always the same? What's your mother say?"

"She sounds like you."

"She's a smart woman, your mother."

"She's a Jewish mother. You're all alike, Sarah. Because I refused to be a doctor for her like her sister's son Maury, now I should tear out her *kishkes* a second time by wearing the same suit on TV every time."

I looked on from the kitchen doorway. They were seated across the table from each other—Benny facing me, my mother with her back to me.

"That's because she's proud of you," my mother said.

"No, that's because her friends ask her, 'Shirley, your son the teacher doesn't make enough money to afford a second suit?'" He shook his head, amused. "You're all *meshuggah*, Sarah. How many Jewish mothers does it take to screw in a light bulb?"

"What?" she said.

Benny caught my eye and winked. He looked back to my mother, who turned to see me standing there.

"How many, Sarah?"

She looked back at him. "A light bulb? What am I? An engineer? I give up. How many?"

"It's okay," he said in a resigned Yiddish accent, "I'll sit in the dark."

"Very funny, Milton Berle. Meanwhile, they have a sale at Macy's. Tomorrow I'll buy you a tie. Next time you go on with that Matthews fellow, you'll have on something new. Your mother will be thrilled."

She turned and gestured. "Come sit, Rachel. I made you tea."

I joined them at the kitchen table, where Benny had already consumed almost an entire platter of my mother's *kamishbroit*, a crunchy Yiddish cousin of the Italian *biscotti*—except that my mother's version would make a Venetian baker jealous.

She poured me a cup of tea. I took a bite of a *kamishbroit*.

"Delicious," I said. "Is this the batch Sam helped you make?"

"We baked them this afternoon."

Sam was only two when Jonathan—his father, my husband—died in a plane crash. My mother, God bless her, quit her job and moved in to help me raise Sam and my two stepdaughters, Leah and Sarah. Eventually, my mother sold her condo and moved into our coach house in back, which Nick Moran had beautifully renovated for her. Leah is now a sophomore at Brandeis University, and Sarah is in her senior year of high school. Although the two girls call me Rachel, all three of my kids call my mother Baba, which is Yiddish for grandmother. Their Baba is hard-headed and opinionated and sets high standards for her grandchildren. Don't ask the girls how many times their red-headed Baba made them rewrite their college application essays. Though she can exasperate me like no other human on the face of the earth, we all adore her. Even me.

Now that Sam was in kindergarten, she's been talking about going back to work part-time or increasing her docent hours at the St. Louis Holocaust Museum. Meanwhile, seemingly endless queues of elderly Jewish suitors await their turn to take the lovely Widow Gold the Elder to dinner and a show. She has gone on record that the developer of Viagra deserves a special place in Hell. I try my best not to think about the implications of that statement.

"So?" Benny said. "Let's have some juicy details."

I checked my watch.

Ten minutes to nine.

My stepdaughter Sarah was at a boys varsity basketball game against her school's big rival. Although a high school senior today knows more about life and sex than I did after college, there were some details I didn't want her to overhear, especially because she had been so fond of Nick Moran.

I probably had enough time before she got home.

I told them about my morning, which I'd spent at the offices of Moran Renovations. Nick's sister had arranged it all. She met me at the office and introduced me to the secretary-receptionist, a pleasant fortysomething woman named Linda who was in the process of closing down the operations.

Linda had been the only other full-time employee of the company and had worked there for almost five years. Nick had a large group of preferred subcontractors and craftsmen that he would hire for particular jobs. On any given day he might have four different painters at four different sites, and three plumbing subcontractors working at three other sites.

I said, "The police talked to Linda the day after they found the body. They asked the usual questions—whether there'd been any recent disruptions or changes in his behavior or the business. She'd noticed nothing like that. She'd never seen him use any drugs. Though he kept a case of beer in the office fridge, he usually drank only on Friday afternoons, and rarely more than a bottle. Although he didn't talk to her about his private life, she had no reason to believe he was gay."

"Did he have a computer?" Benny asked.

"In his office. He didn't have one at home. He didn't use the office one much. Linda told me that days could go by without him even turning it on. I booted it up and poked around some. He didn't use the calendar feature. She kept all his appointments on one of those day planners that he'd take with him. I checked his email. Not much, and nothing that interesting."

"Who did he email?" Benny asked.

"A few of his subcontractors seemed to prefer to schedule jobs by email or to send invoices that way. He mostly forwarded them on to his secretary, who would print out the bills and write the job schedules into his day planner."

"No emails to boyfriends?" Benny asked.

"Nope. And none to girlfriends. Or family. I checked his Sent folder, his Deleted folder and his Saved folder. Nothing personal."

"What about the Internet?" my mother asked.

"Not much there, either. I made arrangements for one of my tech guys to analyze the hard drive, but I didn't find anything promising. He just wasn't a big computer user. He had a high-speed Internet connection, but that was mainly for his secretary's use. I went online and checked his history of Website visits. Pretty run-of-the-mill stuff. Home Depot, Mapquest, plumbing suppliers, Google, a few used car sites."

"No male porn?" Benny asked.

"No porn period. He did go to some fishing sites. And hunting sites. Places like Bass Pro and Cabelas."

"Did he have a cell phone?" my mother asked.

"Same story. Had one but didn't use it much. His secretary said most days he either forgot to charge it or he'd leave it at home. He mostly used pay phones and his customers' land lines."

"Let's pause for a recap," Benny said. "No Internet porn. No salacious emails. No records of cell phone calls to male escort services. Unless I missed something, you've told us nothing that could even charitably be described as interesting, much less juicy."

"True," I said.

"So?" Benny replied. "What else you got?"

I smiled. "For starters, how about a surveillance video of a naked gay housepainter?"

Benny laughed. "Are you shitting me?"

"Do you think I could make that up?"

"A *surveillance* video?" my mother asked.

"The man's name is Bobby Clay," I said. "He was one of Nick's painting subcontractors. Apparently, he preferred to paint in the nude, although Linda didn't know when exactly Nick learned about his painter's quirk. Since Bobby was usually alone in the houses he painted, it hadn't been an issue before."

"Naked?" Benny shook his head in wonder.

"He'd strip down to nothing but his work boots and his iPod, which he wore on a strap around his waist, and he'd dance and paint the day away."

"So what happened?" my mother asked.

"About three months ago he painted a den that had one of those hidden surveillance cameras. When the husband got home that night and reviewed his videotapes, he was not pleased. He fired Nick and dropped off a copy of the surveillance tape with the cops. According to Linda, Nick went down to the police station and got everything taken care of."

"What happened to the painter?" my mother asked.

"Charges were dropped. Nick continued to use him on jobs, too, but only after he agreed to comply with the new dress code."

"You saw the tape?" Benny asked.

"The cops gave it to Nick. Linda showed it to me."

"And?" Benny said, eyes twinkling.

"Interesting." I smiled. "It would have been better with a soundtrack, because he was really swaying those hips."

"And?" Benny said.

I shrugged. "Lots of movement down there. Reminded me of a cowboy doing rope tricks."

"You said this naked painter is gay?" my mother asked.

"According to Linda. And he seemed pretty flamboyant on that tape. Like one of the Village People. And in his emails to Nick."

"What kind of emails?" Benny asked.

"Business, actually. A total of three. Confirming job sites and schedules. But he called Nick 'darling' in two of them, and he signed off once with the phrase 'kisses and misses.'"

"Do you think he and Nick had a relationship?" my mother asked.

"I hope to find out tomorrow. He's working on a job in U City. He agreed to meet me after work at Blueberry Hill."

Benny said. "Anything else?"

"I found five possible girlfriends."

"Nick's girlfriends?" my mother asked.

"Apparently. At least according to his sister. Nick occasionally talked to her about his social life. She was always bugging him to get married. She remembered three names he mentioned to her: Brenda, Ruth, and Barb. She didn't know any of their last names. When I went through his customer files this morning, I looked for those names. I think I identified all three. His secretary gave me two more names. An interesting group. I called them all today and set up meetings with each of them tomorrow."

"Do we know any?" Benny asked.

"You know at least one of them."

"Who?"

I gave him my lawyer look. "This is confidential. You can't tell anyone."

Benny mimed zipping his lips. "Yes, ma'am."

"Especially since these may not be girlfriends. There may be nothing romantic about these relationships. Even if he's heterosexual. And especially if he's gay. These could just be lady friends."

"Fine," Benny said. "I understand. Now which one do I know?"

"Ruth," I said.

"I do?"

"She's on the law school faculty."

"Ruth?" He frowned. "He was banging someone on the—hold on." His eyes narrowed. "'Ruth Parnos?"

I nodded. "Professor Parnos."

"Ruth?" he said, incredulous. "I thought she was a dyke."

"I'll find out tomorrow."

"Ruth Parnos?" He leaned back in his chair. "No way."

"You might be wrong, Benny."

"For chrissake, she drives a Subaru Outback."

I couldn't help but laugh. "What are you talking about?"

"Come on, Rachel. Don't give me that Little Miss Muffet shtick. A chick behind the wheel of a Subaru Outback is one of the two most reliable indicators."

I gave him a weary sigh. "And the other is what? Varsity softball?"

"Bingo. The sport with the highest concentration of carpet munchers in America."

"Carpet what?" my mother asked.

"Never mind," I said to her.

"You played softball, honey," my mother said.

Benny snorted. "That was in law school, Sarah. On a co-ed team at Harvard. Doesn't count."

My mother patted me on the hand. "I'm sure you were an excellent player, even on carpet.

"Oy." I shook my head. "This is a demented conversation."

"Back to Nick," Benny said. "Who were his other four girlfriends?"

"Not necessarily girlfriends," I reminded him.

"Fine. Acquaintances of the female gender, O Princess of Propriety. Who?"

"One of them is Ann's friend."

Ann is my younger sister.

I turned to my mother. "Brenda Gutterman."

My mother put her hand over her mouth. "Oh, my."

"We don't know anything yet, Mom. It could even be another Brenda. But no matter what, your lips are sealed, too. I mean that. Not a word to Ann."

She shook her head. "Never."

"Gutterman," Benny said. "Is she married to a dentist?"

"Actually, an endodontist. They do root canals."

"That's the one. Phil, right?"

"You know him?"

"He gave me a root canal. About a year ago. My idea of a great afternoon. Even more fun than a prostate exam. Nice enough guy, but kind of a *schlemiel.*"

"That's him," I said.

"Who are the others?" my mother asked.

"The third name his sister gave me was Barb. There was just one Barb in his files. Barbara Weiss."

"And?" Benny said.

I smiled. "Small world. You know her."

"How?"

"Her son was on our T-ball team."

I coached Sam's little league baseball team last year. Benny was my assistant coach during spring training but missed most of the games because he was a resident fellow that Spring and Summer at a law-and-economics think tank in Washington, D.C.

"Which one is her son?"

"Barrett."

"Oh, yeah. Nice kid." Benny frowned. "What happened to him?"

"He has some sort of asthma flare-up after our first game. He had to leave the team. Doctor's order."

"Barb?" Benny squinted. "Dark hair, glasses, kind of pretty in a mom sort of way."

"Whatever that means," I said. "Yes, that's her."

"And the other two?" my mother asked.

"Names Nick's secretary gave me. Two women who called the office a lot looking for him. Robin Emerson and Judy Bussman. I've never heard of either one. They both agreed to meet me tomorrow."

The front door opened.

"Sarah?" I called.

"Hey," she answered.

We all turned as my stepdaughter came into the kitchen. Although people mistake Sarah for my biological daughter because we both have dark curly hair, the resemblance ends there. She is taller than me—almost five ten—and is a Mediterranean beauty with huge brown eyes, high cheekbones, and a strong Roman nose. When I take her shopping at the mall, men and boys of all ages turn to stare as we pass. Though she is far more reserved than her older sister Leah, her entrance always seems breathtaking to me. Tonight she had on faded jeans, a red down vest over a white turtleneck, hiking boots, no lipstick, and no makeup. Her cheeks were flushed from the January cold. She could have stepped off the cover of *Vogue*.

"Hey, girl," Benny said.

She gave him a shy smile. "Hi, Uncle Benny."

All three kids called him Uncle Benny.

"Hi, Baba," she said.

My mother stood. "Come give me a kiss, gorgeous."

She leaned over my mother and gave her a kiss and let my mother hug her.

"So?" I said. "How'd we do?"

She shook her head. "We lost."

"Bad?"

"It was close. Like six points, I think."

"How did Corey play?"

She shrugged. "Pretty good."

Corey Stein was her boyfriend. My mother had certified him *A Nice Jewish Boy*, and I agreed. He was a sweet kid. He'd already been accepted to Northwestern, which meant that he and Sarah would be going their separate ways after the summer, since the five schools she'd applied to were Amherst College, Colby College, Miami of Ohio, University of Wisconsin, and Johns Hopkins University. I'd wanted her to apply to Brandeis as well. I loved the thought of the two sisters together at college, but Sarah was determined to go her own way.

"You going to bed, sweetie?" I asked.

"I still have some reading for American history."

"I'll come kiss you goodnight after I walk the dog."

"Okay." She turned to Benny and my mother. "Goodnight, guys."

"Goodnight, gorgeous," my mother said.

Benny gave her wink. "See ya, kiddo."

Off she went.

Benny and my mother followed a few moments later after I promised them both I'd fill them in on tomorrow's meetings.

# Chapter Six

Professor Ruth Parnos made her reputation in the field of conflicts of law, which examines how a court in State A decides which state's laws should govern a case involving litigants from States B and C in a dispute over a defective product manufactured in State D, purchased in State E, and causing injury in State F. In the only conflicts class I took in law school, I fluctuated between the states of confusion and boredom.

Professor Parnos also taught a seminar in special remedies, which focused on the various non-monetary forms of relief a litigant could seek. Several such remedies required decisive and bold action—which also described her relationship with Nick Moran.

"I seduced him," she said. "His second day on the job."

It was mid-morning and we were seated at a small table in Kaldi's coffeehouse in the DeMun area.

She smiled at the memory. "I hauled him into the bedroom, pulled down his jeans, and screwed his brains out."

I took a sip of coffee as I tried to conjure up that scene.

I came up with nothing beyond a deeper understanding of the term cognitive dissonance. Professor Ruth Parnos was no casting director's choice for Salome. Though she was vivacious, she was also short and stocky, wore thick glasses, and had black frizzy hair. There wasn't a hint of sexy or saucy in her outfit, which consisted of a brown corduroy sports jacket, blue button-down dress shirt, loose-fitting khaki slacks, and thick-soled brown-and-white saddle oxfords.

"Wow," I finally said.

"Wow is right," she said. "I have never done that before in my life. Never."

"I can understand, though."

She gave me a curious look. "Oh?"

"I was tempted."

"You knew Nick?"

"He renovated my kitchen and my coach house."

She smiled. "Then you understand."

"I do."

"Most men don't."

"Especially the ones with advanced degrees," I said.

She burst into laughter—a lusty, cheerful laugh.

"Exactly," she said. "They have no conception of the sexual allure of a man who can actually fix a garbage disposal or install a ceiling fan."

"You're right."

"You bet I am. I taught at Kansas before coming to St. Louis. My boyfriend there was a philosophy professor. Sweet guy, but totally useless around the house. As my dad would say, like tits on a bull. I was unscrewing a ceiling light bulb once and it broke off, leaving the metal part in the socket. I asked him to help. He had no idea what to do and no interest in figuring it out. He told me to call an electrician. But Nick"—she paused with a distant smile—"he knew how to make things work. All kinds of things. A tool belt on a good-looking guy is our version of a garter belt on a sexy girl."

I said, "My mother was in love with him, too."

"I'm not surprised. My niece is in high school. She came over one afternoon with a couple of her teammates. By the time the girls left, they were all smitten. High school girls. Jocks, to boot. You'd have thought he was a rock star."

"Does your niece play softball?"

"Actually, yes. Do you know her?"

"No. I saw the bumper sticker on your car."

"Oh, right. How did you know that was my car?"

"I parked right behind you. I saw the Washington U parking permit."

No need to tell her that it was also the only Subaru Outback on the street—or how I came to know about her allegedly incriminating connection to that vehicle.

"She's my only niece," Ruth said. "I adore her. I go to all her games."

We talked some about her niece and then returned to the subject of Nick Moran. Their relationship continued beyond his renovation work, which he had completed almost two years ago. Although the romantic and emotional ties had started to fade by the time he finished the kitchen, they remained "friends with benefits" up until his death. Theirs was a casual sexual companionship which, depending upon the month, could involve anywhere from one to four trysts.

Ruth knew surprisingly little about Nick's life outside her bedroom.

"That was the rule," she explained. "When we got together, it was for sex. Period. We were friendly, but we never ever talked about the rest of our lives. If I called to get together and he was busy, or vice versa, we'd never presume to ask for an explanation. If one of us was busy, so be it. Hopefully, you'd be free the next time the other one called."

"Were you surprised by the circumstances of his death?"

"Absolutely. I'd never seen him use any drugs, and I never picked up any bisexual vibes, but that doesn't mean anything. I had a boyfriend back in college that could have made it into the Guinness Book of World Records. He was insatiable. We used to have sex three or four times a day. He had piles of *Playboys* and *Penthouses* in his dorm room, and he claimed he masturbated to them every day in addition to all the sex we had. Guess what? We broke up at the end of our junior year, and by the start of the next semester he'd already come out of the closet. Remember all those gay marriage licenses they issued in San Francisco a few years ago? It was front page news. And guess whose picture was actually on the front page? With his longtime male companion?" She shrugged. "Who knew?"

Ruth had to get back to campus for her special remedies class, and I had a meeting with the homicide detective who'd investigated Nick's death. She needed to stop in the bathroom, so we said goodbye in the coffeehouse. I thanked her for meeting with me and told her to be sure to tell Benny hello.

As I walked to my car, I passed by her Subaru Outback. I paused to look at the bumper sticker that read "Softballers Rule," wishing that my cell phone had one of those cameras. I would have loved to send the image to Benny with a one-word text message: NOT!

# Chapter Seven

"Oh, Rachel Gold." He placed his hand over his heart. "Light of my life, fire of my loins."

I rolled my eyes. "Good morning, Humbert."

"You know what I think every time I see you?"

"Do I want to know?"

"I think what a cruel twist of irony it is that my wife's older brother is the most vicious divorce lawyer in St. Louis. Unless I want to spend my golden years living in a van down by the river, I am condemned to only admire from afar a face which nature's own hand painted."

"Oh, my God, Bertie." I took a seat facing his desk. "Nabokov *and* Shakespeare. You sure you aren't hiding a Ph.D. in literature?"

"Like I told you, kiddo, only advanced degree I got is in stakeouts. Four hours sitting alone in a car and even a knucklehead like me might be able to get through a chapter of *Anna Karenina*."

We were in the office of Roberto "Bertie" Tomaso, a homicide detective with the St. Louis police department. Bertie and I had known each other for years. I'd met him through Jonathan, who'd had numerous cross-examination encounters with him as a criminal defense lawyer. Bertie and his wife Sue had come to our wedding, and to Jonathan's funeral, and though he is an old-school Catholic raised on the Italian Hill, he came to my house every day during the week we sat *shiva* and somehow got a hold of a Jewish calendar and sent me a condolence card on the first *yahrzeit* (anniversary) of Jonathan's death.

Which didn't change the fact that he was a shameless flirt. But he was also a respected homicide detective and one of the most literate people I'd ever met. Indeed, he was the one who—after listening to one of my interminable paeans to Jane Austen—insisted that I read *Middlemarch*. I loved it so much that I ended up reading all seven of George Eliot's novels.

Tomaso was a burly man in his early fifties. He was about my height and had one of those naturally dark complexions that made it seem like he'd just returned from a week on the beach. He had a warm smile and a pair of eyes that could be playful or severe, depending upon the situation.

"So what brings you down here?" he asked.

"Nick Moran."

"The rehabber we found on Gay Way?"

"His sister asked me to look into his death."

"I talked with her."

"And?"

He gave me a sad smile. "It's always hard on the family, Rachel. Especially when no one suspected he was that way."

"She's convinced he wasn't."

"They always are. People have a serious misconception about the men who visit Gay Way. I worked vice for ten years. We had ourselves a Who's Who of St. Louis married men on Gay Way. Managing partners of law firms, rabbis and ministers, heart surgeons, judges, corporate CEOs, real estate developers. Lots and lots of closet queers. You name it, we had it. And your guy wasn't even married."

"I know, Bertie. She's upset. He was her beloved big brother. She begged me to look into his death. That's what I'm doing."

"I understand, kiddo. I'm just saying this one doesn't look dodgy to me."

"She gave me a copy of the medical examiner's report. I had a couple questions."

"Fire away."

"I'm not sure how they could tell, but the report said that he didn't ejaculate."

"Right."

"Is that fishy?"

"Not really. The drugs killed him, not the sex. And even when the sex kills you, you don't necessarily complete the act. Nelson Rockefeller died having sex with his mistress. New York cop I talked to told me Rockefeller's heart attack beat him to the finish line." He shook his head. "The ultimate coitus interruptus, eh?"

"What about the drugs? According to the report, he didn't appear to be a user. There were no needle tracks on his arms or legs, and no other signs of repeated heroin use."

"True, but you'd be surprised how many first-timers die from an overdose, especially if they're doing it with a user. You build up a resistance over time. An addict can handle over a thousand milligrams in one injection, but just two hundred milligrams can be fatal to a first-timer. I assume that's what happened here."

"What do you mean?"

"Whoever joined him in his pickup truck must have been a user. He convinced Moran to do it with him—or maybe it was Moran's idea. Either way, the other guy probably injected Moran with his own usual dose, which would have been two or three times too high for a first-timer. He wouldn't have died right away, which probably explains why his pants were unzipped. But he would have slipped into a coma pretty damn quick. My read is the other guy panicked and cleared out."

"You have any leads on who the other guy was?"

"All we know is that the dead man was working on a kitchen in Ladue that day. Called his secretary a few minutes before five to check in and tell her he was heading home soon. Left the jobsite about five-fifteen, according to the maid. That's the last contact we know about. We don't know who he met up with." He gave me a sad smile. "And we probably won't turn up anyone. Once we eliminated any homicide suspicions, this case dropped way down on the priority list."

Behind me someone cleared his voice. "Excuse me, sir."

I turned to see a uniformed cop in his twenties.

Tomaso said, "What is it, Henry?"

"Uh, sir, the brass wants to see you."

"Which tubas exactly?"

"Sir?"

"Brass? Get it? Orchestra section? Never mind. Who wants to see me?"

"Captains Carper and Fenley."

Tomaso groaned. "What do those bozos want now?"

"I'm not sure, sir. I think Captain Carper has some questions about the department's numbers. I heard Captain Fenley say something about needing some success stories—his term, sir—needing some for his monthly press conference."

"Great, Henry. Just great. Tell them I'll be there in five."

"Thank you, sir."

Tomaso turned to me and sighed.

"Thanks, Bertie."

"Some days I feel like Barnaby the Scrivener and some days I feel like Joseph K."

"Just don't start feeling like Hannibal Lecter."

"Nah. My life here is more like something out of Kafka."

"I know the feeling. I was once a junior associate in a big law firm. It's why I left life in a big law firm."

He smiled. "Maybe I should do the same."

"I could see you as Lew Harper."

"I'm more Columbo than Harper."

"Either way, I'd hire you for all my cases."

"Don't tempt me, Beautiful." He stood with a grunt. "On this Moran thing, if you turn up anything suspicious, come see me. The case won't be officially closed for another month or so."

"Thanks, Bertie."

"And if, God forbid, my brother-in-law the shark should ever get disbarred, I'm going to reserve a suite at the Ritz that night for us."

"It's a deal. You bring Sue, I'll bring my kids, and we'll have a pajama party."

"You're a riot, Gold. Hey, one more thing—and this is important." He leaned over his desk and lifted his *Post-Dispatch* newspaper, which was folded back to the *New York Times* crossword puzzle. He'd become a *Times* crosswords addict back in his stakeout days.

"Here we go. Eight letters." He was frowning at the clue. "Three word phrase. Sounds legal to me. First two words are '*Res*' and '*Ipsa*.'"

"*Loquitur*," I said, and spelled it for him.

"What a gal. *Res Ipsa Loquitur*. What the hell does that mean?"

"The thing itself speaks."

"Huh?"

"It means that the proof is self-evident. You don't need any additional evidence."

"*Res Ipsa Loquitur*." He grinned. "Like my heart for you, eh?"

"Go to your meeting, Bertie. I'll be in touch."

# Chapter Eight

The credits to the motion picture *Airplane* identify one character simply as Hanging Lady. She is the elderly woman seated next to the gloomy ex-fighter pilot Ted Striker in the scene where he tells her the interminable story of his decline and disgrace. When the camera finally pulls back, we discover the poor woman has committed suicide, hanging herself from the luggage compartment.

After forty minutes of Brenda Gutterman's yakking, I felt like the Hanging Lady's understudy. I'd heard detailed accounts of her children (including dance and French lessons for Rosalind, club hockey for Roland, school musical try-outs for Regan), her husband, her in-laws, her parents, her siblings and spouses and incomes, her last vacation, her physical trainer, her hairdresser, her colorist (source of her blond hair), and other topics of no possible interest to anyone but Brenda. She'd been babbling nonstop from the moment I met her at the entrance to Briarcliff Country Club.

Her choice of venue.

Talk about starting off on the wrong foot.

I am no fan of country clubs. Even so, Briarcliff is the worst of the worst: an exclusive *Jewish* country club—and thus a place where my people, victims of discrimination and exclusion throughout their history, can discriminate and exclude their own people. There are men in St. Louis—accomplished men, wealthy men, otherwise distinguished men—whose membership applications to Briarcliff have languished for years. Even decades. Some eventually give up and join the other Jewish country club in town, Golden Bough (a.k.a. Goldenberg)—land of pinky rings, Mercedes SUVs, and Vegas vacations. Others die with their applications still pending before the dreaded and inscrutable Membership Committee.

Brenda and her husband were members for one reason: she was a legacy. Her great-grandfather, Stanley Fine, was one of the founders of Briarcliff Country Club back in 1919. While I had waited for her in the main hall at noon, I'd perused with amusement the large brass plaque that lists the five esteemed founders:

Jerome Brown
Stanley Fine
Harold Marshall
Yadi Olson
Philip Gold

On the immigration ledgers at Ellis Island, those same five are listed as:

Yacov Bronkowitz
Schmuel Finkel
Heschel Marx
Avram Olshovansky
Pinchus Goldenberg

No matter. The Ellis Island Era is as relevant to Briarcliff as the Jurassic Era. The club strives for a Wonder Bread version of Judaism—where corned beef is available only on St. Patrick's Day, the menu lists lox as smoked King salmon, the Friday night seafood buffet features a full array of shellfish, and the golf course is packed on Rosh Hashanah. As the men in their tennis whites sip their single malts on the veranda after a game of doubles, they can pretend that they aren't stuck in a Yiddish minstrel version of a real country club.

We were having lunch in the Great Hall, a kitsch homage to King Arthur. You could gaze up at the overhanging rows of flags emblazoned with English heraldry and pretend that your family coat of arms was something more regal than, say, a gefilte fish rampant on a field of chopped liver.

"Can you believe that?" Brenda said. "Can you?"

I tried to rewind the last segment of her monologue, to patch together what was apparently so hard to believe. I came up empty.

Assuming that her question was merely rhetorical, I said, "I can't believe it."

"No one could, Rachel. People were so—oh, look, it's Sheri Bronson. Hello, Sheri," she called in a lilting voice a full octave higher than normal.

A red-haired woman—presumably Sheri—paused on her way to her table.

"Love the suit," Brenda said, still in a cheerful falsetto.

Sheri was wearing a dark pinstripe pants suit and pumps. She had an enormous leather purse slung from her shoulder. She smiled and put her hand on her hip in a runway pose.

"Thanks."

"Neiman Marcus?"

Sheri nodded.

After she'd moved on, Brenda leaned forward.

"She better enjoy this lunch," she said in a stage whisper. "Do you know her husband? Jim Bronson? The liquor distributor? He's divorcing her. Once that decree is final" —she made a throat-slicing gesture with her hand— "she's history at Briarcliff."

Our waiter arrived with our lunches—the daily low-carb salad special for Brenda, a turkey club for me. As I watched Brenda issue additional orders to the poor guy, I finally realized what had seemed so odd about her face. The entire upper half, from eyebrows to hairline, was immobile. Presumably the result of a recent round of Botox. Along with the forehead wrinkles, the injections had eliminated all facial expression. Brenda was no plastic surgery novice. Judging from the way she filled out her turtleneck sweater top, I was guessing a fairly recent boob job as well. Her nose job—the turned-up Debbie Reynolds style—had been a popular style during her high school days and mine. I've read that women these days opt for a more natural, less obvious version. I assumed that her blue eyes owed their eerie radiance to tinted contact lens.

I couldn't understand how Brenda and my sister Ann were good friends. But there were many things about my younger sister that I couldn't understand—and I'm certain she was equally baffled by me. Long ago we'd decided to just love one another and forget the rest.

But I also couldn't understand what Nick Moran had found romantic or alluring about this self-absorbed woman. It was like discovering that Prince Charming had been sleeping with one of Cinderella's stepsisters the whole time.

Maybe Nick's sister was wrong about Brenda. Maybe their relationship was not a romantic one. Regardless, I needed to find out.

As Brenda paused to take in a forkful of salad, I said, "I appreciate you meeting with me."

She nodded.

"You knew Nick Moran."

Her face remained blank as she chewed.

"He redid your master bathroom about a year ago."

She stared. "How did you know that?"

"I've looked through his files. His sister retained me to help wrap up some things after his death."

"What kind of things?"

"Just things. We should leave it at that."

I'd realized ten minutes into our meeting that telling Brenda Gutterman anything was the equivalent of broadcasting it on the airwaves.

"Well, well, well," she said with sarcasm. "Top secret, eh?"

"Just attorney-client privilege. The same if you retained me to handle something for you."

"So what *can* you tell me?"

"The reason I asked to meet today. I want to ask you about your relationship with Nick."

"My relationship?"

Judging by her voice, she was trying to feign confusion. Her face, of course, remained blank.

"According to Nick's sister, your relationship with Nick extended beyond his renovation work."

"Meaning exactly what?"

"Meaning exactly what you think it means, Brenda."

"He told her about me?"

"Yes." I decided to gamble. "Everything."

She sat back in her chair and placed her hand over her heart.

"I am shocked. I am outraged. I cannot believe he would do that. That he would betray me. Would betray us. This was our secret."

"Who else knows?"

"How can I say? Apparently, he is a member of the kiss-and-tell club. Serves me right for sleeping with the help."

I wanted to reach across the table and slap her in the face. Instead, I tried to keep my face as blank as hers.

"I don't believe he told anyone," I said.

"He obviously told his sister."

"He didn't tell her about the sex part."

"Then who did?"

"No one."

"How did she know?"

"She didn't. All she knew is that one of the women Nick talked to her about was named Brenda. I figured out that you were that Brenda when I looked through his work files."

"He talked to her about me?" She sounded flattered.

"Yes. And had nothing negative to say about you." Which was true, I supposed.

"So he cared about me?"

"That's what it sounds like. Tell me about your relationship."

She sighed. "There isn't much to tell, I'm afraid. We were lovers for barely two months. When he started working on our master bathroom, it felt like a scene out of one of those trashy romance novels. Phil and I moved into the guest bedroom downstairs because the workers arrived every morning at seven.

I started coming up with excuses to visit with him during the day. I knew he was attracted to me. A girl can tell. I started wearing sexier clothes each time I dropped in on him. Well, it finally happened one morning. I hauled him into the bedroom and—Oh My God—it was unbelievable, Rachel. I had more orgasms that morning than Phil's given me in a year."

*Poor Phil.*

"What happened after that?"

She leaned forward, her voice low. "Imagine your perfect sexual fantasy. That was us. I'd get Phil off to work and the kids off to school each morning, come back upstairs, put on something sexy, and fetch him from the bathroom. If he had other workers there that day, he'd find some excuse to meet me in the exercise room in the basement."

"Every day?"

"In the beginning. But even toward the end we'd do it three or four times a week." She smiled. "He was an awesome lover. He knew what I liked."

"So what happened?"

"It was too good to be true." She shook her head. "He finished the job, got his final payment, and, poof, the bastard disappeared."

"Disappeared?"

"Went on to the next job and that was it. I tried to call him. I went to the new job site. Nothing."

"What did he say?"

"The usual crap. Time to move on. Fun while it lasted. I was deeply hurt. A man like that—a blue-collar worker—doesn't just use a woman like me and walk away."

"What did you say to him?"

"Plenty. I was furious. I even threatened to tell my husband."

"Tell him what?"

"That I'd been taken advantage of. Used and discarded."

"Did you?"

She gave me a look—or at least appeared to be trying to give me a look with that blank face. "Of course not. Oh, I hinted around some. I wanted Nick to feel my pain. But I never came out and told Phil what had happened."

"Do you think he suspected anything?"

"I don't know. Frankly, he isn't the best communicator."

"Did you tell anyone else?"

"My therapist, of course. I had to talk with someone. I felt so demeaned."

"When did your relationship with Nick end?"

"About six months ago. No, seven months. Right before I had my breasts done. That was my gift to myself. After all that pain and suffering, I deserved something special."

She glanced at my boobs.

"You'd be surprised at how good it makes you feel about yourself. Every girl should consider it."

*Poor Phil.*

# Chapter Nine

"It's unlocked," I called.

The door slowly opened, and Barbara Weiss peered into Benny Goldberg's office. I was seated behind his desk.

I stood. "Come on in, Barb."

She was the fifth and final woman on my list. After my lunch with Brenda Gutterman I'd been able to meet with Robin Emerson and Judy Bussman, the two women Nick's secretary had flagged for me. She'd selected them because of the number of times each had called the office looking for Nick. As I quickly determined, however, there was no romantic motive behind those calls. Instead, each woman fit into that category of client dreaded by professionals of all stripes: the obnoxious complainer who feels entitled to call day and night regarding any issue, no matter how trivial. Each woman conceded satisfaction with the renovation work and seemed oblivious to any other aspect of Nick Moran.

Barbara Weiss stepped into Benny's office, closed the door, and gazed around, eyes wide. "Wow. I've never been in a law professor's office before."

"Trust me, Barb, this in not your typical law professor office."

Framed on one wall were tributes to what Benny claimed were his two childhood heroes: a Spiderman poster signed by Stan Lee and a New York Knicks #22 jersey signed by Dave DeBusschere. On the facing wall was a zany array of framed photographs and memorabilia, including the item that Barb was leaning forward to study: the infamous page 127 of a deposition Benny took in the *Allied Chemicals* case many years ago when we were associates in the Chicago headquarters of Abbott & Windsor. Though Benny's years at that firm had included several notable litigation misadventures, the encounter memorialized on page 127 of the Reynolds deposition—eventually reprinted verbatim in a *Chicago Bar Journal* article on the decline of professional courtesy—was, depending upon your perspective, his zenith or his nadir. The exchange occurred after Benny expressed exasperation with his adversary, who had just made his fifty-third objection of the day:

> Mr. Klemper: That's too bad, Mr. Goldberg. As you know, I have a perfect right under the Federal Rules of —
>
> Mr. Goldberg: Forget the Federal Rules, Norman. From here on out we're operating under the Goldberg Rules. Here's Rule Number One: You open that pie hole of yours one more time and I'm going to rip off your head and shit in your lungs. You read me?
>
> Mr. Klemper: I—you—I cannot believe—do you—this deposition is over.
>
> Mr. Goldberg: Excellent. Then get your sorry ass out of here before I throw you through that window.

"Oh, my." Barb straightened up. "He sounds like a real character."

"That he is."

I pointed at the framed photograph of our T-ball team, which was taken right before the first game. "Here's your son."

She stepped over to look. "Barrett just loved being on that team, Rachel. He was so devastated when he had to stop playing because of his asthma."

"Let's hope he's all better by next season." I gestured toward the small round table in front of the bookcase. "Let's sit."

Benny's office was the perfect meeting place. Barb worked in the Center for the Humanities, which was just across the Quad from the law school. While she was willing to meet with me, she was uncomfortable doing so in her building and clearly preferred a more private venue. Her day ended at four o'clock, which is when Benny's antitrust class started. He suggested that we meet at his office.

I had liked Barb from the very first meeting of our T-ball team parents last year. She was unpretentious and unassuming despite her wealth, the scope of which I discovered when I dropped her son off after practice one day. She lived in an impressive Tudor-style mansion in an affluent older neighborhood. Nevertheless, she drove a Chevy minivan, wore little jewelry and less makeup, and dressed in Standard Soccer Mom Attire that could have come off the rack at Macy's, and probably did. Today's outfit was a green long sleeve cardigan sweater over a matching green shell, beige cargo slacks, tan loafers, and simple pearl earrings. She wore glasses and had straight brown hair that she parted in the middle and wore to her shoulders.

"So?" She raised her eyebrows. "What's going on? This all seems mysterious."

"I wanted to talk with you about Nick Moran."

"Nick?"

She lowered her eyes.

"That's why I wanted this to be private, Barb."

She nodded, head still down.

"Nick has a sister. She asked me to look into his death. He had mentioned your name to her."

She looked up, her eyes red. "He told her about me?"

"Nothing private, but enough for her to conclude that you and he were close."

"We were," she said, almost in a whisper.

"According to his secretary, he did work on your kitchen, den, and guest bathroom on the first floor. Took almost three months in total. He finished about two months before he died."

She nodded.

"Actually," I said, "I was a little surprised to discover that Nick had done work on your house."

"So was my husband."

"What do you mean?"

"He's convinced that new is always better than renovating. He wanted to sell our house and move us into one of the new mansions out in Chesterfield. I refused."

"Why?"

"I didn't want to move. I love our house. It just needed some updating. I love our neighborhood. So do the children. I didn't want to be stuck in a gated community twenty miles west."

I smiled. "So you won that battle."

"Hard to say. My husband and I are separated."

"Because of that?"

"No." She sighed. "It's complicated. We've tried to keep it private. He moved out several months ago. Now he's trying to move back in—trying to pretend like everything's back to normal."

"I'm sorry, Barb." After a pause, I said, "Did Nick do a nice job?"

She looked up with a smile. "Oh, Rachel, he was an artist. You should see his work."

"I have, and I agree. He did some work for me."

"I didn't know that."

"That's why I was surprised. I didn't realize you used him as well. Nick was a true craftsman."

She nodded with a distant smile.

"Did your husband agree?"

Her smile disappeared. "He was unkind to Nick."

"How so?"

"We were separated by then. He happens to work with building contractors. He hired one name Rudy to come by the house every few days to check on the work. Since he was paying the bills, he claimed he had the right to monitor the work. I'm convinced he told that man to be difficult. If something wasn't perfect, he'd make Nick redo it. He never had a nice thing to say about Nick's work."

"How did Nick handle that?"

"Like a saint. He never argued, never complained, never acted annoyed. He'd just listen and nod and take notes and when the inspector left he'd assure me that he'd make it right. And he always did."

"That must have been upsetting, though."

"It was. More and more each time. Nick's work was beautiful, Rachel. I felt so bad for him." She sighed. "There was so much strain. I'd get more protective of Nick and angrier at my husband—until one day I couldn't take it any more. I'd just come back from a school meeting and was feeling overwhelmed. I was crying when I walked into the house. I was so embarrassed I ran upstairs to my bedroom. I couldn't stop crying. Nick came into the bedroom. He tried to comfort me. He held me in his arms."

She blushed. "Listen to me. I make it sound like a soap opera."

I offered a sympathetic smile. "Life can be a soap opera."

"Mine certainly seemed that way."

"How long did it last?"

"Until the end." Her eyes welled up again.

I waited.

She shook her head, forcing a smile. "But probably not the way you think. Physically, we never went further than that hug. I was tempted. So tempted. But it just didn't seem right. I was still married—am still married—even if we were separated. Nick understood. He never pushed it, never tried to force anything. We stayed friends. He'd call me sometimes. Sometimes I'd meet him for coffee at a Starbucks. I once met him at the zoo."

She smiled at the memory. "We rode the zoo train together." Her lips quivered. "I miss him."

I took a Kleenex tissue out of my purse and handed it to her. She whispered thanks and pressed it against her nose.

"I'm sorry, Barb. I didn't know it would be so painful."

"It's okay. It feels good to be able to share this with someone."

My cell phone starting ringing. I checked the number.

"I better take this," I said.

I took the call in the hall outside Benny's office—in part for privacy and in part to give Barb a few moments alone. My assistant was calling because she was leaving for the day and wanted me to know about a settlement demand letter I'd received via facsimile from opposing counsel in another case. I had her read it to me and then give me his telephone number. I called him, got his voice mail, and left a message rejecting his settlement demand and informing him that I intended to proceed with the hearing next week unless his client accepted my prior offer, which was non-negotiable.

When I stepped back into Benny's office, Barb had composed herself.

I asked her about drugs. She'd never seen Nick use anything beyond an occasional beer.

I raised the location of his death and what that implied.

"I was surprised, Rachel. I've never actually known a bisexual—or at least one that identified himself as one. Nick seemed, well, totally heterosexual to me. But I guess that doesn't prove a thing." She frowned. "You never really know, do you?"

"You never do."

# Chapter Ten

"My boyfriend?"

Bobby Clay giggled and waved his hand at me.

"Don't I wish, honey. He was definitely a hotty. A boy can dream."

He gave a big exaggerated sigh and shook his head.

"The only relationship we had was contractor-subcontractor. Strictly business. Why do you ask?"

"I wasn't sure," I said. "I looked through his email and saw a few from you. The subjects seemed to be strictly business—arrangements for painting at various jobsites."

"That's how I schedule my jobs. I have one of these things." He pulled an iPhone out of his shirt pocket. "I use it to stay in touch with all my contractors. There are always last-minute changes in my business, honey. This way I can check when I'm on break."

"Makes sense," I said. "I noticed, though, that in two of your emails to Nick you called him 'darling,' and once you signed off with a 'kisses and misses.' I didn't know whether that meant anything."

He giggled. "Good grief, girl, I call everyone 'darling' or 'honey' or 'sweetie.' Men, women, boys, girls. My momma taught me that. Same with 'kisses and misses.' It's just me being friendly. I never kissed Nick except" —he raised his eyebrows— "in my fantasies."

Bobby Clay had to be the most flamboyantly gay house-painter in St. Louis, if not the entire Midwest.

The waitress stopped at our table. "Another round?"

Bobby Clay looked at his empty pint glass and nodded. "Sounds wonderful, sweetie." He gave me a wink and looked back at her. "Thanks, beautiful."

"No more for me," I told the waitress.

The two of us were seated in a booth at Blueberry Hill in the University City Loop. I hadn't known whether I'd recognize him with his clothes on, but apparently I'd paid more attention to his face than I realized because I spotted him the moment he stepped into Blueberry Hill. It helped that he was dressed the way I imagined a painter dressed—oversized faded blue chambray shirt, baggy white painter pants, paint-splattered brown work boots. He was an attractive guy: slender build, early thirties, friendly blue eyes, blond crew cut, matching goatee.

"Nick was a terrific dude." Bobby said. "As my grandmamma would say, a real prince."

"How so?"

"Honey, I got in big trouble on one of his jobs."

"The naked dance?"

He widened his eyes and placed his hand on his chest. "You know about that?"

"Yes."

"Oh, I was mortified."

He fanned himself with his hand.

"Absolutely devastated. I felt that I'd totally betrayed Nick. The poor man had no idea. He could have dropped me, fired me on the spot. I would have understood. Completely. He could have done far more than that. He could have warned other contractors about me. He could have ruined me. But he didn't do any of that. No, sir. He went to the police station, worked everything out, and that was that. I know Nick lost money on that job, but he still took me back on. He said I was a craftsman, and that counted for more than the rest. Of course, he also told me if I so much as even took off my shirt on a job it would be the very last time I ever painted for him. He made me swear, and I swore. On my grandmamma's grave, I swore. And I swear to you, honey."

His voice cracked.

"Nick Moran was an angel," he whispered.

I waited as the waitress set down another pint of beer. He gave her a smile, took a sip, set down the glass, wiped his eyes with the back of his hand, took a deep breath, and nodded at me.

"I'm okay, honey."

I checked my watch. I needed to wrap it up.

"I've talked to some others who knew him," I said. "I've asked every one of them about drugs. No one ever saw him use anything. How about you?"

"We didn't spend much time together, but he never seemed high to me. He seemed like a pretty sober guy all around."

"Did you ever get the sense that he had any homosexual tendencies?"

Billy smiled. "You mean did my Gay-dar go off? Never. I would always kind of flirt with him some. Nothing obvious, of course. If you don't know about a guy's sexual interests, especially a guy you work for, you don't want to offend him. Guys like me—we know how to handle that, to keep it joking but still enough to pick up any signals. I never sensed a thing from him. Never. That's why I was so surprised. I went to the funeral, you know."

"I did, too."

"Oh, how sweet of you. Well, while I was in that funeral home I was checking out the crowd, looking for a possible boyfriend or two."

"And?"

He shook his head. "I didn't see anyone."

He shrugged.

"But you never know. I've had guys come on to me that I never would have suspected in a million years. And there've been one or two guys I was certain about—guys who really triggered the old Gay-dar—and they turned out to be straight as arrows."

"They found his body on that lane in Forest Park."

"Right."

"Do you know that area?"

"Gay Way?" He gave me an amused look. "Not personally. Anonymous sex with closet queens? Not my style, honey pie."

"Do you know anyone who visits Gay Way?"

He thought about it. "Yeah."

"Could you do me a favor, Bobby? Could you ask those guys to ask around, to see whether they know anyone who might know something about what happened that night? I've asked a few of my gay friends to do the same. The police aren't investigating it. They've pretty much closed the case—written it off as an accidental overdose. Maybe that's all it was. But I promised his sister I'd look into his death. I'm not turning up much, but there is a lot traffic on that lane every night. Dozens and dozens of cars stop there. Maybe some one you know—or someone they know—saw something. I promise to keep whatever they saw confidential."

Bobby smiled, his eyes red. "I'll do it for Nick. He took care of me. It's the least I can do."

# Chapter Eleven

The Frankenstein case started off as the Finkelstein case. In the court's files, it remains *Muriel Finkelstein, et al. v. City of Cloverdale and Ruby Productions, LLC.* In my files, however, it has long since morphed into a monster. More specifically, a TIF monster.

The acronym stands for "tax increment financing." It also stands as proof of the law of unintended consequences. TIF statutes were enacted around the country with the best of intentions. Their creators saw them as a way to provide financial incentives to encourage private developers to revive blighted portions of our inner cities. In a qualified blight area, public tax dollars can be used to reimburse a whole range of costs that a developer would ordinarily have to absorb, such as the costs of acquiring and demolishing existing structures, the fees of various professions (architects, engineers, lawyers), and the construction costs for public works on the redeveloped property, such as sewers and streets. The vision of the TIF creators was that these financial incentives would lure developers into the slums.

Instead, clever developers and their lawyers figured out how to exploit the rules by tapping into public funds and the power of eminent domain to construct shopping malls, fancy housing projects and other profitable developments in locations that no lawmaker could have imagined would qualify for TIF funds.

Developers seduce town officials with visions of higher property values (and thus higher tax revenues) while intimidating them with the threat of taking their project to the adjacent town if denied the TIF they want. In metropolitan St. Louis, for example, the inner city slums fester while developers use TIFs to expand already profitable upscale suburban shopping malls into an even larger, more profitable, and more upscale malls and to level entire middle-class neighborhoods in order to replace them with big-box retailer strip malls.

Although TIFs have become, quite literally, money in the bank for developers, for the metropolitan areas and their citizens they have become a textbook example of the zero sum game in which one suburb's gain is exactly balanced by the losses of others.

No one has proved more adept at exploiting TIF laws than Ken Rubenstein, dubbed by *The Riverfront Times* as the Baron of Blight. His specialty is the gated residential community. Through his development company, Ruby Productions, he has used TIFs to level neighborhoods throughout suburban St. Louis and replace them with enclaves of McMansions for the nouveau riche.

My Frankenstein case is aimed at his latest TIF, which in turn is aimed at Brittany Woods. I became involved, as usual with my lost causes, through my mother. Her dear friend Muriel Finkelstein lives in Brittany Woods, a subdivision of 200 modest one-story homes dating back to the late 1940s. Muriel and her late husband Saul bought their home in the 1950s and raised their four children there. Saul owned a small shoe store in the University City Loop. Muriel and Saul were typical Brittany Woods residents of that era—middle-class Jews of modest means. Now the neighborhood is mostly Black families and elderly Jewish couples whose children have long since moved away.

Although the values of the individual homes in Brittany Woods—three-bedroom ranches built on slabs—have not kept pace with inflation, the untapped value of the underlying real estate has grown steadily, principally because the subdivision is located in the suburb of Cloverdale, which happens to be within one of the best public school systems in Missouri. No one grasped that inherent value better than the Baron of Blight, who somehow convinced the local officials to declare Brittany Woods blighted and to grant his company the power of eminent domain to acquire the entire subdivision so that he could bulldoze it and replace it with Brittany Manors.

The profits to Ruby Productions will be astounding. The average home in Brittany Woods is worth $160,000. If you can acquire all 200 at that price—which is possible only if the city gives you the power of eminent domain—the total outlay is $32 million. Even with the fifteen-percent incentive payment Rob Crane offered after court the other day, his total outlay would still be less than $37 million. The plans for the gated community include 90 mansions with an average sales price of $1.8 million, which seems conservative given the other amenities the development plan includes, such as a swimming pool, state-of-the-art health club, jogging paths, and tennis courts—all funded by TIF dollars, along with public funds for sewer lines and other infrastructure improvements. Ninety mansions at $1.8 million each totals $162 million. A pretty good return on your investment.

The unfairness of it all is manifest, especially if you spend any time with the residents. Over 300 children from the subdivision—mostly Black and Hispanic—attend the excellent local schools. All of those children will be forced out of the school system because their parents will have no choice but to move out of the district. Indeed, the housing costs in the next cheapest neighborhood in the school district start at more than three times the appraised value of the Brittany Woods homes. So, too, older couples who have lived in the subdivision for decades would be forced from their homes and neighborhood and cut off from their friends and daily routines.

Which is why the case haunts me. I may have justice on my side, but Ruby Productions has the law. Except in that imaginary state known as Hollywood, the law generally trumps justice.

The headline writer for the *Post-Dispatch* apparently cannot resist the alliterative allure of "Tiff" and "TIF," since the words have been paired four times in headlines for articles about the lawsuit, including an editorial chastising the city council of Cloverdale. But "tiff" is far too gentle a term for a lawsuit that often feels like the litigation equivalent of the Bataan Death March. Tonight, though, I was taking a break from that march to gather in Muriel Finkelstein's small living room with the ten members of the plaintiffs' steering committee. The purpose was to update them on the lawsuit, convey Rob Crane's latest settlement offer, and find out whether they were ready to raise the white flag and accept the offer.

I knew the answer to the white-flag question long before Cletus Johnson leaned back in his folding chair, crossed his arms over his massive chest, and shook his bald head.

"Not gonna happen on our watch, Miss Gold," he said in his deep baritone. "These are our homes. They may not look like much to Mr. Rubenstein but they are castles to us."

"Maybe so," Kianga Henderson said. She was a young mom with three kids. "But how can we just say no without checking with the others first?"

I said, "The settlement offer requires all two hundred households to agree. Rubenstein doesn't want to pay a premium to half and then get stuck in two years of condemnations proceeding against the rest. It's all or nothing."

"Then it's nothing," said Muriel Finkelstein.

I turned to see her standing in the kitchen doorway. She was holding a platter of freshly baked Toll House cookies—the third batch since we'd arrived.

"Anyone need more coffee or tea?" she asked.

There were several murmured "No's" or "No, thanks."

Muriel was a plump, red-cheeked grandmother in her late seventies. She had thick gray hair cut short, sparkling blue eyes, a complexion to die for, and a fashion preference for sweatshirts, sweatpants, and walking shoes. What with her four children and twelve grandchildren, she had ten different colleges and universities represented by her outfits, each of which she wore proudly. Tonight's sweats were from Colby College, which, as she explained to me when I arrived, was where her "marvelous

Joshua was a junior majoring in philosophy—such a smart boy—a regular Maimonides."

From what I'd observed the few times I'd come to see Muriel on weekends, she was the honorary grandmother for most of the kids in the neighborhood, all of whom seemed to stop by for Toll House cookies, a glass of milk, and a chance to tell Miss Muriel their latest adventures. Her refrigerator front and the bulletin board in her dining room displayed an ever-changing collection of paintings and drawings given to her by the neighborhood kids.

Muriel set the platter of cookies on the sideboard.

"I don't understand," she said, turning toward us. "Seven council members. They needed four votes to get this TIF thing approved. Furman, Reynolds—okay, they were goners from the start. You can count on them to say yes to whatever increases tax revenues. But the other five—I thought no way would any of them go for that TIF. Especially Mary O'Conner and Milt Bornstein. Milt grew up right here in Brittany Woods. Two blocks over. I knew his parents, I knew his whole family. Always voted Democrat. Milt even worked for McCarthy in New Hampshire back in 'Sixty-eight. How did those Ruby Production *goniffs* ever convince Milt to go against his old neighbors? It's a *shanda*, I tell you. Same with Mary. She didn't grow up here, but she's a good liberal. I marched with her in Washington at that Moratorium in 1969. We rode up there together on the bus from St. Louis. She thinks Al Gore walks on water. How can you march on Washington and love Al Gore and vote for this TIF?"

She shook her head in angry frustration. "There has to be a way to stop this. What else can we do, Rachel?"

"Our options are limited," I said. "I'm taking Ken Rubenstein's deposition this Friday. The courts don't give us much leeway in those depositions, but I'm hoping to get something out of him. I've also filed a Sunshine request with the City of Cloverdale."

"What's a Sunshine request?" Cletus Johnson asked.

"It's a state law that requires government bodies to turn over copies of all their files on a subject. I served the request on the city clerk last Friday. That means they have to turn over their files tomorrow."

"Nu?" said Jerry Weiner.

Jerry was in his seventies. He was skinny and completely bald with enormous protruding ears. He sat with his cane upright on the floor between his knees, his hands crossed over the top of the curved cane handle, his chin resting on his hands.

"Jerry?" I said.

"What kind of files are we talking about?"

I shrugged. "Hard to say. The city clerk gathers up all the council members' documents after each meeting. You have all the usual stuff—agenda, bulletins, you name it. Sometimes the only other stuff in there are doodles. But occasionally something worthwhile ends up in that pile."

I smiled. "So keep your fingers crossed."

He held up his hand, fingers crossed. "Aye, aye, Counselor."

Jerry Weiner was one of my favorites. Although he was frail and hunched over, he was a Brittany Woods legend for his homegrown tomatoes, which he grew in a fenced-in area that took up almost his entire backyard. During the harvest season he kept two wooden bushel baskets on his front porch, which he replenished with fresh-picked tomatoes each day for anyone in the neighborhood to take. I'd had a few, and they were delicious.

"Rachela," Jerry said with a smile. "I think this is a first."

"A first what?"

He gave me a wink. "When I was in business, Rachela, I learned one thing. When they told you it wasn't about the money but the principle, guess what? It was only about the money. Principle, shminciple. Forget about it. But this crew here?" He looked around. "Cletus. Walter. Miguel. Yolanda. I think when these people tell you it isn't about the money, guess what? It isn't about the money. This crew here, Rachela, these clients of yours, they got moxie. This is a roomful of *mensches*. I'm proud to call them neighbors."

As I say, the case haunts me.

# Chapter Twelve

I placed the gray pebble on top of Jonathan's headstone, right next to the ones that Sarah, Sam, and I had placed there last Sunday when we visited the cemetery. I laid my hand on the granite, which was cold in the morning air, and closed my eyes.

After a moment, I shook my head and said, "Girls are awful, Jonathan. Just awful."

At the foot of the two graves was a granite memorial bench with WOLF carved on the front. I took a seat and tried to get my thoughts and emotions in order. I'd come home last night from the meeting at Muriel's house to find Sarah sitting cross-legged on her bed, eyes red, clutching her teddy bear, a John Mayer song on the radio. I sat down next to her, took her hand in mine, and listened to the music with her. Eventually, she told me what happened.

Raising two stepdaughters served as a constant reminder of how hard it is to grow up, especially if you're a girl. Sarah had once again been caught in what I'd come to call the Toxic Trio. Put three girls together—on an elementary school playground, a high school cafeteria, a Starbucks in the mall—and invariably two of them will gang up to snub the third. Sarah had been the third that day, and it left her devastated. So we hugged and talked and I made her a cup of hot cocoa and tucked her in bed and sang "Puff the Magic Dragon" and told her how much I loved her and kissed her goodnight and turned off her light.

Then I went down the hall to my bedroom and sat alone in the dark for nearly an hour. I'd thought back to my elementary and middle school days, which were the years that I'd been such a determined tomboy. Oh, sure, I loved kickball and soccer, and was lucky enough to be competitive with the boys in both sports. But as I sat there on the edge of the bed in the dark I thought that maybe the whole tomboy thing was a defense mechanism, a way to avoid those awful girl cliques on the playground.

Although Sarah seemed happy again in the morning, I was dealing with my own Toxic Trio by then—my anger over the way her "friends" had hurt her, my frustration over the Frankenstein case, and my yearning for Jonathan. His absence was just a dull ache most days, a piece of my soul that was simply missing, like the missing piece for my father. But this morning I awoke from a dream about Jonathan, and the pain I felt when I realized it was just a dream, that my husband was gone forever, that he would never hug me again or run his fingers through my hair or zip up the back of my dress before a party—well, I felt as if all of the joy had been sucked out of me.

Sam rescued me. He came in the room in his Cardinals pajamas a few minutes later, Yadi trailing behind. He climbed into bed, gave me a kiss, and—paraphrasing my wake-up greeting to him most days—said, "Good morning, Supergirl. Time to rise and shine."

The cemetery was just a few blocks from Sam's elementary school. After I dropped him off I decided I needed to spend some time there before heading to the office. I needed to steel myself for the day, for the week.

For some unfathomable reason, spending time at Jonathan's grave comforted me. I say "unfathomable" because little about the gravesite was comforting, beginning with the side-by-side headstones of my husband and his first wife. The pair of dates etched onto each headstone was solemn evidence of life's unfairness. Robyn Wolf died at the age of 33 of ovarian cancer, leaving behind two young daughters. Jonathan Wolf died at the age of 44. He'd been determined to get home from a two-week trial in

Tulsa in time for our wedding anniversary. Rather then wait for the next commercial flight, which included a change of planes in Kansas City and a one-hour layover that wouldn't get him home until eleven that night, he'd hitched a ride on his client's corporate jet, which took off in a thunderstorm and crashed ten miles east in a oilfield, killing all aboard. He was supposed to be home by seven o'clock. I made dinner reservations for eight o'clock. The call came in around midnight.

Jonathan had been an Orthodox Jew. I was raising his daughters and our son in the Jewish tradition, albeit back at my Reform congregation. I still light the candles and say the blessings on Friday night and go to *shul* to say Kaddish on his *yahrzeit* and on my father's *yahrzeit*. But Jonathan's death—coupled with his first wife's death and the tragedies that have befallen some of my friends—have made me wonder whether the only religion that actually makes sense out of life's nonsense, that reconciles all of the injustices, is the religion of the ancient Greeks. In a world ruled by a mob of unruly, hot-tempered, meddlesome deities, it isn't surprising that good things happened to bad people and bad things happened to good people. Up on Mount Olympus, shit happens because the gods say so.

The other unsettling aspect of the paired gravesites is their location. To the left was a double headstone for Robyn's father (who had died two years before Robyn) and her mother (who was still alive), and beyond that double headstone to the left was an entire line of tightly packed gravesites. On the right side of their pair gravesites stood a large memorial for the Schwartz family, several of whom were buried in a row. The result, when I was seated alone on the memorial bench, was an acute sense of solitude. There was no room for me.

Although I don't typically seek solace from Rebbe Chandler, his wisdom helps me on the subject of burial plots. *What did it matter where you lay once you were dead?* his protagonist Marlowe muses as he contemplates the final resting place of Rusty Regan. *In a dirty sump or in a marble tower on top of a high hill? You were dead, you were sleeping the big sleep, you were not bothered by things like that. Oil and water were the same as wind and air to you.*

Maybe so, I tell myself. Maybe so.

A few moments later, I stood, kissed the top of Jonathan's headstone, and headed down the pathway toward my car. As always after visiting his grave, I felt a little better—and almost serene.

The feeling lasted through the drive to my office in the Central West End and up to the moment I stepped into the reception area of Gold & Brand, Attorneys At Law.

"Oh, Rachel," my assistant said. "I've been trying to reach you."

"My cell phone battery is dead. What's up?"

"Barry Graham called. He says it's important. He needs to talk to you right away."

"Did he say about what?"

"No. He said to call him as soon as you got in."

So I did.

"I found you a witness," Barry said.

"Really?" I leaned forward in my chair and picked up a pen. "Who is it?"

"I can't say."

"What do you mean?"

"That's his condition. He made that very clear. He'll meet with you and he'll tell you what he saw that night—but only if you agree in advance to keep everything absolutely confidential. That means you can never tell anyone—especially the police—who he is or what he saw."

"What did he see?"

"I don't know. He won't tell me."

"Do you think he's legit?"

Barry chuckled. "Most definitely."

"Okay," I said, a bit uncertainly.

"Do you agree to his terms?"

*Do I have a better option?*, I asked myself. *I'd been nosing around for two weeks and hadn't been able to poke a hole—or even a dent—in the official version of Nick's death.*

"I agree."

"Do you have lunch plans today?"

I glanced at my calendar. "No."

"Perfect. Let's meet at Llywelyn's Pub. One o'clock. Okay?"

"I'll be there."

# Chapter Thirteen

Barry Graham was in a booth near the front of Llywelyn's Pub. I gave him a kiss on the cheek and slid in on the opposite side of the table.

"How are you, Counselor?" he asked.

I said, "You're looking quite handsome today."

"And you're looking quite ravishing. As always."

The waitress had followed me to the table and took my order for an iced tea, which is what Barry was already drinking.

With his silver hair, square jaw, and gray eyes framed in elegantly round tortoise-shell glasses, Barry Graham could have passed for a successful partner in a major law firm, which is what he had once been. Three years ago, and just two years shy of his fiftieth birthday, he gave up his practice to pursue his passion by opening the Graham Gallery on Maryland Avenue in the Central West End. Within those three years, he'd become one of the more influential art dealers in town.

We'd met as opposing counsel in a lawsuit back in his litigator days and had become friends by the time our clients settled the case on the first day of trial. I've even represented him in a copyright matter involving an artist. He invites me to his gallery openings, I invite him to our annual client appreciation party, and we try to get together for lunch two or three times a year. Our favorite spot is Llywelyn's, a Celtic pub within walking distance of our offices. We usually try for a late lunch on a Friday, which gives us an excuse for a pint of Guinness or Newcastle. But this was early in the week—and thus the iced tea.

During the early days after my meeting with Nick Moran's sister Susannah, I'd asked several gay friends, including Barry, to put the word out in their community to see whether anyone knew anything at all about Nick's life or death.

"I ordered your lunch already," he said.

"Oh?" I gave him a curious look. "What am I having?"

"I assumed that by one o'clock you'd be nice and famished."

I smiled. "The Famous?"

He nodded. "Of course."

The Famous was Llywelyn's beloved steak sandwich: a marinated flank steak covered in pepper cheese and fried onions and stuffed in a hearty roll. Although it was delicious, it was also too much to eat in one sitting, at least for me.

"What about you?" I asked.

"Nothing. I'm leaving in two minutes."

"What do you mean?"

He leaned forward, his voice low. "The waitress will deliver your lunch three booths back on my left. There's a man in there already. He's waiting for you."

I leaned out of the booth but could see nothing. Whoever was in the booth had his back to me.

"He's the witness?" I asked softly.

Barry nodded.

I leaned back in. "Who is he?"

Barry shook his head. "No names. That's part of the deal. If you happen to recognize him, pretend you don't. It'll only make him more skittish. He'll tell you what he saw, answer any questions, and then he'll leave. The deal is that you will never try to contact him again and you will never tell anyone, including the police, what he told you."

"I understand."

I took a sip of tea and studied Barry.

"How do you know him?" I asked.

"He's a client. I've sold him several paintings and sculptures."

"This part of his life—it's not public?"

Barry nodded.

"Why is he willing to talk with me?"

Barry's expression softened. "Because he thinks it's the right thing to do. As corny as it may sound, that's the type of person he is. He's a deeply religious man. He thought about it and prayed on it and decided to talk to you."

He checked his watch. "Your food should be out any minute. You better go join him."

I reached across the table and squeezed his hand. "Thank you, Barry."

He smiled and stood. "Good luck, Rachel."

I watched him leave.

I took a sip of tea as I peered out the window. A moment later Barry Graham came into view crossing the street. I watched him head down the sidewalk and around the corner.

I stood, picked up my glass of iced tea, and stepped out of the booth. Three booths down I could see the back of a bald man's head. He was wearing a brown suit and sipping a cup of coffee.

I took a deep breath, exhaled, and stepped toward his booth.

# Chapter Fourteen

The man in the brown suit looked up. He was in his late forties, slightly overweight.

"Hello," I said.

He nodded, lowering his eyes.

I slid into the booth across from him. He had thinning brown hair, a pudgy nose, and wire-rimmed glasses. Under his brown suit jacket he was wearing a white dress shirt and a red-and-yellow striped tie.

I said, "I appreciate you meeting with me."

He took a sip of coffee and set the mug down carefully. He was clearly agitated.

The waitress arrived with my lunch. He didn't look up as she set it down.

"Anything else, honey?" she asked me.

"No, thanks."

"More coffee, sir?"

He shook his head, eyes down, and adjusted his tie.

I took a bite of my sandwich and gazed at him.

I recognized him, of course. He was the son of the founder of one of the largest privately held companies in town. He was, as I recalled, the executive vice-president and COO. Two of his brothers were in the business as well, although in less prominent roles. Their father, now in his late seventies, was still the CEO and chairman of the board and still arrived at the office each morning at six-thirty, according to a piece that ran earlier in the year in the *Post-Dispatch*.

Theirs was a prominent Catholic family—prominent in charities and community affairs, prominent in the Church. When Pope John Paul II visited St. Louis in 1999, the entire family had a special audience with the Holy Father. The family name was on a wing of a local hospital, on a science building at a local university, and on a pavilion at the zoo.

He was married and the father of six. In a profile of him that appeared in the *St. Louis Business Journal* last year, the reporter wrote about his deep love of soccer. Although he routinely put in seventy to eighty hours of work each week—arriving at seven in the morning, rarely leaving before seven at night, six days a week—he still found time to coach his kids' soccer teams, often returning to the office after the games. He sat on the boards of the St. Louis Zoo and the Contemporary Art Museum.

He glanced at me and then looked down at his mug.

In a gentle voice I asked, "What can you tell me?"

"I was in the park that night."

He said it quietly.

I sipped my iced tea.

"I didn't know he was dead," he said. "I didn't even know it was him."

"Tell me about it."

"I was…there is this street…more of a lane…in the park, Forest Park…it's near the woods—the lane, I mean, and—"

"I know about the lane."

He nodded, eyes averted.

"Go on," I said.

"I'd worked late that night, until maybe nine o'clock. I was tense and tired. I decided to stop there on the way home. I'd had a rough day, I was feeling tense, and I, well, I was…"

"I understand."

He stared at his coffee mug.

"I'm here because of Nick's sister," I said. "She loved him. She asked me to look into his death. I understand this is difficult for you, sir. I promise that whatever you tell me I will never repeat. Never. You have my word on that."

He nodded.

After a moment, he said, "I first noticed the truck when I got out of my car."

"What truck?"

"A pickup truck. A large one. It was parked directly behind my car. It must have been parked there already when I arrived, because I didn't notice it pull in behind me. I would have noticed. It was dark by then. It would have had its headlights on. So it was there already. I got out of my car and walked back down the lane past the pickup truck. There was no one in it. When I came back, it was still empty."

"How long had you been away?"

"Maybe twenty minutes."

"What happened next?"

"I got back in my car and tried to decide what to do—whether to go home or not. Another pickup truck passed by and pulled into the space right in front of me. As it passed, I saw the words "Moran Renovations" on the side panel. That's why I paid attention. I know—er, knew—Nick."

"How?"

"He did our kitchen and a rec room in the basement. I knew him pretty well—or thought I did. I was surprised."

"Surprised?"

"To see his truck there. I didn't think Nick was, you know—"

"Right."

"Anyway, when I saw it was his truck it was like a jolt of adrenalin. I was confused to see him there and didn't know whether I wanted him to see me or what. I was sitting there trying to get my wits about me when the driver—who I assumed was Nick—turned off the engine and turned off the lights. I could tell there were two people in the cab from the backs of their heads, but that was about all I could tell. It looked like the one on the passenger side was asleep."

"Why do you say that?"

"It looked like he was resting his head against the window. But it was dark. I couldn't tell anything for sure. Then the driver's door opened. I slid down. I didn't want Nick to see me. But it wasn't Nick. I had my head low but I could still see."

"Did you recognize who it was?"

"No. I could just see he was a big man, bigger than Nick. Over six feet—probably six two or six three. He easily weighed more than two hundred pounds. A big man. Bald, I think. Or at least very short hair. It was a dark night. I couldn't see any features."

He was staring at me as he spoke, his eyes intense behind the thick lenses of his wire-rimmed glasses.

He shook his head. "I didn't know what was going on."

"So the big guy," I said, "the one who was driving, he got out of the pickup. And then?"

"Right. He walked past my car and got into the other pickup truck, the one behind me. The one that had been empty the whole time I was there. He turned on the engine, pulled out of space, and drove off."

"What did you do?"

"I did the same. I started my car and drove off."

"Did you look into Nick's pickup as you passed?"

"I didn't pass it. I made a U-turn and drove back the way I came. I didn't want to go past his truck. I didn't want Nick to see me."

"Could you tell whether Nick was the man on the passenger side?

He shook his head. "It was dark. I was anxious to get out of there. I didn't even try to look."

"Could you describe the other pickup? The one the big guy got into."

"It was too dark to tell the color. I'm not real good with pickup truck brands. It was big. I know that much. I've looked at pickup models on the Internet, trying to identify it. It might have been a Dodge. But I couldn't say for sure."

I nodded, trying to mask my frustration. "Anything else happen after you drove off?"

"That was it."

"Okay."

"I did write down the license plate."

I stared at him. "Whose?"

"The one on the big truck. I saw the license plate when it pulled out in front of me. I'm not sure why, but the number stuck in my head. Maybe because I was so nervous. It was still in my head when I found out about Nick, so I wrote it down. I wrote it down on a sheet of paper."

"Do you still have that paper?"

He reached into his suit jacket and pulled out an envelope. "I brought it with me. I hope it helps."

He handed it to me. I put the unopened envelope in my purse.

"Thank you," I said.

He nodded and took out his wallet. "That's all I know. Unless you have any more questions, I'm going to leave."

He placed a five dollar bill near his coffee mug.

"Thank you for doing this," I said. "I admire your courage."

He frowned, staring at the empty coffee mug.

"There's nothing courageous about me, Miss Gold. I've come here today in secret because that part of my life is secret." He shook his head. "This is the act of a coward. A sinner and a coward. I should have gone to the police the very next day. That would have been the right thing to do. But then I would have had to explain why I was there that night, and then my family—my wife, my children, my father—they would have found out about me, about my secret. I took the coward's way. I am a weak man."

"Not to me."

He looked up, his eyes red.

"Not to me," I repeated. "Today took courage."

He stood and shook his head. "You are kind, Miss Gold. May God bless you."

He turned and hurried out of the pub.

I took another sip of tea as I thought over our conversation, over what I'd learned and what it might mean. I took the envelope out of my purse and tore it open. Inside was a folded sheet of bond paper. I unfolded the sheet and placed it flat on the table. Handwritten in blue ink at the top of the page were the words "MO license" followed by a combination of three letters and three numbers.

I took out my cell phone and dialed a number. It was answered on the third ring.

"Detective Tomaso, please. Tell him it's Rachel Gold."

"Yes, ma'am."

Nearly a minute passed before he got on the phone.

"Hello, Gorgeous."

"Hi, Bertie."

"What's up?"

"I'm not sure. I have a license plate number, though. Missouri plates."

"And who do those Missouri plates belong to?"

"I have no idea. I was going to call Miss Cleo, the telephone psychic, but I can't find her number. Then I was going to visit the Oracle of Delphi, but I can't find Delphi on Mapquest."

"It's down near the Arkansas border. Try Google maps."

"I was going to do that, but then I thought of the Oracle of Tomaso."

"Ah, now it becomes clear. You want me to run the plates."

"You're clairvoyant."

"Amazing, eh? If I run these plates today, will you still love me tomorrow?"

"I promise."

"Last question: if and when you have reason to believe that the owner of these plates is somehow connected to a crime, do you promise to call me instead of doing something stupid on your own?"

"I promise to consider that."

"Good Lord. Give me the damn number."

I read it to him, and he read it back to make sure he had it right.

"I'll have them run it," he said. "I'll call you back when I have something."

"Thanks, Bertie."

# Chapter Fifteen

My secretary buzzed. "Benny's here."

I checked my watch. 4:50 p.m.

He'd gone downtown that afternoon for a meeting at the Federal Reserve Bank, which had retained him as a consultant on some trade regulation matter. He'd promised to drop by on his way home.

"It's happy hour, Darling."

Benny stood in the doorway. He had a six-pack of Schlafly's Hefeweizen in one hand and a large white bag in the other. As he stepped into my office the tangy aroma of barbecue filled the air.

"That smells delicious."

"Smoki O's finest."

Smoki O's is a barbecue joint in the warehouse district on North Broadway, a hole in the wall that Benny stops at every time he's downtown.

He took a seat over at my small work table, put the six-pack and the bag on the table, and gestured toward the empty seat next to him.

"Dig in."

I joined him at the table as he lifted two foil-wrapped containers out of the bag.

"What'd you get us?"

"What do you think? Once upon a time, the Rachel Gold I knew could scarf down some real barbecue—back before she turned her home into a pork-free zone. But since we ain't home, I went whole hog, so to speak."

"Which parts?"

"Which parts? Come on. We're talking Smoki O's. That means we're talking two parts."

"Oh, no. Noses again?"

"Not noses, for chrissake. Snoots. And not just any snoots. These are primo snoots. Trust me, if the Rabbis of the Talmud had sampled Smoki O's snoots, they'd have carved out an exception in the laws of kashruth."

He unwrapped the foil on the containers and looked up with a smile.

"Plus rib tips, my sweet. Snoots and tips—best combo on the planet outside the bedroom."

"You wore that outfit to meet with officials of the Federal Reserve?"

He gave me a puzzled frown and then looked down at his clothing. He was wearing baggy cargo pants and a navy blue sweatshirt over a red T-shirt. On the front of the sweatshirt was an official-looking logo that read *Department of Redundancy Department.* Benny was a Firesign Theater fan.

He shrugged. "Actually, the sweatshirt adds a touch of class to what might have been missing with just the T-shirt."

"Which one is it?"

He leaned back and pulled the front of the sweatshirt over his ample belly to reveal the slogan on the red T-shirt: *I AM THAT MAN FROM NANTUCKET.*

I rolled my eyes. "Benny."

"A line from a beautiful poem. My favorite. Meanwhile, it's not like I was down there testifying before Congress. And believe me, those clowns lost all speaking privileges today."

"Oh? What happened?"

"I get on their elevator and guess what's playing over the goddam speakers?"

I couldn't help but smile. "What?"

He opened a bottle of beer and handed it to me.

"The 101 Strings," he said.

"Playing what?

"Brace yourself. AC/DC's 'Highway to Hell.'"

He shook his head in disgust. "Can you believe that? A fucking Muzak rendition of 'Highway to Hell'? On an elevator owned by the federal government?"

"That's pretty bad," I conceded.

"Pretty bad? That shit is so wrong in so many ways that all you do is shake your head and say, 'What the fuck?'"

"Which is what you said to them?"

"For starters. Then I told them the Founding Fathers would be spinning in their graves. I told them if you're going to play AC/DC on government owned and operated elevators, do it the way Ben Franklin would have: electric guitars and all."

"I must have missed that history lesson. I had always assumed Ben preferred the unplugged version."

"Why do you think that crazy dude was out in a thunderstorm with a kite? Old Ben was a heavy metal freak."

"These rib tips are delicious, Benny."

"Where's Jacki? She's my snoot buddy."

"She should be back any minute. She had a court hearing out in the county at two-thirty. Afterward, she was going to stop by the Cloverdale City Hall to pick up my Sunshine documents."

"Oh, yeah. How's Frankenstein going?"

"I'm taking Rubenstein's deposition on Friday."

"Got any decent ammo?"

"Not much. I'm hoping Jacki brings me back something to work with."

"You better hope she brings back a photo of Rubenstein blowing a council member."

"As my father would have said, from your lips to God's ears."

He scarfed down another snoot and took a big gulp of beer.

"How are things going with your dead guy?" he asked. "The one who was banging my Subaru colleague?"

"That's what I've been working on this afternoon."

"Turn up anything?"

"I don't know. I can't figure it out."

"What do you have?"

"A license plate and a name."

"Tell me."

Without revealing the identity or anything else about my source, I told Benny about the license plate number from the pickup truck and its connection to Nick.

"Cops run the plates for you?"

I nodded.

"And?"

"The truck is registered to Corundum Construction Company."

"Which is?"

I frowned. "I can't figure that out."

Benny crunched on another snoot as he thought it over.

"Makes sense," he said.

"What makes sense?"

"Your guy did renovations on homes. That means he dealt with others in the construction industry. We can safely assume he wasn't the only *fegala* doing renovations. He must have met the other guy on a job site."

"That was my thought, too. I called Nick's secretary Linda as soon as I got the license plate information. She told me that Nick never did any work with that company."

"Maybe they were on same job site doing different things."

"It's possible, but Linda did a search of Nick's records. She came up with nothing that indicated that Corundum Construction had ever been on the same job site with Nick."

"What kind of work does the company do? New homes? Rehabs? Commercial? Residential?"

"I have no idea. I can't find any information on them."

"Who owns them?"

"According to the Missouri Secretary of State, Corundum Construction Company is the d/b/a of one R.S. Corundum."

'Who's that?"

"Beats me. I checked the telephone directory. There's no

listing for Corundum in the business section and there's no listing for anyone named Corundum in the white pages."

"Unlisted number?"

"For a construction company? That would be weird. How could people reach them? I did an Internet search, too. Nothing."

"Maybe they're out of business."

"Then how do you explain the license plate?"

Benny shrugged. "Hasn't expired."

I frowned. "I suppose."

"You're saying Moran's secretary had no information on that company?"

"She'd never heard of them."

"Maybe your police buddy can help. What's his name?"

"Tomaso. I can't go to him on this. At least not yet. He was willing to run the plate for me without any other information, but if I want anything more I'll have to tell him how I found out about the plate, and I can't do that."

He belched and gave me a playful grin. "You got yourself what I'd call a real Corundum conundrum."

"Try saying that fast five times."

"Try saying what?" said a familiar voice.

We both turned.

Standing in the doorway—indeed, filling up the doorway—was Jacki Brand, all six feet three inches and 250 pounds of her, dressed in heels, white blouse, and navy skirt.

She sniffed the air. "Barbecue?"

"Snoots and tips," Benny said. "Grab a chair, Sexy."

"Maybe a few nibbles," she said. "I've got a dinner date tonight."

"Freddy?" I asked.

She took a seat and nodded. "Freddy."

Judge Fred Epstein was Jacki's latest beau. They were an odd couple, since he was fifteen years older, eight inches shorter, and a hundred pounds lighter than his lady love. He told me it was love at first sight the day Jacki appeared before him in family court on a motion for protective order in a nasty divorce case. Indeed, the only downside to their relationship was that Judge

Epstein was one of the better judges for divorce cases. Because Jacki specialized in divorce cases, their relationship meant that she could have him in the bedroom or the courtroom but not both. Except for the one time a case of hers got reassigned to Judge Flinch, she'd never regretted the tradeoff.

Benny gave her a Groucho Marx leer. "Freddy's in for a treat tonight. You are looking quite voluptuous, Ms. Brand."

She blushed. "If I didn't know you better, Benny, I'd think you were flirting."

"I am flirting. What do you mean 'know me better'?"

"She means," I said, "that she might think you were flirting if she didn't know that you prefer girls who might ask you to their senior prom."

"Oh, very funny, Rachel Gold. Ho, ho, ho. Such a clever girl." He took a swig of beer.

"You know what your problem is?" he said. "Actually, both of your problems?"

I winked at Jacki and turned to Benny. "Enlighten us, Professor."

"You can't deal with consistency in a man."

"Is that so?" I said. "Please explain, Ralph Waldo."

"By the time I turned twenty-five, I had discovered that I preferred girls who were around that age."

"Hardly a unique discovery."

"Ah, but I didn't realize then that my tastes had fully matured."

"Meaning?" I asked.

"Meaning that I still prefer girls around that age, and probably always will."

"Fully matured?" Jacki chuckled.

I said, "It's not worth it, Jacki. We know the man is a total pig, but he brought you snoots and he brought me ribs and he brought both of us beer. As I've learned, he's much more fun to eat with than argue with."

She eyed the basket of snoots and nodded. "Good advice."

She turned to Benny, pressed her hands together in front of her chest, and bowed toward him. "I thank you and your mature tastes."

He pried the cap off a bottle of beer and handed it to her. "Up yours, Hot Stuff. Have some snoots."

I smiled as I watched them banter.

Jacki Brand and I met nearly a decade ago when she was still a Granite City steelworker named Jack Brand. When St. Louis University Law School accepted his application to the night program, Jack Brand decided to quit his steelworker job and pursue both of this dreams: to become a lawyer and to become a woman.

I hired him as my legal assistant at the front end of those pursuits, when he had just started attending law classes and taking hormone shots and wearing dresses and wigs. The new Jacki Brand helped keep my law practice organized, and I helped teach her to be a woman. The week after she received her law school diploma, she underwent the final surgical procedure that lopped off the last dangling evidence of her original gender.

When she passed the bar exam six years ago, I changed the title of my firm from the Law Offices of Rachel Gold to Rachel Gold & Associates, Attorneys at Law. A year ago, I made her my law partner. I kept it a secret until the new signs and business cards were ready. She left for court that morning from the offices of Rachel Gold & Associates and returned that afternoon to Gold & Brand, Attorneys at Law. You haven't experienced joy and gratitude until you've been swept off your feet in a bear hug by your blubbering six-foot three-inch 250-pound high-heeled partner.

Jacki still acts as if I did her a big favor, but it was—as I keep trying to tell her—a no-brainer. She has become one of the most respected and sought-after divorce lawyers in town, especially by wealthy women. They adore her—and not only for her blue-collar moxie but for the sight of their soon-to-be exes, generally arrogant corporate execs, surgeons, and lawyers, trying not to cringe at the initial settlement conference as they shake hands with a towering attorney whose previous job really did involve bending steel.

I said to Jacki, "Did they have anything for me at the Cloverdale City Hall?"

"Anything?" Jacki said. "Good grief. How about four boxes of documents?"

"Four? I can't believe it."

"That's what I said when the city clerk rolled them out on a hand cart. I was expecting maybe a couple folders."

"Did you look in the boxes?" I asked.

"All four were sealed with packing tape. That's how I had to sign for them. But I asked him about the contents. He told me that their city attorney is very strict. Immediately after each meeting he makes the clerks gather up every single document at every council member's place and file them away in separate folders. They aren't allowed to throw anything out. The clerk told me they made us copies of everything. Everything."

"Meaning?" I asked.

"From doodles to empty candy wrappers."

"Mr. Rubenstein," Benny said in his serious deposition voice, "I've asked the court reporter to mark this Butterfingers wrapper as Plaintiffs' Exhibit Five."

I groaned. "Four boxes."

"When are you taking his deposition?" Jacki asked.

"Day after tomorrow."

She winced. "Ouch. If you need help reviewing the documents, I can call Freddy and tell him something's come up."

"You're a sweetie, Jacki, but I'll be okay. I'm the one who's going to be asking Ken Rubenstein the questions on Friday. It's better if I'm the one who looks through the documents."

"I can help if you need me. I have a hearing at nine tomorrow, and I have to go over to City Hall for a couple hours, but otherwise I'm available."

"What's at City Hall?" Benny asked.

She sighed. "Lots of boring records in one of my cases."

"What kind of boring records?"

"Mostly building permits."

"You got a real estate case?" he asked.

"No, I have a sleazy husband who tried to hide his marital assets by setting up trusts to invest in apartment buildings in the city. Long story short, he'd renovate them, sell them, and reinvest in others—and all the while keeping his name off the records. He made one mistake, though. He got his brother involved. His brother owns a construction company in Iowa, and he was the one who did the renovations on the properties. The good news is that it happens to be the only work his brother's company has ever done in St. Louis."

"Why is that good news?" I asked.

"Because it means I can identify the properties by going through all the building permits issued during the relevant period and match each permit issued to his brother's company to the property involved."

"Awesome." I turned to Benny and smiled. "Why didn't I think of that?"

Benny frowned. "Think of what?"

"Building permits."

"What are you talking about?" he said.

"Think about it, Benny. You need to get a building permit before you can do any work. If Corundum Construction is a real company that really builds things, there's going to be a trail of building permits. Right?"

He raised his eyebrows. "That's good."

"What are you two talking about?" Jacki asked.

I explained my Corundum conundrum.

"No problem," she said. "I'll be sorting through building permits anyway. I'll make copies of any that identify Corundum Construction as the contractor."

"That would be great," I said. "Thanks."

"My pleasure. Maybe you'll get lucky. Maybe we'll find an active site."

"And do what?" Benny asked.

"Check it out," she said. "Maybe spot that big guy that Rachel's source saw."

# Chapter Sixteen

The deposition was actually going to start on time.

Ken Rubenstein was seated at the end of the conference table. To the left along the side of the table were his three lawyers—Rob Crane, a young male partner named Burwell, and a male associate. Seated to the right of Rubenstein was the court reporter. I was seated next to her and thus almost directly across the table from Rob Crane. At the other end of the conference table stood the videographer, her camera mounted on a tripod and aimed at the witness.

I gazed at Rubenstein as the videographer tested our microphone voice levels. There was a coiled intensity about him that made him seem much bigger than his five feet eight inches. He had an angular face, deep-set dark eyes, a sharp nose, and unnaturally white teeth. He wore his thick brown hair slicked back and sported a neatly trimmed goatee flecked with gray.

No bicycle shorts today. He was dressed for the boardroom: dark blue suit, white dress shirt, red-and-gold striped silk tie, and a fair amount of bling, including a gold pinkie ring with a large ruby (of course), gold monogrammed cufflinks encrusted with small diamonds, and a gold Rolex watch, all of which were on display as he rubbed his goatee with his thumb and forefinger and frowned at a message on his iPhone.

Hard to believe he was the son of a small town scrap metal dealer—or maybe not so hard. He was a climber and a striver, an alpha dog who worked long hours but found time to pursue his two passions, triathlons and crossword puzzles. And pursue them he did, with the same ferocity he brought to his business. According to one gossip column item, he played against the clock each morning at the *New York Times* online crossword puzzle site and regularly ranked in the top ten times nationwide. Indeed, Rubenstein's publicist made sure he got press for every triathlon or crossword puzzle achievement.

Watching the court reporter swear in Rubenstein, I decided to change my deposition strategy. I could already tell that Rubenstein was poised. If I had any hope of catching him off balance, of getting beyond rehearsed answers, I needed to skip the usual preliminary questions—the educational background, employment background, current job responsibilities, blah, blah, blah. That standard litany tended to calm most witnesses by giving them thirty to sixty minutes of easy questions to answer—all of which had the effect of bolstering their confidence. Ken Rubenstein's confidence needed no bolstering.

"I do," Rubenstein said to the court reporter.

The court reporter looked over at me. I glanced back at the videographer, who nodded. I turned to the witness, who was gazing at me with just the hint of a smile. He stroked his goatee with the thumb and forefinger of his right hand.

"Mr. Rubenstein, has your company investigated the violent crime rate in Brittany Woods?"

He raised his eyebrows slightly. After a moment, he shrugged. "I don't believe we have, Ms. Gold."

"Is that a no?"

He smiled. "That is a no."

"In your experience, Mr. Rubenstein, can the violent crime rate of a neighborhood be a factor in determining whether that neighborhood is blighted under the TIF laws?"

"I suppose so."

"Did you know that the violent crime rate in Brittany Woods is the lowest in all of Cloverdale?"

"I did not know that."

"Would you agree with me, Mr. Rubenstein, that if the violent crime in Brittany Woods is the lowest in all of Cloverdale, then that crime rate would not support a finding of blight?"

He smiled. "I would agree, Ms. Gold, although, as I stated before, I don't know what that crime rate is."

"Has your company investigated the number of abandoned properties in Brittany Woods?"

"I don't believe so."

"In your experience, Mr. Rubenstein can the number of abandoned properties in a neighborhood be a factor in determining whether that neighborhood is blighted under the TIF laws?"

"I suppose so."

"Did you know that there are no abandoned properties in Brittany Woods?"

"I did not know that, Ms. Gold."

And so it went for almost an hour, until the videographer's equipment went on the fritz. She said it wouldn't take more than twenty minutes to get it running again, so we took a break.

For a lawyer representing a typical client, a break one hour into a deposition is a godsend, a perfect time to meet with your witness out in the hall to go over any problems in his testimony and prepare him for the questions to come. Ken Rubenstein was no typical client. Though he had plenty of lawyers to confer with, he'd waived them all off, and now they were out in the hall on their cell phones while their client remained seated at the far end of the table. The court reporter was down the hall getting a cup of coffee, which left just three of us in the conference room—the videographer tinkering with her equipment, me leafing through my deposition notes and exhibits, and Ken Rubenstein hunched over a crossword puzzle, pen in hand, a ticking stopwatch on the table to his left. This was his second puzzle of the break. He had some crossword tournament coming up.

Our first hour had been a spirited round of deposition ping-pong, and we'd played to a draw. He was good. None of my questions fazed him. He knew—as I knew—that the dictionary definition of "blight" was not the same as the statutory definition, and thus he could concede on point after point that would hurt his case about as much as those little darts thrown into the side of a bull by the banderilleros. A few might sting, and even draw a little blood, but none would bring him down.

By the time the video equipment malfunctioned, I'd moved on to questions about the studies his company, Ruby Productions, had submitted to the Cloverdale council in support of his TIF proposal. Although I had a list of inconsistencies in those reports, none was major, which meant that after the break it would be more little darts. Such is litigation.

He grunted.

I looked up from my notes.

He glanced over at the stopwatch and back down at the crossword. He scribbled in a word.

During the deposition he had tried to put on an air of nonchalance, but the intensity in his eyes and the vein in his temple gave him away. He was too controlled to allow himself to get rattled by my questions. He was also too controlled to be lured into one of my favorite deposition traps, which I call the "accelerated conversation," where you seek to ask questions at a quicker and quicker pace while keeping the lawyer jargon to a minimum. When it works, the witness begins to feel like he is having a conversation with you instead of answering questions that are being taken down verbatim by a court reporter. Everything speeds up, and you have a witness who not only gives you unrehearsed and unguarded testimony but gives his attorney no time to squeeze in an objection or otherwise slow down the pace.

Ken Rubenstein quickly figured out that tactic and, like a basketball coach calling timeout to halt the other team's rally, slowed the pace—listening carefully to each question, sometimes asking the court reporter to read it back to him a second time, pausing several beats before giving me a precise and narrow answer.

He was a formidable adversary.

As he frowned over his crossword puzzle, his left hand fiddled with the button pinned to his suit jacket. All Ruby Production employees wore the button, which was bright yellow and displayed the company's four-letter logo in large red letters:

WSPP

Those initials trace their origin to Rubenstein's first lawyer, Jimmy Hayden. During his rainmaker days at Gardner & Eisner, Jimmy Hayden—hawk-nosed, prematurely gray, elegantly attired—combined a hard-nosed style of advocacy for his clients with a fervent style of proselytism for his transcendental meditation. As he did with other clients, Hayden took Rubenstein up to Fairfield, Iowa for a three-day course in TM at Maharishi University. Rubenstein returned from Fairfield with enough "inner peace" and "universal consciousness" to achieve, by all accounts, even higher levels of ruthlessness in his business dealings.

He also returned with the WSPP logo. According to company literature, the initials stand for the phrase *Work So Peace Prevails*—a mantra that supposedly popped into Ken Rubenstein's head during his sojourn in Fairfield. No one is quite sure what the expression really means. How, for example, does one build upscale gated communities in a manner that will enable world peace to triumph? His critics contend that the initials stand for the company's true mission: *We Screw Poor People*.

Alas, Jimmy Hayden is no longer Rubenstein's lawyer—or anyone else's. As a result of a weekend in the penthouse suite of a downtown hotel with a large supply of crack cocaine, three bottles of Wild Turkey, a video camera, and the nubile fifteen-year-old daughter of one of his clients, Jimmy Hayden now has ample time to practice his mediation without interruption, compliments of the Missouri Department of Corrections.

"Yes!"

I looked up. Rubenstein was holding the stopwatch in his left hand and had his right hand clenched in victory.

"Better?" I asked.

"Oh, yeah. Watch out, boys." He chuckled. "Kenny's got his groove."

◇◇◇

It was almost three o'clock. We were nearing the end of the deposition. We'd been at if for almost five hours.

Rubenstein had refused to break for lunch, preferring instead to grind on. I assumed his goal was to wear me down. Any guy who bragged about all the triathlons he competed in each year no doubt assumed he could wear down a lawyer at a deposition— especially a girl lawyer. And he was probably right, although a glance across the table at his three bleary-eyed defenders confirmed that he was wearing down all the lawyers in the room.

What Rubenstein tried to ignore, though, was the unique pressures of being the witness. His job was tougher than mine, and if you looked carefully you could see effects of five straight hours of carefully answering questions in front of a camera while a court reporter took down his words. His eyes were a little bloodshot, his collar button was undone, and the lines in his face seemed deeper.

I didn't have much ammo, but now was the time to use it.

I flipped back several pages in my deposition notes and pretended to study one of the entries for several seconds.

"Earlier today, Mr. Rubenstein, I asked you whether it was your practice to meet privately with the council members in the cities where you were promoting a TIF. You testified that it was not your practice. Do you recall that testimony, sir?"

"Of course, Ms. Gold."

"Why don't you meet privately with those council members?"

He shook his head with impatience. "Because you're not supposed to."

"Why not?"

"It's improper. Actually, I think it's illegal. Sunshine laws or something like that."

"Don't speculate, Ken,' Rob Crane said. "Stick to your personal knowledge."

"And when it comes to TIF proposals," I said, ignoring Crane, "you and your company do not engage in improper or illegal conduct, correct?"

"Object to the form," Rob Crane said.

I kept my gaze on Rubenstein.

"You may answer. Do you and your company engage in improper or illegal conduct in connection with TIF proposals?"

He gave me a withering smile. "No, Ms. Gold. We don't engage in improper or illegal conduct."

"So you did not meet privately with any of the Cloverdale council members during the pendency of your TIF proposal, correct?"

His eyes narrowed slightly. "Correct."

"Nor did you attempt to meet privately with any of the Cloverdale council members, correct?"

"Correct."

"Therefore, you did not meet privately with Council Member Harry Furman and you did not attempt to meet privately with Council Member Harry Furman. Correct?"

He started to turn toward his attorney, but Crane was jotting down a note.

"Correct?" I repeated.

He met my gaze.

"Correct."

"Because, as you just testified under oath, that would be improper and possibly illegal, correct?"

Another pause.

"Mr. Rubenstein, you need to answer the question."

"Correct."

I reached into my folder and pulled out three photocopies of a telephone message slip. I handed one copy to the witness and one to Crane.

"Mr. Rubenstein, I've just handed you what the court reporter has marked as Plaintiff's Deposition Exhibit 43. I will represent to you that the document was produced to us by the City of Cloverdale. It was in a folder of documents gathered up from Council Member Harry Furman's seat after the meeting of the Cloverdale aldermen last June fifteen, which was one month before your TIF proposal was formally presented to the City of Cloverdale. Exhibit 43 was one of approximately two dozen telephone message slips that Alderman Furman brought to the meeting and left at his seat when the meeting ended. Although we hope to have an opportunity to ask Council Member Furman questions under oath about this document, I'm showing it to you, sir, to see if it refreshes your recollection."

Rubenstein was staring at the exhibit, his jaw clenched.

"Do you see the date at the top of the message?"

Rubenstein stared at the exhibit.

"Mr. Rubenstein?"

He looked up.

"What?" he snapped.

"Do you see the date?"

"Yes."

"What is the date?"

"June thirteenth."

"So two days before the city council meeting, correct?"

"I don't know when they met."

"According to the exhibit, who called Council Member Furman on June thirteenth?"

"This says 'Mister Rubenstein.'"

"And it also lists a telephone number for that Mister Ruben-stein, correct?"

"Yes."

"That's your cell phone number, correct?"

He stared at the document. "Yes."

"So you called Council Member Furman two days before the aldermen meeting?"

"I don't recall."

"Let's see if I can refresh you memory. Read the message, sir. Read it aloud."

He lifted the document.

"'Mister Rubenstein called,'" he read, "'to confirm meeting at four today at St. Louis Club re project.'"

He looked up from the exhibit and stared at me. The vein in his temple was visible.

I said, "Did you meet with Council Member Furman at the St. Louis Club at four o'clock on June thirteenth?"

"I don't recall."

"Was the project you referred to in your message the TIF project involving my clients' homes."

"I don't recall."

"How many times have you met with Council Member Furman?"

"I don't recall."

"More than once?"

"I don't recall."

"But according to Exhibit 43, you had at least one meeting with him before your TIF project was presented to the City of Cloverdale, correct?"

"Objection. Asked and answered."

I turned to Crane. "Asked, Mr. Crane, but not answered."

"He said he doesn't recall."

I turned back to the witness. "Is that your answer to this question, too? That you cannot recall whether you had a private meeting with Council Member Furman at the St. Louis Club just two days before your TIF project was presented to the City of Cloverdale?"

A bead of sweat trickled down the side of his face as he stared at me.

"I don't recall."

I checked my notes to make sure that I'd covered all of my topics. I had.

The only thing left on my list was my wild card. I opened my folder of deposition exhibits and stared at Exhibit 44. It was the only document I had not shown to the witness. It was also the only one I had not known whether to even mark as an exhibit. I had no idea what it meant.

I removed it from the folder and placed it face down on the table in front of me. I looked up at Rubenstein, who glanced down at the document and back at me.

"Mr. Rubenstein," I said, "what can you tell me about the Corundum Construction Company?"

# Chapter Seventeen

I turned on the television, loaded the DVD player, and returned to the chair with the remote in my hand.

"Okay, Jacki," I called out.

The Rubenstein deposition had ended an hour ago. I'd prevailed on the videographer to download a copy of the rough cut onto a DVD before she left.

Jacki Brand came into my office and took the chair next to mine facing the television. She nodded at the screen.

"Roll it," she said.

I pointed the remote at the DVD player and pressed Play. After a moment, the player began to click and whirr.

I'd drawn my own tentative conclusion, but I needed an expert opinion on Ken Rubenstein's handling of my Corundum questions. Jacki was my expert. During her steelworker years, she—or rather, he—played cards with the boys every Monday and Thursday night. Over time Jack Brand became a poker legend in Granite City, Illinois. His ability to read the tiniest gestures and eye movements of his opponents—the "tells," in poker lingo—convinced several of the players that he had ESP. They eventually convinced him—or, by then, her—to enter a Texas Hold 'Em tournament at the Casino Queen on the East St. Louis side of the Mississippi River. Jacki won the tournament. Indeed, she was so good at Texas Hold 'Em that her poker winning helped pay her law school tuition.

The screen flickered and resolved into a head-on shot of Ken Rubenstein seated at the end of the conference table. No one else was visible in the picture.

"The time is ten a.m.," the videographer said off screen. "This is the deposition of—"

I pressed the Fast Forward button, and Ken Rubenstein suddenly started twitching and jerking and talking in silent rapid motion.

"It's at the very end of the deposition," I said to Jacki.

I had come into the deposition with nothing new on Corundum Construction except for an intriguing doodle. Jacki's day of searching building permits at the St. Louis City Hall had turned up zilch. If there really was a Corundum Construction, it had not built a thing in the City of St. Louis during the past decade. But my search through the four boxes of documents produced by the City of Cloverdale had yielded one possible—and unexpected— reference to the mysterious company in the form of a doodle on Council Member Mary O'Conner's copy of the typed agenda for the September city council meeting. There was no agenda item for the Brittany Woods TIF or for any construction project, but there—in the margin of Ms. O'Conner's agenda—was the word Corundum. She had written it in bubble letters and had festooned it with curlicues and arrows and cross-hatches.

I'd come across the document in the fourth box of documents that Jacki had brought back from the Cloverdale City Hall. The first two boxes of documents had yielded nothing of interest. The third had contained that sheaf of telephone messages from Harry Furman, including the one from Rubenstein. Halfway through the final box, trying to pay attention as I leafed through hundreds of pages of financial documents, I came across that agenda with the doodle. I stared at it, and then put it in the pile for possible use at the deposition. There was no reason to connect the doodle to Rubenstein—or, for that matter, to any aspect of the TIF battle. But, I had mused, Ken Rubenstein knew a heckuva lot more about the St. Louis construction industry than I did. Maybe, just maybe, he had heard of Corundum

Construction. A pure fishing expedition, of course, but I brought it to the deposition anyway.

I hit the Pause button.

Ken Rosenfeld froze on the screen, a frown on his face. His lawyers were off-screen to the left. I was off-screen to the right.

I turned to Jacki. "Ready?"

She nodded.

I pressed Play.

"Mr. Rubenstein," my voice said.

"Stop," Jackie said.

I pressed Stop.

"What's he staring at?" she asked.

Rubenstein was looking down to the right—his left.

"The doodle document," I said. "I had it face down in front of me."

"Okay."

I pressed Play.

"—what can you tell me about Corundum Construction Company?"

He leaned back.

"Who?"

"Corundum Construction Company."

He chuckled. "Corundum? Why are you asking me that?"

"Just answer the question, Mr. Rubenstein."

He glanced over at the document in front of me and raised his eyes to mine. He frowned.

"What was the question?"

Off screen, my voice: "Would the court reporter please read the pending question to the witness?"

During the pause, Rubenstein looked toward his attorney with a tight smile.

"Mr. Rubenstein," the court reporter read in a monotone, "what can you tell me about Corundum Construction Company?"

He shrugged. "Nothing."

"Do you know of the company?"

"Nope."

"Have you ever heard of the company, sir? In any context?"

He glanced over at the document in front of me, which was still facedown.

"I don't recall."

"You don't recall the name Corundum? Is that your testimony?"

He smiled. "Unless you mean the sapphire."

"What sapphire?"

"Corundum." He chuckled. "You're talking to a crossword puzzle nut, Ms. Gold. When I hear corundum, I think clue. It's a scientific term for sapphires."

He glanced over at his attorney with a grin.

"I'm not asking you about sapphires, Mr. Rubenstein. I'm asking you about a construction company named Corundum."

"Objection," Crane said. "Asked and answered."

"Then answer it again," I said. "Is it your sworn testimony that you have no information or knowledge concerning Corundum Construction Company?"

He stared at me a moment and then leaned back.

"That is my testimony."

"I have no further questions."

Rubenstein crossed his arms over his chest and nodded at the camera.

I pressed Pause, and the image froze.

I turned to Jacki.

"Well?" I asked.

"My, my." She raised her eyebrows. "You struck a nerve."

"That question about Corundum—it was a shot in the dark. I had nothing on the company. Not even a listing in the phone book. I was just hoping a big developer like Rubenstein might have heard of the company."

"Oh, he definitely heard of them."

"You think?"

"I know. Did you see the way he kept eying that document you had face down? You were freaking him out, Rachel. He didn't know what you had there. That's why he started riffing with all that crossword puzzle nonsense."

"What do you make of it?"

"He was treading water, trying to get you off topic. You told me he was real disciplined for most of the deposition."

"Definitely. He was careful to just answer my question. He never volunteered a thing."

"Not there at the end. You had him rattled. He knows something."

I sighed. "Maybe."

Jacki gave me a puzzled look. "What do you mean?"

"Let me show you the mystery document."

I leafed through the deposition exhibits and pulled out the final one, the one I kept face down and never showed Rubenstein, the one with the word Corundum doodled on Council Member O'Conner's agenda.

"Look." I handed it to Jacki. "She didn't write Corundum Construction Company. Just Corundum. For all I know, she was doing a crossword puzzle during the meeting."

"Maybe she was, but he wasn't. You going to ask her why she wrote it?"

"If the judge lets me, which is doubtful. So far, Flinch has denied all of my requests to depose council members. He claims I'm trying to pollute the sanctity of the legislative process."

Jacki snorted. "What a moron. Maybe you should file a motion anyway."

"And argue what? That I need to depose her to find out why she wrote the word Corundum at the bottom of the agenda? I have no basis to connect her or Rubenstein or anyone involved in that TIF with any company named Corundum. But Rubenstein's reaction gives me a new idea for the Nick Moran situation. It certainly seemed to you that Rubenstein recognized Corundum Construction Company, right?"

"Right."

"Ruby Productions does all of its projects in the suburbs. So maybe Rubenstein ran across them on a job site. Maybe that's how he knows the name."

"And?"

I smiled. "Building permits. You need them in the suburbs, too."

"True."

"I have a hearing out in the county tomorrow. I'll drop by a few town halls before coming back to the office. Maybe I'll get lucky."

"Might be worth a shot."

"It's the only lead I have. I owe it to his sister."

As Jacki stood, I said, "Does he look familiar?"

She looked down at me. "Who?"

I nodded toward the frozen image of Ken Rubenstein on the screen.

She frowned. "You mean does he look like someone else?"

"No. I'd never seen him before today—or at least that's what I thought. But when he was sitting there across from me today, there was something familiar about him. Like I'd seen him before."

Jacki shrugged. "You said he's a publicity hound. Maybe you saw him on TV or in the paper. Doesn't look familiar to me. I'll see you later."

I stared at the screen and searched for a connection.

Nothing.

# Chapter Eighteen

I turned off the engine and checked my watch.

5:20 p.m.

There was a blue Ford Expedition SUV in the driveway. A good sign.

I glanced over at Benny. "Ready, my darling husband Nick?"

"Absolutely, my darling wife Nora."

We were seated in my car, which was parked at the curb in front of 22 Dielman Way, a colonial-style red-brick four-bedroom home in Asbury Groves, a suburb of St. Louis.

I smiled at him. "I have to say, you are looking quite dapper in that outfit."

"And I have to say, I am feeling quite the douche bag in this outfit. All that's missing are a pair of Topsiders and a prep school accent."

"I think you look cute."

And he did. He had on a blue button-down dress shirt, khaki slacks, and cordovan loafers. He'd even shaved for me.

Of course, getting him to put on nice clothes was almost as difficult as getting Sam to put on nice clothes. Benny had finally conceded that his standard attire—which was somewhere south of rock band roadie—clashed with our cover story: a married couple trying to decide which contractor to hire to add a family room and deck to our house.

My review of the building permits files at the Asbury Groves town hall yesterday had turned up two permits issued to Corundum Construction Company in Asbury Groves, both about three years ago. One was for the construction of a back porch and deck at 22 Dielman Way, which is where we were parked, and the other was for construction of a swimming pool and deck at 723 Noyes. The owners of 22 Dielman Way, according to the permit file, were Harold and Mary Carswold. The owners of the other home were Jeffrey and Cynthia Kirkland. Unfortunately, the telephone numbers for both were unlisted. Because I didn't feel comfortable asking Bertie Tomaso for another Moran-related favor, I came up with the married-couple-checking-out-contractors pretext.

My plan was to visit the two houses on my own. I would be the married woman with a husband too busy to join her. But when I told Benny my plan, he insisted on joining me.

"You think I'm letting you go there alone? No fucking way, girl. It's a goddam murder investigation."

"Benny, I'm not visiting a suspect's house. I'm just trying to get a lead on a possible suspect—or just the person who was with Nick Moran that night. We don't know it's a murder. We don't know anything. I'm just looking for some closure."

"You aren't going there alone. Period. Anyway, your lame-ass story will be a lot more believable if your husband is with you. No guy is going to spend a hundred grand on home improvements without checking out the contractor's work."

So it was settled. Benny would join me for the two house visits, and then we'd go back to my house, where my mother was cooking up a feast. He also came up with our married names: Nick and Nora Charles. Given his girth, Benny liked the reference to *The Thin Man*.

He opened the passenger door and gave me a wink. "Let's do it."

◇◇◇

A woman in her thirties opened the door. In the background were the sounds of a television cartoon—the boings, boinks and accompanying music—at high volume.

"Yes?"

She had the slightly-harried look of a mother with young children.

I gave her a sympathetic smile.

"We're so sorry to bother you, Mrs. Carswold. My name is—"

"—I'm not Mrs. Carswold. They don't live here anymore."

"Oh. I didn't realize—"

"—they moved about a year ago. We bought their home. I think they moved to Florida. That's what I've heard."

"I didn't know that."

"Do you need to contact them?"

"Actually, we were—" I paused and looked toward Benny with a wifely smile.

"We're not here to sell anything," he said to her in a reassuring voice. "And we're not missionaries. I promise. My wife and I are planning to build an addition to our house. One of the contractors we talked to did your addition. We tried to call to see if it was okay to come over and look at their work, but your number—or, actually, the Carswolds' number—wasn't in the phone book. But we happened to be in the neighborhood anyway, so we thought we'd drop by to see if anyone was home."

She smiled. "No problem. I'm Joanne Clark. Go around back. I'll meet you there and show you the deck and porch."

Corundum Construction Company did quality work. That was obvious the moment we reached the back. The redwood deck was on three levels and included a hot tub, a wet bar, hanging gardens, and a beautiful dining area. Joanne Clark showed us around the enormous enclosed porch, which featured a ceramic tiled floor, beautiful woodwork, heavy oak beams overhead, and a dramatic stone fireplace. Having been through my own renovation projects, I could tell this one had cost plenty.

"Have you met the contractor?" I asked.

"I don't even know who it was."

"Does Corundum Construction ring a bell?'

"No." She gave me a sheepish smile. "I'm sorry."

"They do nice work," I said. "Thanks for letting us see it."

"Oh, my pleasure."

"I'm sorry we weren't able to call in advance. If they moved to Florida, that explains why their telephone number wasn't listed anymore."

"Actually, I don't think they were listed even when they lived here. I remember our realtor had to give us their phone number. But you would have had just as much trouble reaching us."

"You're not listed either?"

"My husband is a doctor. A psychiatrist. Can you imagine the calls we'd get in the middle of the night if he was listed?"

"I understand," I said. "Was one of the Carswolds a doctor?"

"Worse. He was an alderman. Can you imagine the crazy calls those people must get?"

A gray-haired man in his late fifties opened the front door to 723 Noyes. He was stocky but fit, had a thin mustache, and wore a pair of reading glasses perched on this end of his nose. He was holding a section of the newspaper in his hand.

"Yes?"

"Mr. Kirkland?" Benny asked.

The man glanced at me and back at Benny. "Who are you?"

"Nick Charles, sir. And you are Jeffrey Kirkland?"

"I am. What do you want?"

"We would have called, Mr. Kirkland, but your number is unlisted. So we decided to drop by."

"Why?"

Benny gave him a friendly smile. "Corundum Construction, sir."

Kirkland's eyes narrowed. "What about them?"

"Your thoughts about their workmanship. What kind of people they were. Mainly, I suppose, whether you feel like you got your money's worth."

"What are you trying to imply, sir? I paid in full. With my own money." He looked at me. "Who is this woman?"

"She's my wife Nora, Mr. Kirkland."

He stared at us. "What's going on here?"

"We don't mean to disturb you, Mr. Kirkland. Nora and I are thinking of doing an addition to our house. One of the contractors we talked to is Corundum Construction. We wanted some references, and you were one of names they gave us. Apparently, they built you a pool and deck."

"You're dealing with Corundum Construction?"

"Not yet," Benny said. "We're trying to decide between them and two other companies."

"Who did you speak with at Corundum?" he asked.

Benny frowned and look at me. "Do you remember the name, Sweetie Poo?"

*Sweetie Poo?*

But I played along, pretending to try to remember.

"I'm not sure," I said. "I talked to so many contractors."

Benny turned to Kirkland. "Who was your contact person?"

The question seemed to catch him off balance. "I don't remember. It's been a long time."

"Were you happy with their work?"

"Yes. No complaints. I have to go. Good-bye."

He closed the door. There was the clunk of the deadbolt lock.

Benny turned to me. "What the hell was that all about?"

# Chapter Nineteen

On the way home from the office the following afternoon I stopped at the supermarket to pick up three items: a gallon of milk, a carton of eggs, and two pounds of apples. I ended up with six bags groceries, and had to run back to the dairy section for the eggs while I was checking out.

I pushed the shopping cart out to the parking lot, parked it alongside my minivan, and started transferring the grocery bags from the cart to the back of the van.

"Well, lookee here. The great and wondrous Rachel Gold—live and in person."

I turned to see Ken Rubenstein, his arms were crossed over his chest and his head was tilted, as if he were appraising a new car. Though it was overcast, he wore reflecting aviator sunglasses. He had on a black silk shirt and a tan suit. We stood at eye level to one another.

"Hello, Ken."

"And hello to you, Rachel." He grinned. "So?"

I put the last grocery bag into the back, pulled down the tailgate, and turned to face him. "So what?"

"Are we going to make love or make war?"

"Pardon?"

"Your lawsuit. We going to settle?"

"That's an issue for me to discuss with your attorney."

"He's not here. How about we cut out the middleman and get it done?"

"Can't do that."

I started pushing the cart across the traffic lane toward the cart rack. I paused and looked back.

"I'm a lawyer, and you have a lawyer. Under the rules of professional responsibility, I can only discuss your case with your lawyer."

"What if I'm a consenting adult?"

"Not to me. Only to *your* lawyer, and then he has to authorize me to talk to you."

"No problem."

I shoved the cart into the rack and started back to my minivan. He'd already flipped open his cell phone and was holding it against his ear.

I checked my watch. "I need to get home."

"Give me five minutes."

"In the parking lot?"

He held up his hand, palm toward me. "Hey, Crane, what's up?…Yeah?…Guess who I'm standing out here with?…Supermarket parking lot. Your beautiful adversary in our Cloverdale case…Yep, the one and only…Huh?…Chatting, dude. Just chatting…'Cause she won't talk to me. Says she can only talk to you about the case…Hey, Robby, there's nothing to worry about."

He raised his sunglasses and gave me a wink.

"I'm a big boy," he said into the phone. "Huh?…Listen, I'm not some illiterate beaner getting asked to sign away his personal injury claim for a case of Schlitz and a lottery ticket, okay?"

His features darkened as Crane said something to him.

"Zip it up, Rob. Listen carefully: I am the client. You are the lawyer. I have now listened to your advice and I have decided not to accept it. I want to talk to her. Make it happen…Sure, here she is."

He handed me the phone.

"Hello," I said.

"Rachel?"

"Correct."

"I understand you want to talk with my client."

"Actually, no. I'd prefer to go home. This is his idea."

"Fine," Crane said. "Here are my ground rules. Number one: whatever is discussed between the two of you is off the record and inadmissible. That means that it can never be used in any—"

"—Nope."

"What do you mean nope?"

"Nope, as in no deal. You want to let your client talk to me, fine. Tell me you consent, and I'll talk to him. If not, not. I couldn't care less. But no ground rules. Understand?"

"That's ridiculous."

I handed the phone back to Rubenstein.

"Your attorney says no. Good-bye."

I turned toward the car, trying to keep a straight face.

"Wait a second," he called to me. "Rob, what the hell is wrong with you? Huh? Bullshit. I instruct you to consent. You either consent or find yourself a new client. Understand?"

"Rachel," he said as I was opening the car door.

I turned. He was walking toward me and holding out the phone.

"Here."

I took it and held it to my ear.

"Yes?" I said.

"I consent. You can talk to my client."

"No ground rules?"

A pause. "No ground rules."

I handed the phone back to Rubenstein. He chuckled as he slipped it into the inside pocket of his suit jacket.

"Sometimes I think Tony Soprano had the right idea," he said.

"About what?"

"That line of his: 'First thing we do is kill all the lawyers.'"

"Actually, Dick the Butcher said it."

"The Butcher?" Rubenstein frowned. "He was in *The Sopranos*?"

"Henry the Sixth."

"That series on Showtime? The Tudors? That's Henry the Eighth, not the Sixth."

"What did you want to say to me?"

"Can we go somewhere first? Somewhere to talk?"

"We can talk here."

"In a supermarket parking lot? How 'bout a little privacy?"

"You want privacy, get in the van and we'll roll up the windows. They're tinted."

He got in on the passenger side and closed the door.

"You're a tough gal, Rachel Gold."

"I need to get home to make dinner. What is it?"

"Our case. Let's get it settled. Let's roll up our sleeves, get it done, and move on."

"I'm listening."

"I'm the one listening. Tell me what you want. What will it take to get this case settled?"

"Drop the project."

He laughed. "Come on. What do you really want?"

"For you to drop the project."

His smile became a frown. He shook his head.

"Not gonna happen. But I am prepared to do something I have never done before. When I instructed Crane to raise my settlement offer to fifteen percent above the appraised value, that was my final offer, as I'm sure he told you. I have never budged off a final offer. Never. You understand what never means?"

I gave him a weary look. "Yes, Ken."

"Today is a first for me. I am prepared to up my final offer."

"To what?"

"Work with me here, Rachel." He smiled. "I need a demand. I know how to budge off my final offer, but I don't know how to negotiate with myself."

"I made you an offer."

"I want a money offer."

"I may not have a money offer, Ken. I'll check with my clients."

"Let's get it done. Time's a wasting. How 'bout I call you tomorrow night?"

"I may not have an answer by then."

"I'll call the day after tomorrow."

"I have a better idea. How about when I have an answer I'll call your lawyer."

"Just call me."

"Ken, that's not how it works. You have a lawyer. Unless he wants to withdraw from representing you, I need to deal with him."

He laughed and shook his head. "All of a sudden you have scruples, eh?"

"What's that supposed to mean?"

He opened the car door.

"You know exactly what it means. When I want to talk directly with you, that's a—" he paused and used the first and second fingers of both hands to make air quotes "—violation of the sacred rules of professional responsibility. But when *you* want to talk directly to someone who *should* have a lawyer there, it's suddenly okay to sneak around."

"What are you talking about?"

He shook his head. "See you around, Counselor."

# Chapter Twenty

Benny paused, a forkful of stuffed jalapeño suspended between plate and mouth. He frowned. "What the fuck?"

"My thought exactly."

He put the forkful in his mouth and washed it down with a swallow of Dos Equis Ambar.

"And that's it?"

I nodded. "He got out of my car and left."

"You think that dickhead has you under surveillance?"

"Seems a stretch. More likely someone he knows happened to see me talking with someone else he knows."

The waitress arrived with my lunch—a chicken enchilada—and two more courses for Benny: a large beef burrito slathered in guacamole and green chili sauce and a bowl of posole soup with enough pork and hominy to feed a Mexican family. We were meeting for lunch on Cherokee Street at El Bravo, Benny's favorite Mexican restaurant. Whether he was there for lunch, dinner, or one of his between-meal "snacks," his order always included posole soup, which the staff at El Bravo's served to El Señor Benny in an extra large bowl.

He scarfed down the rest of his stuffed jalapeño, chased it with another gulp of Dos Equis Ambar, and used his other fist to partially smother a belch rumbling up from the depths of a digestive system that could go one-on-one with any metropolitan sewage treatment facility.

He leaned over the soup, inhaled, closed his eyes and sighed. "Heaven."

I shook my head in wonder. The only thing more remarkable than the size of his appetite was the size of his waist. Given the sheer volume of food that Benny shoveled down his gullet every day and his disdain for any form of physical exertion outside of the bedroom, he should have long since reached a poundage level measurable only by a truck weigh station. Instead his weight remained steady somewhere just north of two-fifty. While that still qualified as obese, his intake-to-girth ratio left you in awe of his metabolism.

"Have you ever seen him?" I asked.

"Rubenstein? Not in person. Maybe a photo in the newspaper. Why?"

"Something about him—he looks familiar, like I've seen him before."

"Ah." Benny grinned. "Another shitty high school date?"

"No. He's not from around here."

"You going to finally give him a settlement offer?"

"Muriel and Cletus are coming by the house tonight to talk." I shrugged. "We'll see whether they want me to make an offer."

"They'd be fools not to."

He paused to take a slurp of his soup and smother another belch.

"You're a great lawyer, Rachel, and by the term 'great' I include more than your tush and your legs. But let's face reality here, kiddo. The law on your TIF case sucks. Ultimately—either at trial or on appeal—that blight bastard is going to win, and that means when this crappy case is finally over, your clients' homes are history. Every last one of them."

"And your point is?"

"My point is that the trial and appeal process could take years. Time is money in the real estate development world. That prick will pay your clients a premium *today* to bulldoze their houses tomorrow."

"This case is not completely hopeless, Benny."

He set down his spoon. "Yes, Rachel, it is completely hopeless. Read my lips. Completely. Hopeless. In the shitter. The sooner you make your clients realize that, the better. Trust me on this, woman. Your clients are screwed. Totally screwed. Upside down, inside out, from the front and from the rear."

"Thank you, Dr. Pangloss."

"Hey." He shrugged and gave me a sad smile. "All is for the best in this best of all possible legal systems."

"Howdy, gang."

We looked up to see Jacki Brand approaching. She'd had a prior commitment for lunch but had promised to stop by afterward. She looked sharp in a gray three-button suit jacket and skirt with a black scoop-neck top beneath the jacket, and black sling-back pumps.

Jacki pulled up a chair and surveyed Benny's array of food—the plate with remnants of the stuffed jalapeño, the plate with remnants of the giant burrito, the half-empty bowl of posole.

"What's going on, Slim?" she asked. "You on a diet?"

"Just getting warmed up, hot stuff."

As if on cue, the waitress arrived with Benny's main course—a large platter of Carne Guisada, a hearty Mexican stew.

I watched Benny tuck into the stew.

"The boy has a capacity," I said to Jacki.

"Speaking of boys," she said to me, "how was the zoo?"

"It was so much fun."

Sam's class had a field trip to the zoo that morning and I went along as one of the parent volunteers.

"Even the snakes?" she asked.

"Yuck." I shuddered. "They give me the creeps."

Sam's class was doing a unit on reptiles, which was thus the focus of the field trip. We spent most of our time in the reptile house, where we met with one of the zookeepers and a pair of docents. The high point for the kids, and the low point for me, was when the docents took out a few reptiles for the kids to touch. I didn't mind the iguana, but as for the black snake—well, the best I can say is that if I'd been Eve, we'd all still be living in the Garden of Eden.

Benny said, "Did Rachel tell you about her charming encounter in the supermarket parking lot yesterday?"

"Yep." Jacki shook her head. "Guy knows no boundaries."

"Rachel thinks that final jab about sneaking around is just the result of a coincidence—that someone he knows happened to see her with someone else."

"Maybe, but that guy seems way too controlling for coincidences." Jacki turned to me. "Meanwhile, I found some more permits."

"Corundum?"

She nodded. "Five in all. Two from two years ago, two more from last year, and one that's barely a month old."

"One month," I said.

"My thought exactly," she said. "It's the first suburb over. I'm thinking we could drop by after lunch, maybe catch them at the work. Maybe spot that pickup and the big guy your witness claims he saw that night."

"Time out, ladies," Benny said. "I can't go after lunch. I'm teaching a seminar this afternoon."

"We'll be fine," Jacki said. "We're just going to do a little surveillance."

"But what if that big guy's there? What if he tries something?"

"We're not going to approach anyone on the site. And don't forget—" she paused and smiled. "—I was once a big guy, too. A helluva lot bigger than you."

"But—"

"—no buts," Jacki said. "And, frankly, in light of what you've eaten for lunch today, there is no way on earth I would spend any time this afternoon cooped up with you inside a car."

# Chapter Twenty-one

We stared at the Colonial house at No. 5 Berkeley Drive in the Town of Edgewood. The only indication of any planned construction was the red and white building permit taped to one of the pillars on the front porch. From our parking spot at the curb we were too far away to read the permit that, according to the permit information Jacki had obtained from the Edgewood City Hall, authorized construction of a new deck and family room at the back of the house. According to the permit, the house was owned by Brett and Lucinda Annis.

"Maybe they'll start next month," Jacki said.

I sighed in frustration, thinking of Nick's sister Susannah. "I guess."

"Let's see if anything's going on in Glenview Heights. It's not too far."

I checked my watch. "Sure."

Jacki had found two permits issued to Corundum Construction by the City of Glenview Heights, both about two years ago—the first for the build-out of a basement that included a movie theater, rec room, wet bar, exercise room, sauna, and bathroom, the second for construction of a backyard pool and deck.

Although no one was home at either house, we quickly confirmed that we were too late to see anyone from Corundum. At the first house, the listing information sheets in the plastic box attached to the For Sale sign on the front lawn featured "a new basement" with all of the amenities listed on the building permit. At the second house, we confirmed from the sidewalk that the backyard pool and deck were already in place.

There was a campaign sign on the front lawn of the second house, which, according to the building permit, was owned by Clyde and Elizabeth Bennett. The sign read RE-ELECT COUNCILMAN CLYDE BENNET, 3rd WARD.

"These guys must have political connections," I mused.

"What guys?"

"Corundum."

"Why do you say that?"

"This isn't the only city official's house they've done work on."

"Who else?"

"An alderman in Asbury Groves. Guy named Carswold."

"That could be good. Maybe it'll give you some leverage."

"How so?"

"They're public officials, Rachel. Think what that means. If you actually spot that big guy at some other Corundum construction site, you're still going need to find a way to get the cops involved, right? If one of these public officials finds out that he has someone working on his house who might be implicated in a death, he should be happy to get the police involved."

"Maybe."

"Hey, it's something."

I shrugged. "I hope you're right."

# Chapter Twenty-two

"Rachel?"

I was staring into the dark when my stepdaughter called my name. It took a moment for her voice to register.

I turned. She was standing in the doorway, silhouetted by the light in the hallway, her school backpack slung over her shoulder.

"Hi, sweetie," I said. "How was rehearsal?"

"Okay." She stepped into the den. "Why don't you have a light on?"

"I wandered in here after I took Yadi for his walk. I guess I forgot to turn it on."

"Forgot?"

She shrugged the backpack off her shoulder and let it drop onto the carpet. She came over to the sofa and sat on the arm.

"What's wrong?" she asked.

I've just been thinking about one of my lawsuits."

"That Brittany Woods case?"

"That's the one."

"What now?"

"I had a settlement meeting here with the clients tonight."

"How did that go?"

"They aren't willing to compromise. They see it as a matter of principle."

"That's a good thing, right?"

"Not always. They might lose their homes."

"You won't let that happen."

"There's only so much I can do. The law is tough."

She leaned over and kissed me on the forehead. "So are you."

I slipped my arm around her waist. "You're a sweetie, Sarah."

"Was Muriel here tonight?" Sarah asked.

"She was."

Sarah knew Muriel through my mother's Mahjong games, which had been taking place in my dining room on the first Wednesday of the month since Sarah was little.

I said, "She told me to tell you that she already had her ticket to the musical. She's coming to opening night with your bobba."

Sarah was playing the role of the Good Witch in her high school production of *The Wizard of Oz*.

I added, "I'll make sure they don't bring an air horn to the show."

She laughed. "Good."

After a moment, she asked, "So no settlement?"

"Probably not. They just don't want to move."

"What's Uncle Benny say?"

"That we're all crazy. He thinks we should take the money and run."

"Do you think he's right?"

"I hope not."

We sat in silence for a few moments, and then I hugged her against me.

"I love you," I said.

She put her arm around my shoulder. "I love you, too."

She kissed me on top of my head. "Good night, Rachel."

"Good night, Sweetie. I'll be up in a few minutes."

After she left, I sat in the dark.

Sometimes I wonder if my own mourning period will ever end, if I will always be the grieving widow. There are moments when my longing for Jonathan is so intense that it seems unbearable. But most of my sadness and compassion are focused on my son and two stepdaughters. It pains me to know that they will grow up without their father, that they will graduate and get married and have children and gather together on special family occasions—and always without their father. The ache I feel for my two stepdaughters is even more crushing, since they will graduate and get married and have children and gather on special occasions—and always without their father *and* without their mother.

I vowed to Jonathan when we got engaged—and then I vowed to him again on the morning of his funeral—that I would nurture and protect those two girls as if they were my own. I've kept my vow, but that doesn't help ease the sadness.

# Chapter Twenty-three

Benny pulled over to the curb and grinned.

"Well, well, well," he said.

He shifted into Park and turned toward me.

I nodded. "Bingo."

Up ahead on the right was 1825 Brandywine Drive—a modern Cape Cod style home with white siding, green shutters, and a red shingle roof with two dormers. The home of Barry and Susan Haven. According to the building permit that Jacki had located at the Brookfield City Hall, Corundum Construction Company was building an elaborate two-level cedar deck in the backyard that would include, among other things, a hot tub, several foliage cutouts, a wet bar, and a screened-in dining gazebo. According to the vehicles in front of the house and in the driveway, construction was underway.

There were two pickup trucks in the driveway—a late-model Toyota and a newer white Ford. Of more interest, though, was the enormous Dodge Ram 2500 parked along the street. It was dark blue and had a flatbed trailer hitched to the back.

Benny turned off the engine and pointed toward the Dodge.

"Is that it?"

"I'm checking."

I flipped through the file and found my notes on the pickup that my Gay Way witness had described. I checked the license plate number in my notes and then stared through the windshield at the Dodge pickup.

"I can't make it out. The trailer is in the way."

"So let's have a closer look. We're getting out anyway, right?"

"I guess so."

Benny opened his door and gave me a wink. "Showtime, Mrs. Charles."

It was mid-morning the day after our lunch at El Bravo's. Jacki and I had left from there to check out the houses with Corundum building permits in Edgewood and Glenview Heights. We'd gone back to the office after the Glenview Heights house because the remaining two permits Jacki had located were in Brookfield, a northern suburb and thus on the far opposite side of the city.

Both of the Brookfield permits had been issued about a year ago. When Benny found out I was planning to visit the sites this morning, he insisted on coming along.

Work on the first house in Brookfield—a two-story addition consisting of a family room below and an extra bedroom above—had not started. According to the permit, the owners were Jack and Mary Prince. Work on 1825 Brandywine had not only started but was still in progress. Better yet—at least according to Jacki's theory—the house was owned by a Brookfield city official: the names on the green mailbox near the foot of the driveway read ALDERMAN AND MRS. HAVEN.

We walked toward the house, pausing along the sidewalk near the back of the Dodge pickup.

"Well?" Benny asked.

I shook my head. "Different license plate."

"Maybe we'll find him back there anyway."

But we didn't.

There were five workmen in the backyard of the Haven's house—two short Hispanic men working on the gazebo, a black man of medium build working a backhoe, and two slender white guys, one in his twenties, the other in his forties.

The older white guy came over to us. He was about six feet tall with a sun-wrinkled face and squinty eyes. He wore a battered St. Louis Rams cap with a frayed brim, a blue short-sleeve work shirt over a white t-shirt, faded jeans and construction boots.

"Can I help you folks?"

He spoke with a rural drawl, out where they pronounce the last syllable of Missouri as "uh" instead of "ee." *Missouruh* .

"Nick Charles," Benny said, reaching out his hand.

The guy hesitated a moment, and then shook his hands. "Good to meet you, sir."

"And who might you be?" Benny asked. He said it with a bit of a twang I'd never heard before and that he'd surely not picked up coming of age in South Orange, New Jersey.

Another hesitation. "Charlie."

"Glad to meet you, Charlie. You the foreman on this here job?"

"I suppose so. At least I'm the one in charge. Is there some problem, sir?"

"None at all, my friend. We admire your handiwork. Mighty fine stuff. This here is my wife Nora. Nora, say hi to Charlie."

"Hello, Charlie."

He nodded and touched the rim of his cap. "Ma'am."

"The wife and I just bought a house in this area," Benny said. "It's got just about everything you could ask for in a house 'cept a deck. We heard y'all were building one for the Havens and thought we might just come over and check her out."

"Not much to see, yet. We're only about halfway through."

Benny shaded his eyes with his hand and glanced over at the work. "It's looking good."

"Thank you."

"You gotta card on you?" Benny asked.

"Card? What kind of card?"

"One of them business cards. Contact info, Charlie. Case we want to get a bid from y'all."

"No, I don't have a card."

"You guys are with Corundum, right?"

Charlie pursed his lips and then nodded. "Yes, sir."

"What's the best way to reach someone over there who can answer my questions? Who do I call, Charlie?"

Charlie scratched his chin. "I'm not exactly sure. We get involved after all the preliminaries, if you know what I mean."

"What preliminaries?"

"Technical stuff. Contracts, architecture drawings, permits, you name it. We don't come in 'til they're ready to break ground."

"Who's involved before that?" I asked.

He turned to me and frowned. "Ma'am?"

"You said you and your crew don't get involved until all the technical stuff is worked out. Who handles that stuff at your company? Would that be Mr. Corundum? Or someone else?"

"I'm not exactly sure, ma'am."

"If we wanted to talk with someone at Corundum about a deck," I said, "who should we contact?"

He pondered the question and finally said, "I'm not exactly sure, ma'am."

"Can you find out?" Benny asked. "We're talking about doing a big deck. Nice piece of change for your company. You might even get some credit for bringing in the business, if you know what I mean, Charlie."

"I suppose I could take your name and have someone give you a call."

"Just tell us who to call, Charlie," Benny said. "We can do the rest. I promise to mention your name."

"Let me check first. I don't know that we do any business off the street. I think it comes other ways."

"What other ways?" I asked.

He shrugged. "I don't rightly know, ma'am. But if you'll give me a name and phone number, I'll have someone get back to you."

"Is this the only crew?" Benny asked.

Charlie looked over at the men and then back at Benny. "We don't have a specific crew, sir. We hire what we need to get all the pending jobs done. Sometimes we have just one crew of men. Other times we might have two crews, or even three. All depends on the workload and the deadlines."

"Is there another crew out there now?" Benny asked.

"There might be. I don't exactly know."

Benny said, "But if we hired your company and wanted you to get started right away and your crew was already on this job, the company would still be able to get our job done, too, right?"

"I believe so, sir. But I'd have to confirm that. If you can give me a way to reach you, I can run it down and get back to you."

"You've been very kind, Charlie," Benny said. "Mrs. Charles and I will talk it over. If we decide we want a get a bid from your company, I'll drop by with some information for you. Okay?"

"That's fine, sir. Whatever you prefer."

"Good talking to you, Charlie."

"Same here. Have a good day." He turned to me and touched the rim of his cap. "And you, too, ma'am."

I smiled. "Thank you, Charlie."

# Chapter Twenty-four

We drove in silence for awhile.

"There's another big pickup truck out there," Benny said.

I gave him a curious look. "Out where?"

"Don't know where, but there's one somewhere out there with Corundum license plates."

"It may not be the only one. I'm going to see if Bertie Tomaso will run the plates on those three pickup trucks. I'm guessing at least one of them has Corundum plates as well."

"Meanwhile," Benny said, "we still have that other one out there. That could mean they have another crew on some other site. We find that site and we just might find your big guy."

"Assuming he is out there," I said, "it's not going to be easy to find him. Jacki and I have searched the files in twelve city halls to come up those five permits. There are close to a hundred other towns and villages in suburban St. Louis. Each one has its own city hall and its own zoning code and its own building permit requirements and its own building permit files. There's no central data base. That means you need to drive from city hall to city hall. It could take a month to search all those files, and by then the crew we just saw might have moved on to another site."

"That's all the more reason we need to get in contact with whoever's in charge of Corundum," Benny said. "Find out who the hell that big guy is. Speaking of which, what's up with that?"

"What's up with what?"

"That redneck out there at the job site. He wouldn't tell us shit about his company. Who's he think he works for? The goddam CIA?

"Speaking of rednecks, Benny, where do you come up that accent? Sounded like you were channeling Merle Haggard out there."

"I got mad skills, woman. They extend far beyond my legendary prowess in the sack."

"My hero."

"Meanwhile, what's up with Corundum? They're not building nuclear weapons for the government, for chrissake. They're building family rooms and fucking patios but we can't find any trace of them. Makes no sense."

"Maybe they don't market themselves to the public."

"That's nuts. Their customers *are* the public."

"Maybe not the whole public. Maybe they're a niche outfit. Maybe they're one of those operations that gets all its work from referrals. Like your root canal last year."

"Like my root canal? That's a helluva segue. Forgive me if I'm not following your line of reasoning here."

"Your dentist told you that you needed a root canal, right? He didn't send you off to find your own endodontist. He gave you a referral. Why? Because lots of endodontists don't advertise. They get their patients on referral."

"Yeah, but guys doing home improvement aren't like guys doing root canals. I think most of them advertise."

"I bet some work off referrals."

"From who?"

"Maybe from satisfied customers. Maybe from real estate agents. Maybe from homebuilders. Maybe from places like Home Depot. Look at what goes on in our profession. There are plenty of lawyers in this town—appellate lawyers, tax lawyers, other specialists—who get all their work on referrals from other lawyers."

"Maybe. But you gotta admit that redneck's behavior made you a little suspicious, eh?

"What makes me even more suspicious is why I can't find them in the phone book. I can understand building your business on referrals, but why have an unlisted number? Even so, we still have to take this one small step at a time. No jumping to conclusions."

"Why the hell not?"

"Because we still have no hard evidence that Nick's death was anything but an accidental overdose. Bertie Tomaso does this stuff for a living, Benny. He took a look at Nick's file and didn't find anything incriminating."

"Something's not right here."

"I agree."

We drove in silence until we reached my office in the Central West End.

"So what next?" Benny asked.

"I have a few things I want to run down."

"What kind of things?"

"Just some loose ends."

"But no home visits on your own, right?"

"Right."

"Promise?"

"I promise."

I leaned over and gave him a kiss on the cheek. "Thanks."

"My pleasure."

"Don't forget about dinner tomorrow."

"You kidding me? Your mom told me she's making stuffed cabbage and kasha. I've got that date circled in red on my calendar. I'm so psyched I may just paint my face and chest and bring along a recording of one of those let's-get-ready-to-rumble chants."

I smiled. "There's an image."

"Don't mock me, woman. No act of homage is too much when we're talking about your mom's stuffed cabbage."

# Chapter Twenty-five

"It is a lovely home," she said.

"It sure did look lovely from the outside," I said.

"When would you like to see it?"

"I'll have to check my husband's calendar. He travels so much, Ms. Crowe."

"Please call me Melissa."

I was on the phone with the real estate agent for the home at 23 Del Ray Avenue in Glenview Heights. That was the home Jacki and I had visited with the For Sale sign on the front lawn. No one had been home that afternoon, but I'd taken one of the information sheets out of the plastic box in front of the sign. The sheet identified Melissa Crowe of Coldwell Banker as the listing agent

I studied the sheet. "I do have some questions, Melissa."

"Certainly. Fire away."

I asked her a few innocuous ones about the age of the furnace, the arrangement of the second floor bathrooms, the fixtures in the guest bathroom on the first floor.

She was a good agent. She had detailed answers to each of my questions, usually with a few extra tidbits, such as which of the upstairs bathrooms had been renovated and when and how.

"Let me ask you about the finished basement," I said. "I read the description twice. It sounds pretty amazing."

"It is totally fabulous. You have to see it to believe it. There's a movie theater that can seat twenty with a soda dispenser and one of those popcorn poppers like you see in a real theater. There's a workout room you'd swear was a mini-health club. All top-of-the-line Nautilus equipment—an elliptical, a treadmill, a stationary bike, weight machines—plus a flat screen TV and an amazing sound system. If you like to work out, you will totally love that room."

"When was the basement done?"

"Barely a year ago. Almost all of the equipment is still under warranty."

"Who did the work?"

"Let me check the file. I'm sure it's in there. This'll take just a minute."

I could hear the sound of her setting the phone on her desk and rustling of papers.

"Ah, here we are. It says the basement work was done by the Corundum Construction Company."

"Corundum?"

"That's what it says."

"I'm not familiar with them. Are you?"

"I think I've heard that name," she said.

"Do you know anything about them?"

"Actually, no. But that doesn't mean much. In my line of work, you're more familiar with the homebuilders. The remodelers—well, there are lots and lots of them. It's hard to keep track."

"Is there a warranty on their work?"

Another pause as she looked through the paperwork. "It doesn't say one way or the other—or at least I can't find anything about warranties. But I'm sure they're a reputable company."

"I could call them myself. Do you have a phone number there?"

"Not in the file."

"I have a phone book here. Let me see." My voice trailed off as if I were actually looking through a phone book. "That's odd. There's no listing. Are they local?"

"I'll find their number, Mrs. Charles. Tell me the best way to reach you and I'll call you with the number."

"I'll have to call you," I said. "My cell phone is on the fritz. Should I call back later today?"

"How about in the morning? That way I'll be sure to have the information. Everything will be fine. Those O'Sheas were fine, upstanding people."

"O'Sheas?" I asked. "Who are they?"

I already know the name, of course. The building permit listed the owners of 23 Del Ray Avenue as Walter and Elizabeth O'Shea.

"The sellers," she said. "Dr. and Mrs. O'Shea. He's a dentist, I believe. Or maybe an orthodontist. Something with teeth. As for Mrs. O'Shea, I don't know if she had a job during the day, but she was a very respectable member of the community."

"Really? How so?"

"She was on the city council."

My second call that morning was to Paul Rogers.

In his late sixties now, Paul Rogers remains one of the top municipal lawyers in Missouri. A former president of both the Missouri Municipal Lawyers Association and the St. Louis County Municipal League, his roster of clients includes several suburban St. Louis towns. For many of those entities, he serves as City Attorney. I'd become friendly with him a few years back while working on a zoning matter involving a city he represented. Although we'd been on opposite sides, it was virtually impossible to spend time with Paul and not become friendly.

"How is that TIF case coming along, Rachel?"

I had consulted with Paul before filing my Frankenstein lawsuit. He'd counseled me against filing it, warning that I'd be fighting a losing battle and would likely end up with a dismissal order and frustrated clients.

I sighed. "Not so great."

"Oh, dear. I am sorry to hear that. Who is it before?"

"Judge Flinch."

"I am surprised your opponents didn't take a change of judge."

"Actually, they did. That's how we ended up before Flinch."

"I see. And you elected not to a change, eh?"

"You were the one who told me I had bad facts and bad law."

He chuckled. "You may have made an astute decision, Rachel. Perhaps under the circumstances the best possible judge for your clients is Howard Flinch."

"To quote my late father, Paul, from your lips to God's ears."

Another chuckle.

"But," I said, "I'm calling you about something different. I'll treat you to lunch if you can help."

"Lunch with you is treat enough, Rachel. I'm happy to help."

"I'm trying to find out some information about a contractor. A small company that does home improvements."

"Which company?"

"Corundum Construction."

"Corundum? Hmmm. It doesn't ring a bell."

"I didn't think it would, unless one of your cities had a building permit dispute with them."

"I do not recall any such disputes. Where are they located?"

"That's the problem," I said. "I can't find out anything about them. No listings in the phone book or in any other directory. Nevertheless, we found several building permits issued to them, including two in Glenview Heights. You're the City Attorney there, aren't you?"

"I am, but permits tend to get issued as a matter of course by the city's department of public works. They do not contact me unless there is a dispute."

"That's what I assumed. The reason I'm calling is that I may have found a pattern with the type of people hiring Corundum. At least half—and maybe more—of the houses that Corundum worked on are owned by city officials."

"Really?"

"Both of the houses in Glenview Heights are owned—or were owned—by city council members."

"Which council members?"

"Clyde Bennett and Elizabeth O'Shea."

"That's interesting. And there are others?"

"Yes."

I gave him the other names and permits we'd found.

I could hear Paul taking notes.

I said, "So one possible reason that Corundum doesn't advertise is because it gets lots of business from referrals from aldermen and other city officials."

"You would like me to approach one or more of these folks regarding Corundum?"

"If you wouldn't mind."

"Why are you so interested in this company?"

"I'm investigating a matter for another client. Nothing to do with my TIF case. I have a witness who saw something suspicious involving a man in a vehicle. I ran a trace on the license plate and came up with Corundum Construction. But I can't locate them."

"Is this an automobile accident case?"

"No. It might be much worse than that, but the less you know about it the better. I'm just trying to find how to contact them."

"You have me intrigued, Rachel."

"I'll tell you more at lunch."

"You have a deal. I shall go find my old fedora, brush up on my Humphrey Bogart impression, and get right on it."

"Thank you, Mr. Spade."

"You are quite welcome, Effie."

# Chapter Twenty-six

I pushed the intercom button.

"Yes?"

"You have a visitor," my secretary said.

"Who is it?"

"Ken Rubenstein."

I stared at the speakerphone.

"You can let him come back," I said.

A moment later, Ken Rubenstein appeared in my doorway.

"Good afternoon, Counselor."

I gazed at him.

He grinned back. He was dressed today in a navy blazer, beige pleated slacks, and crisp blue dress shirt unbuttoned at the neck.

"Where's your lawyer?" I asked.

"Don't know. Haven't talked to him today. But don't fret."

He stepped toward my desk, reached into his blazer, and removed a folded sheet of paper.

"Here." He handed it to me. "This should take care of your concerns."

It was a sheet of stationary with the letterhead of Rob Crane's law firm:

Dear Ms. Gold:

In accordance with Rule 4.2 of the Missouri Rules of Professional Conduct, I hereby consent to direct settlement communications between you and my client,

Ruby Productions, Inc., including its Chairman and
CEO Kenneth C. Rubenstein.

Sincerely,

*Robert Crane*

Robert L. Crane II

I looked up from the letter and gestured toward one of the
chairs facing my desk. Rubenstein took a seat, tilted back in the
chair, crossed his arms and smiled.

"Well?" he said.

"Well what?"

"Where's my settlement demand? I told you I was willing to
go above the fifteen percent premium I've already offered your
clients. I also told you time was a wasting. You promised to talk
to your clients. I assume you have by now."

"I have."

He rubbed his goatee with his thumb and forefinger.

"And?" he said.

"Our original demand is still our first choice."

"That's the one where I walk from the project?"

"Correct."

"But now you have a second choice, eh?"

I nodded.

"What is it?"

I opened my briefcase, removed an unsealed legal-sized
manila envelope, and slid it across the table to him. "It's in there."

Inside were two sheets of blueprint paper. The first was a
copy of the aerial view of his proposed redevelopment plan
showing the location of the homes and the various amenities in
the proposed Brittany Manors. He flipped to the second page
and studied it. He looked up at me with frown.

"What is this?"

"One of my clients has a brother who's an architect. That
second drawing is based on his calculations. There are 201
homes in Brittany Woods. You can apparently fit four modest
townhouse units onto each of those home plots. That means you

can tear down all 201 homes and replace them with townhouses on just one-fourth the space. So instead of paying my clients thirty million dollars, you can use that money to build them new residences."

"Build them where?"

I pointed at the blueprint. "Right there. Your plans show ninety homes. Under our proposal, you'd still have room for sixty."

He gave me an incredulous laugh. "That's a settlement proposal? I drop thirty homes from my project and replace them with two hundred little townhouses? On my property?"

"It's *their* property now, Ken. All of it. They're willing to give you three-quarters of it as part of this deal."

He looked at the blueprint and shook his head. "You call that a compromise?"

"Absolutely. My clients love their neighborhood, their location, and their school system. This is a way they can keep their neighborhood, their location, and their school system while you still make a ton of money."

His face was flushed. He tossed the plans on my desk and shook his head. "This is a joke. A complete joke."

"I take that as a no."

"Take it as hell no."

"Then this meeting is over. Please leave."

He stood, his face flushed. "They're fools. They could have made a killing here."

"They're not looking to make a killing. They're just looking to keep their neighborhood."

"That's never been an option."

"Wrong. It's always been an option. And it'll be a reality if we win the lawsuit."

"Win the lawsuit?" He snorted. "You're as crazy as your clients."

"We're done here. Good-bye."

He started toward the door, shaking his head. "Unbelievable."

He paused and turned back to me. "You are going to regret this day, lady. You and your knucklehead clients. For the rest of your lives." He pointed a finger at me. "This is war. World War Three."

After he left, I gazed at the empty doorway for a long time.

# Chapter Twenty-seven

I stepped through the entrance to Woofie's and smiled at the sight of Paul Rogers, who was seated on a stool facing the door. It was a bit like stepping into a dimly-lit roadhouse bar and realizing that the gal standing by the jukebox sipping from a longneck Bud and swaying to the beat of Hank Williams' "Lovesick Blues" is Margaret Thatcher.

I shook my head. "Hard to believe."

Paul had his back to the counter that ran along the side wall in the tiny dining area. He smiled.

"What's not to believe?"

"I made us reservations at Acero. When your secretary told me you'd meet me instead at Woofie's, I thought I misheard her. When I promised to buy you lunch, Paul, I meant a fancy lunch. Not hot dogs."

"Ah, but these are no ordinary hot dogs, Rachel." He gestured toward the Vienna Beef poster on the wall.

"I agree. I love this place. But still."

He waved his hand dismissively. "I've had enough fancy lunches to last two lifetimes. This is far more fun. As I recall, you got your professional start in Chicago. I was hoping that you'd been in the Windy City long enough to learn the joys of the Chicago hot dog."

"Are you kidding? I lived there long enough to get in fights over who had the best dogs."

"And your favorite?"

"Wieners Circle."

"On North Clark. A fine establishment. But my personal shrine is a bit further north. I went to college at Loyola."

I tried to recall the Rogers Park eateries. "Flukys?"

"Yes. Did you know that the founder of Woofie's trained at Fluky's."

"Really?"

"A fine gentlemen named Charlie Eisner. May he rest in peace." He gestured toward the front counter. "Shall we place our orders?"

I smiled as I watched the dean of Missouri municipal lawyers and the current chair of the American Bar Association's Committee on Land Use Planning study the menu on the wall and then order a Big Daddy with extra grilled onions, chili cheese fries and a lemonade. I opted for pure Chicago—a Woofie dog with mustard, neon-green relish, and sport peppers, an order of fries, and a Coke.

We took our trays of food over to a pair of stools along the side wall counter just beneath framed signed photographs of Bill Cosby and Bob Costas.

I raised my cup of Coke toward Paul.

"Bon appetit."

He rubbed his hands together in anticipation as he eyed his meal. "Oh, boy."

Paul Rogers is so mild-mannered, good-natured and unpretentious that he could pass for the bald older brother of the late Fred Rogers of PBS fame, right down to the cardigan sweater and blue sneakers he favors when, as today, he does not have to appear in court or before one of his boards of alderman or city councils.

We ate our meals with relish—Paul figuratively, me literally.

"Another lemonade?" I asked.

"Oh, I am quite full. But thank you, Rachel. That meal was delicious."

"You're a cheap date."

"I am afraid that today I am overpriced even at Woofie's rates." He sighed. "I do not have much information to report."

"Tell me."

"I was able to reach most of the aldermen and city council members you found listed on those building permits. I spoke with Clyde Bennett and Elizabeth O'Shea in Glenview Heights. Barry Haven in Brookfield. Jeffrey Kirkland in Asbury Groves. I even spoke with the mayor and the city attorney for Asbury Groves."

"And?"

"Not much. The mayor had never heard of Corundum. Nor had the city attorney. The city officials who had had Corundum do work on their homes were hardly any better."

"What do you mean?"

"They had virtually no information on the company."

"Really?"

He nodded. "I told each of them I was helping a family member select a contractor for an addition to her house. I explained that someone had mentioned that Corundum had done work on their house. Each one told me he or she was pleased with the work and had no complaints, but when I asked how to get in touch with the company, they simply did not know. When I asked them who their company contact had been, they claimed they did not remember. When I asked if they could check their records, they gave me vague answers about having to locate the files and getting back to me if they could find any contact information. No one has gotten back to me."

"This is maddening."

"And a little fishy. Tell me more about this witness you mentioned."

"This is confidential, Paul."

"I understand."

"A man died of an apparent drug overdose. That's what the police concluded. His sister doesn't believe it. She asked me to look into his death. I did some poking around. I found a witness who can connect another man and a pickup truck to the dead man."

"Connect in what way?"

"Just that they were together in the dead man's truck on the night the man died. The other man left him in the truck and drove off in another pickup truck. I have the license plate of that truck. Turns out it's registered to Corundum."

Paul tugged at his earlobe pensively. "That doesn't mean that other gentlemen committed any crimes."

"True, but it does mean that he was with the dead man shortly before he died. If nothing else, he knows something about the dead man's last night."

"I am so sorry. I wish I could have found you something."

"I appreciate your effort."

"What will you do?"

"Keep looking."

"How?"

"I found one pickup truck at a Corundum job site, but it had a different license plate. That suggests there might be another crew out there. I'll do some more digging for building permits."

"Good luck."

I smiled. "Thanks."

"Speaking of luck, how is that TIF case going with Ruby Productions?"

I shrugged. "It's going."

"Any settlement prospects?"

"Not really. My clients don't want to move."

"Even if they were willing to move—" he shook his head "—Ken Rubenstein is one tough cookie."

"Actually, Rubenstein claims he wants to settle."

"Really?"

"He's even offered a nice premium over the appraised value of their homes."

Paul leaned back on the stool, his eyebrows raised. "Rachel Gold, I am impressed. I knew you were good, but I had no idea."

"You're too kind, Paul. Any credit here goes to Judge Flinch. I'm guessing they're willing to pay a premium to avoid a spin on the Judge Flinch Wheel of Fortune."

He chuckled. "You are too modest, Rachel. I was involved in the TIF dispute with Ruby Productions in Glenview Heights. That was a hotly contested litigation as well. The City Council approved that TIF by just one vote—four to three."

"Which one was that?"

"Wycliffe Palisades. Several of the neighborhood residents filed a lawsuit to stop the project. I represented the city, so we were on the same side as Rubenstein. I was able to watch him and his lawyer Rob Crane up close in court, and those are two sturdy warriors. They refused to make a settlement overture to the homeowners. I know that for a fact because I tried to mediate the dispute."

"How did that case come out?"

"The homeowners surrendered on the second day of trial. The resulting settlement agreement paid the homeowners exactly one percent over the appraised values of their homes."

"That is tough."

Paul asked, "What kind of premium has he offered your clients?"

"Fifteen percent, and he claims he's willing to go higher."

He raised his eyebrows. "My goodness."

"I know, Paul. It's a good offer. But my clients love their neighborhood and love their school system."

"They may lose both." He gave me a sympathetic smile. "The TIF law is a tough one to overcome."

"The case is giving me ulcers."

# Chapter Twenty-eight

I stared, my heart racing, unsure of what to do next.

A black Dodge Ram 2500 was in the driveway. The license plate matched the one my Gay Way witness had written down the night Nick Moran died.

*The* pickup truck.

Parked in the driveway of 359 Dorantes Avenue.

*Now what?*

I'd driven out to Amity, a far western suburb, with expectations so low that it would have been a stretch to call them expectations. Paul Rogers had given me a list of eleven suburban towns whose searchable electronic databases included building permit information. My secretary Dorian spent yesterday afternoon on the phone with a series of reluctant city clerks, one from each of the towns, trying to cajole them into searching their data bases. Six clerks relented, and one of them—from the Town of Amity—turned up two building permits issued to Corundum Construction, both within the past six months.

When Dorian marched into my office with a big smile and a MapQuest printout of driving directions to the two houses, I had to pretend to share her excitement. Having already been through the drill with the other Corundum building permits, it was hard to be enthusiastic about the prospect of a ninety-minute roundtrip to the edge of the boonies for the opportunity to drive past two houses on which renovations had not yet commenced

Nevertheless, I rearranged my calendar for the following day and, at three that afternoon, left the office with the MapQuest printout sitting on the passenger seat. I got off Highway 70 somewhere beyond the Missouri River and followed the map along streets and avenues I'd never before driven through a suburban town founded a decade ago on the promise of pastoral vistas for blithe spirits and which had morphed into strip-mall congestion for weary commuters.

At five minutes to four that afternoon, I drove slowly past the redbrick contemporary ranch house at 525 Chouteau Lane, pausing long enough at the edge of the property line to confirm that the in-ground swimming pool and patio listed on the building permit had not yet been installed. I sighed in exasperation and returned to the driving directions.

I turned right on Edgewood, left on Mapleleaf, left again on Bonhomme, and then right onto Dorantes. And there—parked in the driveway of 359 Dorantes—was the black Dodge pickup I'd been looking for. I braked to a stop and stared at the truck.

Then I drove around the block as I tried to figure out what to do next. I eliminated any thought of actually getting out of my car and going around back to the jobsite to see whether the big guy was there—in part because I didn't know what to say to him if he was there and in part because, well, the concept was a little scary, especially if the big guy was culpable in any of the events leading to Nick Moran's death.

As I drove around the block at about ten miles per hour I recalled that my digital camera was in the trunk, where I'd left it after Sam's last basketball game. I wasn't exactly sure what I could do with it, but I stopped the car just before the Dorantes intersection, popped the trunk, retrieved the camera, and turned onto Dorantes.

There were three other pickups, all older models, parked in front of the house. I pulled my car against the curb across the street one house up from No. 359. That gave me a good view of the house and the black pickup in the driveway.

*Okay, Miss Marple*, I said to myself, *now what?*

I checked my watch. 4:16 p.m.

I took my camera out of the case and framed a shot of the black pickup in the driveway with the address visible on the mailbox in the foreground. I took the shot. I zoomed in on the back of the pickup, close enough to make the license plate legible. I took the shot.

I checked my watch. 4:18 p.m.

I took a shot of each of the other pickups. Because of the angles, the only visible license plate was on the back of the pickup closest to me.

According to the permit, Corundum was building an enclosed back porch and an elaborate redwood deck. I rolled down the window and heard what sounded vaguely like construction noises.

At 4:24 p.m., a short, stocky black man in overalls and work boots came around from the back, got in the middle pickup of the three on the street and drove off. I took a photo of him as he opened the driver's side door and a close-up shot of the back of his truck as he pulled away from the curb.

At 4:29 p.m., my cell phone rang. I looked at the caller ID. My secretary.

"Dorian?"

"Sorry to bother you, Rachel, but that attorney for Ruby Productions—Rob Crane—he's called twice. He says he needs to talk to you. He says it's very important."

"Is he calling about the depositions?"

Yesterday I'd served on Crane notices to take the depositions of eight of Ken Rubenstein's underlings, two a day beginning the following Monday morning. Given Rubenstein's litigation threat at the end of our last meeting, I had decided to launch the first missiles. I assumed Rob Crane was calling to announce the litigation equivalent of the Normandy Invasion.

"He didn't mention depositions. He didn't mention any reason. He just said he needed to talk to you. He asked me to tell you to call him. He said it's important."

"Okay."

"Do you need his number?"

"I'm sure it's in my BlackBerry."

Just then a pair of Hispanic guys came around from the back.

"Gotta go, Dorian. Thanks."

They were heading toward the pickup closest to me. I put down the phone, grabbed my camera, and snapped a hurried shot of one of them climbing into the driver's side. I took another one, better framed, of the back of the truck as it pulled away.

I checked my watch. 4:33 p.m.

I looked up to see a tall, lanky black man in jeans and a t-shirt stride toward the last pickup on the street. He was unhooking a tool belt. I took a photo of him as he slung the tool belt into the bed of the truck, and I took another one of the back of the truck as he pulled away.

I glanced over at the pickup in the driveway and then toward the back area where all of the other men had emerged. Nothing.

My cell phone rang. The caller ID showed ROBERT CRANE.

I looked out toward the truck and back down at the phone—irritated that he'd called me on my cell phone, then recalling that my cell phone number was listed on my letterhead along with the office phone.

I clicked the Answer button.

"Yes?"

"Rachel? Rob Crane."

"What is it, Rob?"

"I need to talk to you."

"Go ahead."

"Not over the phone. In person."

"Why in person?"

"I'll explain it then."

"Is this about the deposition?"

"I'd rather talk to you in person."

"If you have a minor scheduling problem, fine. Otherwise, I'm not budging. You have any other problems with the depositions, file a motion. I'll see you in court."

"Wait."

"What?"

"I'm not calling about the depositions, Rachel."

"Then what do you want?"

"I have to tell you in person. You free for a drink after work?

"No."

"How about lunch tomorrow? You're in the Central West End. I can meet you at Herbie's."

I frowned in disbelief.

"You want to do this over lunch?"

"Why not? I think you're going to like what I have to tell you."

I clicked over to the calendar screen on my BlackBerry. I had no lunch plans for tomorrow.

"I'm out of the office now," I said. "I'll have to check my calendar in the morning."

"Fair enough. Meanwhile, I'll have my secretary make reservations for noon. If I don't hear from you in the morning, I'll assume we're on for lunch."

A man came out from around the back of the house. He was a white guy in his forties—average height, powerful build, close-trimmed beard, smoking a cigarette. He wore jeans, a short-sleeve Hawaiian-print shirt, construction boots, and a faded St. Louis Blues hat.

"Rachel?" Crane said.

"That's fine, Rob. I'll call you in the morning if there's a problem. I have to go."

I clicked the disconnect button, set the BlackBerry on the passenger seat and picked up the camera. The guy was already in the pickup by then. I tried zooming in on the truck cab, but the angle was bad and the glare off the passenger window distorted what little of his profile was visible.

He appeared to be talking on a cell phone. I waited, glancing from the pickup toward the rear area of the house, hoping to see some large white bald guy emerge from back there.

Five minutes passed. No one else joined him. He started the engine and backed out of the driveway. Still not sure what I was doing, I started my engine. I waited until he turned the corner and then pulled away from the curb in the same direction. I stayed a block back as we wended our way out of the subdivision and back toward Highway 70.

I checked my watch as we approached the highway entrance. 5:20 p.m.

My mother had her mahjong tonight, which included dinner with her girlfriends as well. That meant I needed to get home to make dinner for Sam and Sarah.

He had on his left turn signal, which meant he was getting on the highway heading west—the opposite direction that I needed to go. He slowed the pickup to get behind the long line of vehicles in the left lane. As I passed him on the right, I glanced over. The cab was too high to see anything but the top of his hat.

# Chapter Twenty-nine

Lunch with Rob Crane.

Our first meal together since our one date back in high school. That meal—dinner—had also been here, back when it was Café Balaban, although I doubt that Rob Crane remembered that connection when he had his secretary make the lunch reservation. Judging from the reaction of the attractive young hostess at the front desk—"Oh, Mr. Crane, good afternoon to you, sir!"—Rob was a frequent guest.

Our first meal here, more than two decades ago, had started awkwardly—and, as the night wore on, grew increasingly uncomfortable.

This one—well, the only word that came to mind was weird.

Our only interaction since high school had been as increasingly hostile adversaries in the Ruby Productions TIF case. While I'd occasionally fantasized about breaking his neck, I'd never fantasized about breaking bread with him. In light of the depositions of his witnesses that I'd scheduled for next week, which would no doubt trigger notices for the depositions of half of the Brittany Woods neighborhood during the following weeks, I was having trouble figuring out why we were seated in these elegant surroundings—me with an asparagus omelet with Gruyère cheese and a glass of chenin blanc, he with a hanger steak, fries, and a pale ale—talking about the current exhibit at the Contemporary Art Museum.

He was on the museum board, and clearly proud of that fact. Fortunately, I happened to have seen the current exhibit—a series of Maya Lin landscapes. I had dragged my stepdaughter Sarah with me for an hour of forced culture after we'd gone shopping for shoes last weekend. Thus I could make semi-intelligent comments about the exhibit.

All well and good, I supposed, except—I kept wondering— why were we having lunch? And why did he choose the Contemporary Art Museum as our topic of conversation?

For one creepy moment I thought this might be a date. According to the gossip columns, he was single again, having recently divorced his second wife.

But he wasn't in date mode. There was nothing flirtatious or playful about his words or mannerisms. Instead, he appeared to be doing the power lunch equivalent of throwing warm-up pitches on the sidelines. At some point soon, he'd be ready to take the mound. But, to continue the metaphor, I was growing impatient in the batter's box.

"Speaking of Maya Lin," I said, "let's stop speaking of Maya Lin."

He gave me a quizzical look. "Pardon?"

"Enough about landscapes. Let's talk about why you asked me to lunch. This is our first meeting outside of a courtroom or a conference room. Given that we have eight depositions scheduled for next week, I suspect you asked me here today to discuss something other than Maya Lin's latest work."

He smiled. "This is actually our second meeting outside of a courtroom or conference room, although it's been more than twenty years since the first time."

"Same restaurant, though."

"You remembered, eh?"

I nodded. "As did you."

He smiled. "I think this one will end better."

"Oh? For whom?"

"You and your clients."

"Does that mean you have a new settlement offer?"

"Yes." He took a sip of beer. "To paraphrase Don Corleone, I have an offer you can't refuse."

"Try me."

"How does a walkaway sound?"

"A walkaway from what?"

"From the redevelopment project."

I frowned. "Are you telling me that your client is offering to drop his redevelopment plans?"

"He is."

"Entirely?"

Crane nodded.

I stared at him, trying to make sense out of what I'd just heard. "What's going on here, Rob?"

He shrugged. "It's a business decision. Dollars and cents. Ken Rubenstein has decided to move on. He has other pending deals, and he believes some of those projects will be more lucrative than the Brittany Woods deal."

"So what's the catch?"

"What do you mean?"

"Rob, your client stood in my office last week and told me he was declaring World War Three. Now he's giving up? That doesn't sound like your client to me."

Rob leaned back in his chair and contemplated his answer.

"Ken is a complex man, Rachel. He can be hotheaded at times, but at heart he's a rational bottom-line businessman. Here he's made what he believes is a prudent financial decision, and he's decided to move on."

"So what are the settlement terms? What does he want from my clients?"

"Not a thing beyond dismissal of their lawsuit. The only person he wants anything from is you."

"What can I give him?"

"A clean break."

# Chapter Thirty

"A clean break?" Benny repeated. "What the fuck is that?"

"My question as well—although I phrased it slightly different to him."

I'd been filling Benny in on my lunch meeting with Rob Crane. We were seated at my kitchen table, just the two of us. Benny had come over for dinner with Sam and my stepdaughter Sarah. My mother was out on a date.

I'd put Sam to bed while Benny and Sarah washed the dishes. Sarah was up in her room now working on her paper on *Macbeth*. Benny had apparently given her some topic suggestions while I was putting Sam to bed, which meant I'd need to review her paper before she handed it in. Benny's take on Shakespeare—like his take on most things—tended to be as eccentric as it was brilliant. Sarah's A.P. English teacher was neither.

"So what did he say?" Benny asked.

"He said his client didn't want to have to deal with me again."

"He won't anyway. Once you dismiss the case, it's fucking history."

"He meant never having to deal with me *ever* again in the future."

"As in some other lawsuit?"

"Apparently."

"Damn, girl. That boy must have decided you had him by the short hairs."

He held his fist out in front for me to tap.

I rolled my eyes.

"Come on," he said, grinning.

"Benny."

I tapped his fist with mine.

"Never again, eh?" Benny leaned back in his chair. "Is that even legal? Can a lawyer agree in advance not to represent an unidentified future client on a specific type of case?"

"Probably not, but we never got that far. I told him I had no current interest in suing his client again, but that I couldn't rule it out in advance—just as his client wouldn't rule out some future deal involving Brittany Woods or some other subdivision in the city."

"Sounds reasonable."

"I thought so. But he kept pushing it. He said he wanted me to turn over all my files on the case."

"And you said?"

"I said no. I told him I couldn't. I told him the obvious, namely, that there were attorney-client communications and other privileged documents in those files. I couldn't give him those documents without my clients' permission, and I wasn't going to ask for that permission because I didn't see any reason to. So then he proposed that I destroy the documents and any electronic copies on my computer and give him an affidavit certifying that I'd destroyed them."

"That's crazy."

"And irresponsible. I've never destroyed a client's file, and, I reminded him, neither has he. And the reason is obvious: what if something unexpected comes up a year or so down the road and the key document is in the client's file?"

"So did you guys work something out?"

"Sort of. I told him I would be willing to state in the settlement agreement that I was not currently representing any other party adverse to his client and that I have no present intent to do so."

"Jeez," Benny said, grinning. "You got Rubenstein so rattled he wants Rachel Gold insurance. Not bad."

"Maybe." I frowned. "The result is wonderful for my clients, but the reason doesn't make sense. Rubenstein goes from all out war to total surrender in a matter of days? Because he suddenly decided he could make money on another TIF deal?"

"Maybe he was nervous about one of those witnesses you were going to depose."

"So he drops the entire project?"

"Could be nothing more than the old time-is-money thing. He's a real estate developer. They're like hookers looking for johns with money, except their johns are cities with TIF funds and tax breaks and other forms of corporate welfare. He probably found a new one with a fatter wallet, and now he wants to make sure you don't fuck up that deal by suing him again."

"More coffee?"

"I'm good."

I refilled my cup.

"Meanwhile," I said, "my clients are in heaven."

"I bet they are.

"I called Muriel right after my lunch with Crane. She was so excited she started crying on the phone. Crane said he would send me a draft of the settlement papers by tomorrow afternoon. I told Muriel to set up a meeting with the steering committee tomorrow tonight so we can go over the settlement terms and get the papers finalized."

"This'll be a load off your mind."

"This case has been driving me crazy."

He winked. "Dr. Frankenstein bids farewell to her monster."

I smiled. "I can't wait."

"Meanwhile, what's the deal with your little jaunt out to Amity yesterday? On your own? All of a sudden you're Dirty Harry?"

"I never got out of the car, Benny. But it was definitely worth it. I was able to ID that pickup truck. I even took some pictures of it. Same license plate. No question. Same truck."

"But not the same guy."

"True, but I'm getting warm."

"Just don't get burnt."

"Don't be such a worrywart. I'm a big girl."

"I believe 'girl' is the operative term."

"I'll be fine."

"So who owns those two houses in Amity?" Benny asked. "More city officials?"

"Good question. I have no idea."

"If they are, you ought to be able to confirm that pretty fast."

"How?"

"If the town has decent electronic records, it probably has a decent website, too."

"Good idea." I stood. "Let's go check."

Benny followed me into the den, where the computer was already on. I did a Google search for towns named Amity, turned up more than a dozen, and found the St. Louis suburb on page two of the search results.

I clicked on the link and the screen opened onto the Amity home page, which featured a bright collage of flowers, a fountain, a red-brick home, a pair of smiling boys in soccer uniforms, and a maple tree in full autumn red.

"There," Benny said, pointing to the **City Government** icon, which was one of several along the top of the page.

I clicked on the icon, which opened a drop-down menu of links, including one entitled **Mayor and City Council**. I clicked on that one, which opened yet another set of links:

> Bios of Mayor and City Council
> Current Agenda
> Recent Minutes
> Public Hearings

I clicked on the first link, which opened a page with a photo and brief biography of the mayor and each of the four council members.

"Bingo," I said.

"Which one?"

"Both. These two." I pointed. "Randy Gunn and Kathy Perkins."

"Amazing. You got to give Corundum its props. Those bastards must have a lock on city pols."

"Where do you think these council members find out about Corundum?"

"Maybe at those annual conventions for city officials. Maybe Corundum has a booth there."

"Maybe."

As we talked I clicked my way back the town's homepage. The other icons across the top of the page included **City Services**, **Boards & Commissions**, **Calendar**, **History**, **Maps**, **Contact Us**, and **News**. I clicked on **News**, which opened to a page of what appeared to be headlines of Amity press releases in reverse chronological order, the most recent at top. Each headline was also a link to the full piece. The sixth one down, about three months old, caught my eye: **RUBY PRODUCTIONS BREAKS GROUND ON STONY GLEN ESTATES**.

I clicked on the story:

> With a pair of shiny new shovels in hand, Amity Mayor Phil Kirkton and Ruby Productions President Kenneth Rubenstein officially broke ground this morning on Stony Glen Estates, a 40-home gated community whose amenities will include a health club, swimming pool and hiking trails. Mayor Kirkton heralded the new development as "the feather in the Amity redevelopment cap."
>
> The land for the new development, which will occupy the site of the former Southwest shopping district and the long-shuttered Amity West strip mall, was cleared and leveled after the City Council granted powers of eminent domain to Ruby Productions. Although some citizens had questioned the special real estate tax waiver granted to Ruby Productions during the construction phase of the project, Mayor Kirkton assured the crowd of onlookers that the city's treasury would be more

than replenished once Stony Glen Estates
was complete.

"Well, well," Benny said. "Your boy is everywhere, eh?"
"But no TIF this time."
"Yeah, but sounds like the city gave him a sweet deal on taxes."

Later that night—after I took Yadi for a walk, got ready for bed, checked on both of the kids, and turned off the reading lamp on my nightstand—I started thinking again about the Town of Amity and Ruby Productions and that Stony Glen Estates development.

Eventually, I turned on the lamp, put on my robe and slippers, and padded back downstairs to the den, followed by Yadi, who'd come out of Sam's bedroom as soon as he heard me on the stairs. I turned on the computer, logged onto the Internet and went to the Town of Amity's website. I clicked on the **City Government** icon, clicked on the **Mayor and City Council** link, and clicked on the **Recent Minutes** link, which opened to a column of dates—one per month stretching back for twenty months.

I clicked on the oldest month, which opened a document entitled: "MINUTES OF A REGULAR MEETING OF THE CITY COUNCIL." According to the date and time at the top of the page, the meeting started at 7 p.m. on a Tuesday twenty months ago. The meeting opened with the Pledge of Allegiance and the Invocation, which was given by Mayor Kirkton. Next came the roll call. All four council members were present. The meeting moved through a variety of city business—approval of an application for a retail liquor license for a tennis club, approval of a resolution authorizing the Mayor to execute an agreement with a nearby city for the purchase of 300 tons of salt for winter road maintenance, approval of a proclamation to a local Catholic girls' high school declaring a particular day Math Day, consideration of a series of bills for ordinances approving annexations of properties or issuances of permits for other properties, and various other seemingly routine city business.

I closed that set of minutes and clicked on the next one, skimmed the minutes, closed it, clicked on the next one, skimmed the minutes, and closed it. The meetings appeared to be held on the second Tuesday of each month. I kept opening and closing the minutes until I reached the meeting thirteen months ago. Under New Business was an entry in which the Mayor described a proposal from Ruby Productions for the creation of a redevelopment district comprising the Southwest shopping district and the closed Amity West strip mall. Under the proposal, the existing structures would be removed and replaced by a gated residential community. Ruby Productions was requesting certain real estate property tax relief and a commitment from the city regarding the costs of certain road and sewer line construction.

According to the minutes, Ruby Productions had already submitted the proposal—which included a lengthy set of drawings and specifications and a detailed pro forma—and was requesting approval of its proposal at the next regularly scheduled city council meeting. One of the council members—Patricia Welch—spoke against the proposal, but the Mayor ruled her out of order, since the only issue before the council was whether to place the matter on the agenda for the next council meeting. Council Member Norm Presberg moved that the proposal be placed on that agenda, Council Member Randy Gunn seconded the motion, and it passed four votes to one.

I closed the minutes for that meeting and opened the next one. As with the others, it opened with the Pledge of Allegiance, the invocation and a series of relatively routine matters. The rest of the meeting, according to the minutes, was devoted to the consideration the Ruby Productions proposal, which was now identified as Ordinance No. 4098. Present on behalf of Ruby Productions with Kenneth Rubenstein, two of his employees, and Rob Crane. They answered various questions posed to them by different member of the city counsel. Patricia Welch, the council member who had opposed even putting the proposal on the agenda, asked the most questions. After the Ruby

Productions officials answered all the questions, the council members each had an opportunity to express their own observations. Once again, Patricia Welch spoke at great length against the project. And finally, the vote. As set forth in the minutes::

MAYOR KIRKTON CALLED FOR A VOTE ON BILL NO. 5057. COUNCIL MEMBER GUNN MOVED, SECONDED BY COUNCIL MEMBER PERKINS, APPROVAL OF BILL NO. 5057 AS ORDINANCE NO. 4098, WITH THE VOTE UPON SUCH MOTION BEING AS FOLLOWS, TO WIT:

MAYOR KIRKTON—AYE

COUNCIL MEMBER GUNN—AYE

COUNCIL MEMBER WELCH—NAY

COUNCIL MEMBER PRESBERG—NAY

COUNCIL MEMBER PERKINS—AYE

THE VOTE ON THE MOTION BEING 3 AYES AND 2 NAYS, ORDINANCE NO. 4098 WAS APPROVED.

I stared at that roll call vote for long time before shutting down the computer and going back upstairs.

# Chapter Thirty-one

I didn't fall asleep until after three that the morning, but at least by then I had a plan. I needed to bring this Corundum investigation to a head one way or the other—more for Nick Moran's sister than anything else, but enough was enough already. I had to find the mysterious big guy and find out what he knew—or didn't know—and wrap it up.

By two in the morning, I had my plan. By three, when I finally rolled over in bed and closed my eyes, I had my partner. And by nine-thirty the following morning, I was parked across the street from 359 Dorantes in Amity, Missouri. In the driveway was the same black Dodge pickup, and along the curb in front of the house were the same three pickups from the day before.

To be safe, I restarted the engine, drove to the end of the block, and parked far enough around the corner to be out of the sightlines from 359 Dorantes.

I turned off the engine, angled the rearview mirror, and checked my appearance. I had on one of my mother's oversized sunglasses, bright red lipstick, and a pink scarf that covered my hair. Not bad.

I turned to my partner, who was seated on the passenger seat, head out the window, panting slightly. He was not as tough as Benny or as intimidating as Jacki, but he was every bit as brave and dependable as either of them.

"Shall we?" I said.

Yadi turned toward me, his tongue hanging out of his mouth. He wagged his tail. I clipped the leash onto his collar and opened my door.

Time to get into character. With my best version of a rural Missouri twang I said, "Ready, y'all?"

He closed his mouth and tilted his head.

"Let's get her done," I said.

We got out of the car, walked around the corner and down the street to 359 Dorantes. We went around to the back, where the construction crew was at work on the enclosed porch.

As we approached the work area, one of the Hispanic guys straightened up, stared at the dog and me, and called out, "Yo, Rudy."

From somewhere inside emerged the guy I'd seen get into the black pickup yesterday—the guy with the close-trimmed rust-colored beard. As yesterday, he was dressed in jeans, a short-sleeve Hawaiian-print shirt, construction boots, and a faded St. Louis Blues hat. Rudy, presumably.

"Can I help you, ma'am?" he asked.

"You folks are Corundum, right?"

He paused.

"Yes, ma'am. We work for Corundum."

"Where's the big guy?"

"What big guy would that be, ma'am?"

"The one that stole my money, that's who."

"Stole your money, ma'am?"

"You got that right, mister. He took my money and he ain't been to my house and he ain't done any work like he promised. I'd call that stealing, wouldn't you?" I peered around. "So where is that fat sneaky bastard?"

Rudy glanced down at Yadi, who was seated at my side and staring right back up at him. His tail was not wagging. Rudy looked back at me. He frowned and scratched the back of his neck.

"What money are you talking about, ma'am?"

"To do my patio is what money I'm talking about. He told me it would cost me two grand and he could get her done in

under a month on weekends and I says that sounded just find
and dandy to me and he says he needs a downpayment to get
me scheduled and I says what kind of downpayment and he says
seven-hundred fifty would do it and I says that sounds kind of
steep to me but he says that's what his company requires so I
went to my bank and took out that money and give it to him
in cash and guess what? I never seen him again. Never."

"Did he tell you his name, ma'am?"

"No, sir."

"So how do you know he works for us?"

"That license plate, that's how."

"What license plate?"

I gestured with my thumb back over my shoulder. "The one
out there on the Dodge pickup in the driveway."

"I don't understand."

"It was parked at the other job, too. The one where your guy
got my money. Well, sir, I copied down that plate before I give
him my money. I got me a cousin on the police force. When I
couldn't find your guy, I talked to my cousin and he ran them
plates and guess what? That there truck in the driveway is registered to Corundum Construction Company, which means you
are the sleazebags that pocketed my money. So where is he? I
got to talk to him. Either he does my job next week or I want
a full refund plus interest."

They guy was clearly flustered. He looked at Yadi and then
at the jobsite and back at me.

"Well," he said, scratching the back of his neck, "we did have
a big fellow who did some work for us once, but he's been gone
at least two months."

"Gone with my money is what you mean. What's his name?"

"Gene."

"Gene what?"

He frowned. "Ma'am, we don't have your money."

"According to my attorney, you do. And guess what else? If
I don't get that work done or get my money back, I'm going to

my cousin on the police force and get them boys to come out here and arrest all of you crooks."

"We didn't take your money, ma'am."

"One of your employees did, and according to my attorney, that's the same as your company taking it. Let me tell you, it wasn't easy tracking you fellas down, but now that I know the name of your company I can make sure I get some justice here. So let me ask you again. What's big Gene's last name and where does he live?"

"Let me talk to my boss, ma'am. What's your name?"

"I'm not telling you my name until you tell me his name."

"If I don't know your name, ma'am, how am I supposed to get in touch with you?"

"You don't get in touch with me, that's how. I got me a lawyer, and a damn good one at that. Her name is Jacki Brand and she's about as big as that Gene guy of yours who took my money and, believe me, she'll either sue his butt or kick his butt. Here's her card."

I handed it to him.

He studied the business card.

I said, "So here's the deal."

I waited until he looked up.

"You got two days," I said, "to find that Gene fellow and get him to contact my attorney. He's the only one we want to talk to, and he sure as heck better be ready to talk turkey. Understand me?"

He glanced down at the card and back at me.

"I'll pass it on," he said.

"You be sure you do." I looked down at Yadi, who was seated on the grass next to me. "Let's go, Tex."

He gave me a puzzled look as he got up.

We walked in silence back down the sidewalk. As we rounded the corner, I checked to make sure no one was looking. I unlocked my car door and let Yadi go in first. He jumped up onto the seat and moved over to the passenger side. I got in, closed the door, started the engine, and turned to him with a smile.

"Dang, Yadi, that there felt mighty good. Maybe we need to trade in this girly car and get ourselves a pickup. Maybe with a hemi, huh? Dang."

Yadi stared at me as I put the car in gear and drove off.

# Chapter Thirty-two

The rest of the week passed in a flurry of activity, mostly involving other lawsuits in dire need of attention. As for the Frankenstein case, the settlement agreement with Ruby Productions was finalized and signed by all parties Friday morning. Attached to the agreement as Exhibit A was the form notifying the City of Cloverdale that Ruby Productions was withdrawing its TIF development proposal. Attached as Exhibit B was the stipulation of dismissal of the lawsuit. Attached as Exhibit C was my signed statement that I was not currently representing and did not have any present intent to represent any parties challenging a Ruby Productions project. Although that exhibit was a first for me, it seemed almost trivial within the weird context of the abrupt end of the lawsuit.

Nevertheless, all parties to the Frankenstein case, and especially me, were pleased with its resolution. Indeed, the only sour note came from Judge Flinch. He had greeted Rob Crane and me in his chambers with a big grin, apparently anticipating yet another nasty pretrial fracas to preside over. The grin faded when we told him we had come to submit settlement papers.

"These are important matters," he told us, his voice laced with disappointment. "They deserve a public airing."

I tried to reassure him. "This won't be your only TIF case, Your Honor. I'm sure you will get one suitable for TV. Perhaps there will be a starring role for Mr. Crane here."

Flinch sighed. "Ah, let's hope so, Miss Gold, let's hope so. As Judge Ito would say, 'The big wheel keeps on turning.'"

Later that Friday afternoon—after swinging by the house to pick up my mom, Sam, and Sarah—I drove over to Muriel Finkelstein's home for the celebration party. Jacki Brand had promised to drop by later. She was working late drafting a property settlement agreement in one of her divorce cases.

The party was on Muriel's front yard, which was festooned with bright holiday lights. The sounds of Frank Sinatra singing "Young at Heart" came from a boombox sitting on her front porch. There were three long tables laden with a pot luck feast, the highpoint of which was a platter stacked with slices and chunks of Cletus Johnson's legendary deep-fried turkey.

The neighbors cheered when we got out of the car, and several came over to shake my hand or give me a hug. I smiled and thanked them, but felt a bit unworthy of taking credit for the result. It's one thing to attend a client's victory party after obtaining a huge jury verdict or a stunning reversal of one on appeal. It's another to do a victory lap after your opponent has—apparently for unrelated financial reasons—decided to fold his cards and walk away from the table.

Even so, it was wonderful to see the joy and relief in the eyes of Muriel and her neighbors. Better yet, my kids were having a wonderful time. One of Sarah's friends lived in Brittany Woods, and the two of them eventually went back to the friend's house. There were several kids Sam's age, and before long they were playing a game of tag in Muriel's backyard. I chatted with the neighbors as my mother and Muriel moved from group to group. More than once I heard my mother's voice uttering that familiar mantra of hers: "My daughter the Harvard lawyer."

Jacki Brand arrived around six thirty. She'd changed at the office and was wearing a red half-sleeve cowl neck sweater over dark jeans and leather boots. Muriel gave her a big hug.

"Hey, partner," I said. "Plenty of good eats."

"I can't eat much. We're going out to dinner tonight."

She looked around and smiled. "This is wonderful, Rachel."

"These folks are so happy."

"They should be. You got them a great result."

"I don't know how much credit I can claim."

"Hey, if you hadn't filed suit and driven them crazy, this whole neighborhood would have been bulldozed by now. You're entitled to take credit."

"Let's just say I'm not planning to look inside the mouth of this gift horse."

"Good idea."

"So did you finish your drafting?"

"Almost." She raised her eyebrows. "I was interrupted."

"By who?"

"Gene Chase."

I frowned. "And he is?"

"One pissed off redneck, as near as I can tell."

"Pissed off about what?"

"About some—and I quote—lying bitch who claims he took her money for some bullshit job."

"Awesome." I was grinning. "So he went for the bait."

"Yep. Now we have to land him."

"What did you say to him?"

"I told him that last time I checked, stealing money from a young widow constituted a felony in this state. I told him that if he kept insulting my client I'd just have to turn the matter over to her cousin on the police force. I also told him he ought to think long and hard about his employer, Corundum Construction. He told me he didn't work there anymore. I told him it didn't matter, because he sure as hell worked there on the day in question, and that's all that counted under the law. I told him to take the weekend to think it over, because if he forced me to bring a lawsuit, I'd be seeking a whole lot more than seven-hundred-and-fifty dollars. I told him I'd name Corundum and the owners and make sure it got in the newspapers and on TV and by the time I got done with them, I'd own their company and their personal assets, including that pickup."

I was grinning.

"You said all that?"

"It was fun."

"What did he say?"

"Not much. He kind of hemmed and hawed. I told him he had until the close of business on Monday to get me the money. If I hadn't heard from him by then, I would assume that he and Corundum had no interest in getting this matter amicably resolved. And then I hung up."

"Nice."

"Let's hope it works."

From across the lawn came Sam's voice, "Jacki!"

We both turned. Sam was running toward us, his face lit up with a big grin. Jacki was one of his favorites.

She got down on one knee, and Sam ran into her open arms.

"Hey, big man," she said.

He disappeared inside her arms as she hugged him. I looked on, smiling.

# Chapter Thirty-three

Gene Chase beat the deadline. At five minutes past four on Monday, Jacki Brand stuck her head in my office.

"Guess who's here?"

I checked my watch. "Alone?"

"Yep."

"Does he match the description?"

"He's big and fat. And a slob." She shrugged. "Seems like Nick could have done a lot better."

"Maybe he's got a scintillating personality."

"Yeah, and maybe I'm the quarterback for the New England Patriots."

"So that's what Tom Brady looks like in a dress."

"Ho, ho, ho. Where should we meet?

"You're the one he called," I said. "Let's do it in your office."

"Go on in. I'll go fetch him."

I took a seat off to the side in Jacki's office, over at the worktable. Though there were two chairs facing Jacki's desk, I didn't want to make him uncomfortable by sitting that close. He'd be plenty uncomfortable without having me up in his personal space.

Jacki entered the office, followed by Gene Chase. He was definitely big: maybe an inch taller than Jacki. And definitely fat: a big gut that bulged over his belt in front and on the sides, arms thicker than my thighs, and a chin that disappeared into a neck thicker than my waist. He had on a faded Cardinals t-shirt, sagging Wrangler jeans, and scuffed work boots. He was bald on top with scraggly brown hair on the sides that flared out into long sideburns. There was a lizard tattooed on his right arm and a scorpion on his left.

Jacki's observation mirrored my own: Nick could have done better than this sluggo. A whole lot better.

"Have a seat," she said, gesturing toward the chairs facing her desk. "That's my law partner over there."

Chase glanced over at me as he took his seat. He was holding a manila envelope in one fat hand.

"Where the girl?" he asked in a rural twang.

"She's not here," Jacki said.

"That's just crap. She's the one made all them BS charges, not me. I got a constitutional right to confront my accuser."

Jacki leaned forward in her chair and gave him a sub-zero stare. "Gene."

"Huh?"

"I'm getting tired of your routine."

"Hey, I'm just saying—"

"Gene."

"What?"

"Cut the bullshit."

He stared back her, eyes blinking.

She nodded toward the envelope. "What's in there?"

"One of them legal documents."

"What legal document?"

"It's what you call a release."

"Who calls it a release?"

"The lawyers, I guess."

"Whose lawyers?"

"The ones for the company."

"You mean Corundum?"

"Yes, ma'am."

"Who are those lawyers?"

"I got no idea. But I think they is the ones that wrote this thing up."

"Let me see it."

Chase seemed momentarily flustered. "Well, she's the one gotta sign it. Like I say, the money thing is bullshit, but I'm supposed to give it to her anyway even though I told them it's bullshit but I got orders and them orders says give her the money but she don't get no durn money unless she signs that there release."

Jacki said, "I'm not letting my client sign anything until I see it. Hand it over."

"Well, okay, but you understand the rules?"

"Yes, Gene. I understand the rules. Here's my rule: either give me that piece of paper or get the hell out of here."

He hesitated, eyes blinking, mind apparently in vapor lock, and finally placed the envelope on the desk. Jacki pulled it toward her, opened it, and removed a single sheet of paper. She skimmed it and turned to me.

I stood. "I'll make copies."

I took the document before Chase could react, stepped out into the hall, made two copies, and returned to Jacki's office.

"Here you are," I said.

I handed the original to Jacki, a photocopy to Chase, and took the other back to my chair.

I read my copy as Jacki read hers. It was a fairly standard belt-and-suspenders release form in which the person (whose name was to be written in on the blank line), on behalf of herself and "her heirs, executors, administrators, trustees, agents, attorneys, insurers, representatives, successors and assigns, and anyone claiming through or under them," in consideration of the payment of $750.00, "completely and irrevocably releases, remises, acquits and forever discharges Eugene Roy Chase and Corundum Construction Company its officers, directors, subsidiaries, successors, predecessors and otherwise affiliated entities, regardless of the form by which the entity is or was doing business, attorneys, agents, employees, subcontractors, assigns, past, present, or future, as the case may be, from any and all actions, causes of action, losses, damages, attorneys fees and claims, of any nature whatsoever, whether arising in law, contract, equity or otherwise, from the beginning of time to the date of this Release, regardless of whether such claims are asserted, alleged, known, unknown or unknowable."

I raised my eyes to meet Jacki's gaze.

*Interesting*, her expression seemed to say.

I nodded.

She turned to Chase. "So you brought the money?"

"I got it here with me but I'm telling you again this whole thing ain't right. I didn't make no promise to your client. I never took no money from her. I'll swear on a Bible. Maybe she got me confused with someone else, but—" he shook his head, resigned "—I guess that ain't no matter now. I'm supposed to give her the money and she has to get that release signed in front of one of them notary republics. Those are my instructions. So if you can get your client over here on the double we can get this thing done and get out of here."

"Is that money your money, Gene?" Jacki asked.

"Pardon?"

"Is it your cash or did you get it from Corundum?"

"I don't see why that matters."

"I don't give a rat's ass what you see. Just answer the question."

He looked down. "It's the company's money."

"Who gave it to you?"

"Rudy."

"Who's Rudy?"

"He's the man your client talked to on some job site. Rudy used to be my foreman."

"What's Rudy's last name?"

"Hickman."

"So Rudy Hickman gave you the money?"

"Yes, ma'am."

"And he gave you the release?"

"Yes, ma'am."

"And he gave you the instructions?"

"Yes, ma'am."

"You don't work for Rudy anymore?"

"No, ma'am."

"You work for Corundum?"

"No, ma'am. Not for a couple months."

"Where do you work?"

"At the Chambers Warehouse on North Broadway."

"Doing what?"

"Loading dock."

Jacki leaned back in her chair and glanced over at me. I nodded.

"Gene," I said.

He turned to me, eyes narrowing. "Yeah?"

"How'd you like to keep that seven fifty?"

He frowned. "What do you mean by keep it?"

"What if we could get you a signed release to give to Rudy but you could pocket the money? Does that interest you?"

"Well." He seemed both confused and tempted. "I'm not following your drift here."

"You can keep the money if you can give us the information we need."

"Information? About what?"

"Nick Moran."

The way his head snapped back, eyes wide, you'd have thought I tasered him.

"Moran? What do you mean?"

"Tell me about you and Nick Moran."

"I don't understand."

"Just tell me."

"About what?"

I sighed and shook my head, more for effect than anything else. "Gene, we have a witness."

His eyes widened. "Witness? To what?"

"In Forest Park. The night Nick died."

"I didn't kill him."

"I didn't say you did. But you were with him, Gene. We have a witness who saw you drive his pickup truck. He saw you park it on that lane in Forest Park. He saw you get out of Nick's truck and get into the one that belongs to Corundum. Next morning the police found Nick dead in that pickup, which was parked exactly where you left it."

"I didn't kill him."

"He died that night, Gene. You were the last person to see him alive."

"No way. I never saw him alive."

"What does that mean?"

"He was already dead."

"He was already dead when?"

"When I got in that truck."

"Which truck?"

"His, I guess. That one I drove."

"In the park?"

"No. Before."

"Where did you get in his truck?"

Chase's eyes were blinking rapidly, his face flushed. He leaned back in his chair and looked down at his thighs. He was tugging at his earlobe.

"Where was his truck, Gene?" I asked in a gentle voice.

No answer.

"Gene?"

"Hold on." He held up his hands and shook his head, still looking down. "Gimme a second."

"How long had you known Nick?" I asked.

"I didn't know him. Not at all."

"Then how do you know his name?"

"It was in the news."

"What news?"

"The next day. After they found him."

"You're saying you didn't know his name until then?"

He held up his hands. "This is going way too fast."

"We can slow down," I said.

"No, I got to think this over." He stood. "I got to go off and think this over real good before I say anything more."

"Don't you want to do this deal?" Jacki said. "We're talking seven hundred and fifty dollars. Just give us the information about that night, keep the money, take back a signed release, and no one will ever know the difference."

He seemed torn as he stood there, shifting from leg to leg.

"This wasn't supposed to happen," he said, to no one in particular.

"What wasn't?" I asked.

"This here. I didn't do nothing wrong that night. They asked me to come over and pick him up and drive him to the park and I done it and that was supposed to be all. And now this? Well, it's gotten a little too complicated for me. I gots to think this over."

"You can tell us about it," I said.

"I don't know about that." His voice was almost an octave higher. "I got to go. I just do. I'll talk to you all later."

And with that he dashed out of Jacki's office. We heard him lumber down the hall.

# Chapter Thirty-four

Jacki and I stared at each other.

"So he was already dead," she said. "Not what we were expecting to hear."

"Nope."

"Maybe it's time to pay another visit to your police pal."

"Not yet."

"Why not?"

"Bertie's convinced this was just a routine drug overdose."

"Now we know it wasn't."

"All we know for sure—or think we know for sure—is that Nick OD'ed on heroin somewhere other than Forest Park and was already dead by the time Chase got into Nick's pickup to drive it Forest Park."

"I'd call that some major new information, Rachel."

"True, but there's still a semi-innocent explanation."

"Which is?"

"That Nick died of an accidental overdose somewhere else. Maybe at someone's house. Or in his pickup with someone else. And that someone panicked and called Chase and somehow convinced him to drive the pickup with Nick inside back to Forest Park."

"That's still pretty shady, and probably illegal."

"But not a homicide—and it might not be enough to get Bertie to reopen a closed case."

"What about the other truck? The one from Corundum that was parked on the lane? How is that innocent?"

"I'm not saying it is, but maybe the truck got there because Nick hooked up with some guy from Corundum who was driving the truck at the time. Maybe they met in the park and then drove somewhere else in Nick's pickup."

"That's a lot of maybes."

"That's all we have so far."

"Do you really believe the innocent scenario?"

"No." I shrugged. "But I need to find evidence that would at least suggest to a cop that it might not be innocent from the start. Until I do that, Bertie isn't going budge."

"How are you going to find that evidence?"

"Gene Chase obviously knows something important."

"How do we make him tell us?"

"He seemed tempted by the money. He might come back on his own."

"What if he doesn't?"

"He's confirmed the Corundum connection. That's important. I'll just keep poking around, see what else I can find out about them." I held up the release document Chase had brought. "This is a first step."

"To what?"

"To Corundum's lawyer. Sometimes a lawyer will talk when a client won't."

Jacki frowned at the document. "How is this a clue to Corundum's lawyer?"

"You see that number at the bottom left corner of the page?"

"The document ID number?"

"Exactly."

Jacki looked up with a frown. "And that tells you something?"

"Read it aloud."

"Okay. S—T—L—D—O—C—S—dash—1—3—5—9—1—7—4."

She gave me a puzzled look. "So?"

"That's the ID number that the law firm's document management system assigned to that document when it was created."

"Okay."

"All we need to do is match that document ID to the lawyer who created it."

"Good Lord, Rachel. Do you know how many lawyers and law firms there are in this city? Matching a lawyer to that ID number could take years."

"I bet I can do it in less than a week."

"How?"

"Look at the first three letters: S—T—L. What's that tell you?"

"It's an abbreviation for St. Louis."

"Exactly. And?"

"And what?"

"When I was a lawyer at Abbott & Windsor, the firm opened branch offices in about six American cities. Each office had its own document dataset maintained by the server in that location. Thus the document IDs always identified which office created the document. If it was the New York office, the first three letter were N—Y—C. Washington was W—D—C. Chicago was C—H—I."

"And St. Louis was S—T—L."

"Exactly," I said. "But the only reason you needed those three initials was because the firm had offices in more than one city. That way, if you were in the Los Angeles office and you were looking for, say, an example of a motion to dismiss and your document search came up with one that started A—T—L, then you knew that if you wanted to review that document you had to open the document dataset for the Atlanta office."

Jacki stared at the lower left corner of the release. "Okay."

"The document ID on this release tells me that it was created at a law firm that has offices in more than one city. Otherwise, there's no need to indicate the city on the ID number. That means the lawyer for Corundum who drafted this document works at a law firm that has multiple offices."

"Ah." She smiled. "So that cuts the list of firms down to fifteen or so."

"Exactly."

"But what are you going to do? Serve them all with subpoenas?"

"Never. We couldn't anyway. We don't even have an existing case to issue a subpoena from. And even if we had a case, the firms would fight a formal subpoena. They'd claim attorney work product."

"So what are you going to do?"

I'm sure I know at least one lawyer at each of those firms."

"You think they'll just tell you?"

"It's worth a try." I checked my watch. "But not today. I'll start calling them in the morning."

"And tell them what?"

"I don't know. I'll think of something."

# Chapter Thirty-five

For old times' sake, I started with my former law firm, Abbott
& Windsor. When I'd joined fresh out of law school fifteen
years ago, A & W had about 300 lawyers—a behemoth of that
era—with 270 lawyers in the Chicago office and a handful each
in Washington, D.C. and London. Now the firm had about
2,000 lawyers and offices in most of the major business centers
of North America, Europe, and Asia. Though I still knew dozens
of lawyers in the Chicago office, I decided to start with a junior
partner in the St. Louis office named Jeffrey Ames. He possessed
three qualities that made him an excellent prospect: he was vain
and pompous and a horndog.

His secretary answered his phone—of course. Jeffrey Ames
was too important to answer his own phone. She asked my
name and I told her. She asked me about the nature of the call
and I told her it was personal. Thirty seconds later, Jeffrey came
on the phone.

"Ah, the lovely Rachel Gold. How are you, my dear?"

*My dear?*

"I'm doing good, Jeffrey."

"Delighted to hear that. Long time no chat. To what do I
owe this distinct pleasure?"

"Possibly your skillful legal drafting."

"Is that so? Pray tell me more. I am most intrigued."

"I have a corporate indenture document in my form file, but
I have no idea where I got it. It's a nice piece of draftsmanship,

Jeffrey, which is what made me think of you. I thought it might be your work."

"Perhaps it is. Who are the parties?"

"Don't know. The names have been redacted. But there is a document ID at the bottom of the page. It looks like a St. Louis document."

"We can confirm that in a moment. Let me get into the document search mode on my computer." A pause. "Okay. Give me the number."

I read it to him.

He repeated it as he typed it in. "Let's see what we turn up."

After a moment, he said, "An indenture?"

"Yes. Is it your document?"

"Unfortunately, no. We most definitely have a document bearing that identification number, but I am afraid it is a notice of appeal, and the author is Roger Bakker of our office."

"Oh, well. Thanks for checking, Jeffrey."

"My pleasure, Rachel. We really should get together. Perhaps you would allow me to buy you a drink after work one day."

"Maybe later in the year. My schedule is pretty crazy these days."

"I perfectly understand. I shall make a note to call you in a few weeks. It is always a delight to chat with you, Rachel."

Between client meetings, drafting a motion to compel, and other tasks that filled up the rest of the day, I was only able to reach lawyers from four of the other possible firms. All four had a document in their St. Louis datasets with the same ID number, but none was the Corundum release. Instead, the ID number matched, in order of my four calls, an assignment of copyright, a software license agreement, a loan guarantee, and a set of interrogatories—and none for a client named Corundum Construction Company.

*Five down, eleven to go*, I said to myself as I hung up after call number five, which had been to a friend at Armstrong Teasdale, where the document ID matched the set of interrogatories.

I checked my watch.

5:25 p.m.

Enough for today. I'd start calling again in the morning and keep at it until I made the match. What I'd do once I made the match—well, I'd cross that proverbial bridge when I reached it.

I stood and gathered my stuff to leave. The rain had increased during the day from a morning drizzle to a steady downpour that seemed to be growing stronger.

I noticed a manila envelope on the carpet by my office door, which I'd closed an hour ago to make a conference call on my speaker phone. There was a yellow Post-it on envelope. I recognized my secretary's handwriting as I bent over to pick up the envelope:

**Rachel, I finished up the research.
Guess what? You were 7 for 7!! Congrats!**

**See you tomorrow.**

**Dorian**

The envelope was sealed. From its heft I estimated there were thirty or so pages of documents inside, which was about what I expected. But not seven for seven. I was hoping for—or perhaps dreading—maybe three out of seven. That would suggest the possibility of a pattern. Seven for seven suggested much more.

As I stared at the envelope, a wave of raindrops drummed against my window.

I checked my watch again.

5:33 p.m.

I needed to get home. Dorian's packet of information could wait until later.

# Chapter Thirty-six

By the time we finished dinner, the rainstorm had intensified into a thunderstorm. The flashes of lighting and explosion of thunder so terrified poor Sam that I stayed with him in bed, singing lullabies, until he finally fell asleep with Yadi curled up at the end of his bed. Even Sarah, who usually did her homework holed up in her bedroom with the door closed, was studying in the den off the kitchen.

By the time I came back downstairs, my mother had already cleaned up the kitchen, brewed tea, opened the manila envelope, and examined the packet of documents, which were now spread across the kitchen table in separate piles. She looked up as I came in the room.

"Is Sam asleep?" she asked.

"Finally."

The window behind her flickered with a flash of distant lightning.

I gestured toward the documents. "Well?"

She shook her head, eyes wide. "You were right."

"All seven?"

The rumble of thunder shuddered the house.

"All seven," she said.

I took a seat across from her.

She said, "How did you know?"

"A lucky guess—or maybe unlucky, depending how this plays out. Benny was over here last week and we were trying to figure out whether the two Corundum building permits in Amity were issued to members of their city government. We went onto the Amity website and found a list of council members."

"And?"

"Both were on the city council. But we also discovered something else: Ruby Productions had a project in Amity. Another one of those gated communities. At the time I just thought it was an odd coincidence—Corundum building permits in the same town as a Ruby Productions development. But it kept gnawing at me. Later that night, I got out of bed, went down to the den, and got back onto the Amity website. I found the minutes for the city council meeting where they approved the project. They were posted on line. The project passed by a vote of three to two. Guess who voted in favor of Ruby Productions?"

"Both of them?"

"Yep."

"But the third vote?" My mother frowned. "There was no Corundum building permit issued to that one."

"Right."

"What's that mean?"

"I don't know. His name is Kirkton. He's actually the mayor. I had Dorian do a title search on his house. There were no building permits on his house. In fact, he hadn't had any work done his house that required a permit for the entire eighteen years he'd owned the house. But that Amity stuff got me thinking about whether there might be a similar pattern in any of the other towns where we'd found Corundum building permits. We had a list of seven city officials with permits—two each in three cities and one in the fourth. I asked Dorian to do some research—to figure out whether there'd been a TIF project in that city in the past few years, and if so, the name of the developer and the votes of the city counsel on the motion to approve the TIF."

"The evidence is all here," my mother said, looking toward the documents.

"All four towns?"

"All four. And the developer on all four projects was Ruby Productions."

"So we're five for five." I leaned back in my chair and frowned. "That sure sounds like more than a coincidence. And the seven city officials? Did each vote in favor of their city's TIF proposal?"

"They did." She stood. "Take a look for yourself. I'll pour tea. I made us some fresh cookies."

It didn't take me long to confirm what my mother had told me. Four cities, four TIFs, all involving Ruby Productions. Four city council approvals, with all seven of the city officials with Corundum Construction building permits voting in favor of the TIFs. But just as in Amity, the city officials with Corundum permits were in the majority but did not constitute the entire majority. In the three cities where we'd identified two city officials each, the vote had been three to two in one of the cities and four to three in the other two. As for the city of Edgewood, where only one city official had a home renovated by Corundum, the vote had been three to two in favor of the TIF.

My mom poured us each a mug of tea and set down a plate of her oatmeal raisin cookies.

Another flash of lightning, another crack of thunder. The rain was coming down so hard now that the gutters above the kitchen windows were overflowing. A translucent sheet of water cascaded down the eaves outside the window.

"So?" my mother said.

I sighed. "This is not what I wanted."

"What do you mean?"

"I'm not an investigative reporter here, Mom. I'm just trying to find out what happened to Nick. That witness from Forest Park helped make the Corundum Construction connection through a license plate number, and since then I've just been trying to follow that trail to someone in the company who can tell what, if anything, they know about Nick's death. This—" a gestured toward the documents "—is entirely different."

"But maybe part of the same trail," my mother said.

"I don't see it."

"What did Corundum and Nick Moran have in common, Honey? They both did renovations. Maybe Nick had some connection to that Corundum outfit. A friend, maybe. A boyfriend. Someone he did drugs with."

"Maybe."

"Maybe that big fat guy will give you the answer."

"Maybe."

"You don't think so?"

"He was panicky when he left the office yesterday. Freaked out. I was hoping we'd hear from him today. Nothing."

"Maybe tomorrow?"

I shrugged. "With each day it gets less likely."

"What then?"

"If we can't get him to talk, we have the name of his supervisor. We could try to track him down, see what he knows, but he's probably the wrong guy. We need to get higher up in the company."

"How do you do that?"

I shrugged. "Since we can't find any information about the company, we need to find someone who had dealings with the higher ups. Like those city council members."

"Who won't talk to you."

I sighed. "Correct."

"Which means you need to figure out a way to convince one of them to talk to you. You need to find some…what do you call it?"

"Leverage?"

"Exactly. So, how can you get some leverage?"

The idea arrived in synch with a flash of lightning outside.

"You're a genius, Mom."

"What?"

"Leverage."

"So?"

"Cloverdale."

"What about it?"

"The vote on the Brittany Woods TIF. It was four to three. We never searched the Cloverdale City Hall records for Corundum building permits."

My mother's eyes widened. "Oh, my God."

"If the pattern holds true in Cloverdale, there should be at least one."

"You might be right."

"I'll know tomorrow."

"What if you are? What will you do?"

I smiled. "Use a little leverage."

# Chapter Thirty-seven

In addition to his seat on the Cloverdale city council, Milt Bornstein was a professor of journalism at one of the local community colleges. The information posted on his faculty web page stated that he had office hours every Thursday morning from 10:30 to noon. I drove over to the college after a morning court hearing and arrived about 11:30. His office door was closed. I could hear muffled sounds of conversation inside.

According to the bumper stickers and other detritus affixed to his office door, Professor Bornstein was a card-carrying member of the ACLU and PETA, a fan of *New Yorker* cartoonist Roz Chast, a lover of vegans and organic produce, a hater of SUVs and Wal-Mart, a big fan of U2, and a bigger fan of Bono. His door, in short, suggested that its owner could risk great physical harm at a cocktail party if he ran into Benny Goldberg.

I knew one key fact about Milt Bornstein beyond the contents of his door—a fact that added a touch of irony to his office hours, which followed a class he taught in ethics. I'd learned that fact at the Cloverdale city hall during the two hours I'd spent yesterday afternoon searching the city's building records. The only building permit issued to Corundum Construction over the past five years was for the construction of an in-ground swimming pool at 1220 Columbia Avenue. The building permit had been issued almost two months to the day before the final vote of the Cloverdale city council in favor of the Brittany Woods TIF project. One of the four yes votes on that motion was also one of the owners of the home at 1220 Columbia Avenue. According to the title records, those owners were Dr. and Mrs. Milton S. Bornstein.

I took a seat in the chair against the wall next to the closed door. Across the hall was a large window with a southern exposure that looked out on a sight not visible in St. Louis for almost four days: the sun. The rain finally ended sometime last night after midnight. Yadi and I had headed out this morning on our three-mile jog under a welcome blue sky.

The door to Bornstein's office opened.

"Next Friday will be fine," he was saying from inside.

An Asian-American woman was backing out of the office, her hand on the door. She had a backpack slung over her right shoulder.

"Thank you, Professor."

A male voice from inside said, "Just email me the outline by Monday."

"I will do that, sir. Thank you."

"No problema."

She nodded at me and then walked quickly down the hallway.

I stood and moved over to the doorway. Milt Bornstein was seated behind his cluttered desk, jotting something onto a yellow legal pad. I knocked against the door.

"Come in," he said without looking up.

He was still writing as I took the seat facing the desk. He was bent over the legal pad, giving me an unobstructed view of his bald head. He wore a blue chambray shirt rolled up to his elbows and a red and blue striped bowtie. On the wall behind him were three framed posters: Che Guevera in his beret, Bob Marley in his dreadlocks, and the advertising poster for *All the President's Men*—the one with the young Dustin Hoffman and Robert Redford in sports coats and loosened ties staring into the distance below the tagline *The Most Devastating Detective Story of this Century.*

"Yes?" Bornstein said, raising his head. His eyebrows arched in surprise. "Miss Gold?"

"Professor."

"What are you doing here?"

"I need to talk to you."

"Are we allowed to do that? I mean, didn't you sue us?"

"That case is over. It's been settled and dismissed."

He nodded and scratched his neck. Milt Bornstein was a skinny, fidgety man in his late forties with a high bald forehead, long ears, and big brown eyes. He had a sharp nose, thin lips and an almost scrawny neck.

He said, "Your clients must be delighted."

"They are."

He shrugged. "Life marches on, Counselor. We on the city council shall seek other means to grow our city's future." He glanced at his wristwatch. "So what is it we need to discuss?"

"Corundum Construction Company."

His eyes narrowed. "I beg your pardon?"

"Who do you know there?"

"What are you talking about?"

"Who did you deal with?"

"What makes you think I deal with anyone at…what's that company name again?"

"Corundum."

He frowned. "Corundum? Who are they?"

"The company that's building your pool."

"Oh, yes. That Corundum. Yes. Of course. Who did I deal with?"

"That's my question."

He leaned back in his chair and rubbed his chin.

"Tell me, Miss Gold, why is that of any interest to you?"

"That's confidential."

"Oh, really." He gave a cold smile. "Then I'm afraid that my contact information is confidential."

"Perhaps not for long."

"What is that supposed to mean?"

"Are they still going to build your pool?"

"Why wouldn't they?"

"The TIF fell through."

He leaned forward in his chair and glared at me, his nostrils flared. "What exactly are you trying to imply, Miss Gold?"

I gazed back. "Come on, Milt. You know exactly what I am implying."

"I am deeply offended. This meeting is over." He stood. "Please get out here."

"Not yet." OF

"Go."

I gazed up at him. "Sit down."

"What?"

"Sit down, Milt. I'm not done."

He stared at me, eyes blinking. After a moment, he took a seat and started strumming his fingernails against the desktop at a staccato pace.

"This is an absolute outrage," he said.

"Relax, Milt. I'm not an investigative reporter."

"What is that supposed to mean?"

"It means I'm not here today to expose you and your sordid little deal. I'm not here to dig up dirt."

He drummed his fingers as he stared at me. "How am I supposed to know that's true?"

"Because I say it is."

He snorted. "And that's supposed to make me feel better?"

"Frankly, Milt, I don't care how it makes you feel. I'm looking for some specific information about Corundum Construction Company that you should have. My suggestion is that you talk to me."

"Why should I talk to you?"

"Because what I care about is a lot different than what a cop or an FBI agent will care about. Okay?"

He was rapping his fingernails against the desktop, his lips pursed, staring at his desktop.

He looked up and met my gaze. "What is it you care about?"

"A death."

His eyes widened. "Someone was killed?"

"I didn't say killed, Milt. Just a death. Maybe it was an accident, maybe it wasn't."

"Who?"

"That's not your concern."

"I don't know anything about a death."

"I didn't say you did, Milt."

"Then what do you want from me?"

"Some information about your contractor. For reasons that you understand better than I do, Corundum Construction Company is a secretive organization. It appears to be a shell corporation that has done a careful job of concealing its owners from the public. I'm here for their names. I want to know who you dealt with."

"Why?"

"Because one of those people will have information about that death."

"What kind of information?"

"That's not your concern, Milt."

"I don't understand."

"You don't need to understand. All you need to do is give me the names of the people associated with Corundum that you dealt with."

"And if I don't?"

I shrugged. "To paraphrase Bette Davis in *All About Eve*, 'Fasten your seatbelt, Milt, it's going to be a bumpy ride.'"

"Are you threatening me?"

I stared at him. "Yes."

He lowered his eyes.

"Well?" I said.

"I need to think this over."

I took out a business card and slid it across the desk toward him. "You have twenty-four hours."

"And then what?"

I stood and gazed down at him.

"And then this is no longer a private conversation." I checked my watch. "Noon tomorrow. I'll look forward to your call."

I turned and walked out.

# Chapter Thirty-eight

Back in the office that afternoon I returned to my list of sixteen St. Louis law firms with offices in more than one city. The first day I'd tracked down the document ID number in the databases of five of those firms and came up 0 for five. I'd hoped to finish the list yesterday but had only been able to reach lawyers at two more firms, which left nine.

Next on the list was Beckman & Boyce, a 100-lawyer St. Louis firm with smaller Missouri offices in Kansas City, Jefferson City, and Springfield. I knew several lawyers at the firm, including Rob Crane and his litigation entourage, but considered only one of them—a young trusts-and-estates partner named Roberta Bronson—a friend. We served together on the board of a local arts organization.

I dialed her number. She answered. After some small talk, I shifted to the point of the call. Since she was a trusts-and-estates partner, I described the mystery document as a power of attorney.

"No names?" she said.

"They've been redacted. But there is a document ID at the bottom of the page. It looks like a St. Louis document. I'm hoping it's yours."

"Let's check. What's the number?"

I gave it to her.

I could hear the clicking of her keyboard.

"A power of attorney?" she asked. "Is that it?"

"No. It's some sort of release."

"What do you mean 'some sort'?"

"The document title is 'Corundum release.'" Trying to sound nonchalant, I said, "Oh, well."

"Sorry."

"No problem. I appreciate you looking, Roberta. By the way, does the document profile show the author?"

"Let's see. R.L. Crane."

"Rob Crane?"

"Yes, Mr. Crane."

"What a coincidence. I may have seen that very release in a case I had with him. Does the profile have a Create Date?"

"Last Wednesday."

"What about a client?"

"That's odd. It just says Firm Miscellaneous."

"It must be another case."

"I can open it and—"

"—No. Don't do that."

"Uh, okay."

"Your system probably records every time someone opens a document. I don't want Crane thinking you're snooping around in his documents. Thanks again, Roberta."

"Sure thing. If you need a power of attorney, I'll be happy to send you one of mine."

"Thanks. If I can't trace this document down, I may take you up on that offer."

I hung up, leaned back in my chair and stared out the window.

"Jeez," I said.

"I'll say."

I turned to see Jacki standing in the doorway.

"Huh?" I said.

"You heard already?"

"Heard what?

"You are not going to believe this. Go to the *Post-Dispatch* website."

Jacki came around the desk to stand behind me as I typed in the Internet address—www.stltoday.com—and clicked Enter."

The page opened.

"Look at the Top Headlines section," Jacki said over my shoulder. "Check out what's new."

On the upper right side of the page was a bullet-point column entitled Top Headlines. The first three items were tagged in red as NEW:

**NEW** One-car crash kills Hillsboro man

**NEW** Court reverses sitter's conviction in infant's death

**NEW** Body found in River Des Peres drainage ditch

"Click on the third one," Jacki said.

I did. It opened on the following story:

Police Investigating Body Found
In River Des Peres Drainage Ditch

St .Louis Post-Dispatch
     St. Louis, Mo. — Metropolitan Sewer
District employees discovered a body this
morning in the River Des Peres drainage
ditch just south of Forest Park near the
entrance to the underground portion of the
river. The MSD workers were driving through
the area at Macklind and Berthold, where
they were checking on pipes in the aftermath of the heavy rainfall. They spotted
the male body facedown in the receding
storm waters and called the police.
     Based upon identification materials found
on the body, including a Missouri driver's
license inside a wallet in the dead man's
pants pocket, the police have tentatively
identified him as Eugene Chase of University City.
     The police are not yet saying how the man
died and are unwilling to label the death
suspicious until after a complete autopsy.

Although there were signs of trauma on the
body, the police cautioned that such signs
are not inconsistent with the man having
fallen into a drainage ditch near his home
in University City during the recent thunderstorms and drowned while being swept
downstream by rising floodwaters through
the underground portion of the river.

I turned to Jacki. "My God."

She nodded.

I reached for the phone. "That was no accident."

# Chapter Thirty-nine

Bertie Tomaso was out when I called. He returned my call thirty minutes later from the Central West End, where he was about to interview a witness. He got off duty at five. I promised I'd take no more than fifteen minutes of his time if he let me buy him a cup of coffee before he went home. He agreed.

I arrived at Coffee Cartel first and got us each a coffee and a scone.

My eyes widened when he walked in.

"Oh, my goodness," I said.

He grinned.

"You like?"

"I love it, Bertie."

Though he was wearing his usual wrinkled-dark-suit-white-shirt-loosened-tie outfit, he'd added something new on top: a grey fedora. He wore it pushed back on his head with the front of the brim bent down over his eyes.

He gave me a wink. "I got that noir thing going, eh?"

"You look terrific. When did you get it?"

"For my birthday. Susie Q got me the hat, a trench coat, and the New American Library edition of Hammett. You should have seen me in the outfit during that rainstorm. I could have passed for Sam Spade—or at least a dago version."

He took a sip of coffee.

"So?" he said. "What's on your mind, gorgeous?"

"That body in the River Des Peres."

"Okay."

"What do you know about it?"

"Not much. The detective assigned to the case—he and I had a late lunch today after he got back from the morgue. We talked some about it."

"Why?"

He shrugged and dunked his scone in the coffee.

"Just shop talk."

He took a bite of the scone.

I said, "I met the dead guy last week."

"Where?"

"In my office."

"Really? For what?"

"He knew something about Nick Moran's death."

"Nick Moran?"

"The body in the pickup truck on Gay Way."

"Oh, right." He leaned back and studied me. "You thought this Chase guy knew something?"

I nodded.

"What?"

I explained how I got to Chase—from my confidential witness on Gay Way that night to the license plate trace to my crazy story at the Corundum job site about the $750 downpayment.

Bertie dunked his scone in the coffee, took another bite, and chewed it slowly.

"Interesting," he finally said.

He reached into his suit jacket, pulled out a small notebook, flipped it open and set it on the table. He took the ballpoint pen out of his shirt pocket, clicked it open, and jotted something down. He looked up.

"This Chase guy," he said, "he told you Moran was *already* dead when he picked him up?"

"Yes. But he wouldn't say where he picked him up. He was really rattled, Bertie. He said he needed to think it over. He practically ran out of my office. Next thing he's dead."

"Not exactly next thing."

"So a few days later."

"A few days can make a big difference, Rachel."

"He was killed, Bertie."

"Because he talked to you?"

"Look at the timing."

"Rachel, we've actually looked at the evidence."

"And?"

"It's consistent with an accidental death by drowning."

"How so?"

"The autopsy ought to help us pinpoint the time of death, but the medical examiner thinks he died no more than twenty-fours before that MSD crew spotted him that morning. That means it had been raining for two days by then. He lived in one of those little shotgun houses in U. City. His house was less than a hundred yards from the River Des Peres stormwater ditch. After those kids fell in and drowned during a storm a couple years ago, they were supposed to fence it off, but there are still gaps. The stormwaters would have been at least three feet deep after two days of that rain. That's deep enough to carry a corpse downstream all the way through that big tunnel that runs beneath Forest Park. There's a lot of debris where it exits onto the riverbed near Macklind—old shopping carts, big branches, car fenders, other crap. That's where the body got snagged when the waters ebbed."

"How do you know he fell in back near his house?"

"We don't know for sure yet, but we know enough to draw some inferences. His car was in the driveway. The front door of his house was unlocked. The body had on a windbreaker, which suggests he'd been out in the rain. The animal pound picked up his dog last night. It had been running free and still had a leash attached to its collar. So the likely scenario is that he's out walking his dog in the thunderstorm, gets too close to the edge of the drainage ditch, slides down the bank, conks his head on the cement and drowns."

I shake my head. "He just falls in?"

"It's pretty slick and muddy over there. Also, he was probably drunk at the time. We don't have the blood work back yet, but the guy liked to drink. The house was filled with empties, and his garage was stacked with cases of Busch."

"Are there any witnesses?"

"Don't know yet. We have two cops taking statements from the neighbors. Could be hard to find a witness, though. Not many people go out walking at night in thunderstorms."

I frowned. "Still, all these coincidences bother me. A guy with no history of drug use and no known homosexual tendencies is found dead of a drug overdose at an infamous gay meeting spot. The last guy to see him alive—or at least to see his body—drowns in a stormwater sewer a couple of days after he gets questioned about his connection to the dead guy. I'm telling you, Bertie, you need to find someone from Corundum. That's what I've been trying to do. Someone there ought to know about Gene Chase and Nick Moran."

I watched him write *Corundum Const. Co* in his notebook.

"You say they do renovations, this Corundum outfit?"

"As far as I can tell."

I couldn't decide how much more detail to give Bertie about the pattern of city officials and TIFs and Ruby Productions. He'd resisted my efforts to get him to reopen Nick Moran's death, and he seemed pretty dubious about the criminal aspect to Gene Chase's death. Moreover, the TIFs were all out in the suburbs—and thus outside the jurisdiction of the St. Louis police department. And I'd far exceeded fifteen minutes of his time this afternoon. I needed to get home, too.

I said, "When will you have the autopsy results on Chase?"

"Another day or so."

"Will you at least call me when they come in?"

"Sure."

"Thanks, Bertie."

He stood, pinched the front of his fedora, put it on, and angled the brim over his eyes. Doing his best Humphrey Bogart impression, he gave me a wink and said, "Here's lookin' at you, kid."

"We'll always have Paris."

He winked. "I'll call you."

# Chapter Forty

The week that began in darkness and rain ended in warm weather and glorious sunshine. Being a blue sky junkie, I packed a picnic basket Saturday morning, loaded Sarah and the dog and a Frisbee into the minivan, picked up Sam from religious school, and drove us all over to one my favorite quirky spots, the Compton Hill Reservoir Park. Although Sarah might have opted for an afternoon at the mall and Sam for an afternoon of videogames, some of Yadi's enthusiasm and mine had rubbed off on the kids by the time we'd spread out the picnic blanket on the grass near the fountain pond.

I'd packed everyone's favorites—a peanut-butter-banana-and-honey sandwich and Cheetos for Sam; hummus, toasted bagel chips, sliced granny apple and cheddar cheese wedges for Sarah; Milk-Bone treats for Yadi; turkey and Swiss on rye with pickles and Stadium mustard for me; and my mother's kamish-broit for us all.

We ate our lunch in the shadow of that outlandish structure known as the Compton Hill Water Tower. Having grown up in St. Louis, I had no idea how unusual our three water towers were. A century ago, there were more than five hundred of them around the country. Now there were just seven—and we had three. Like its two counterparts on the north side of the city, the Compton Hill Water Tower had been erected to help equalize water pressure in the fast-growing city of the eighteen-hundreds.

It was a huge standpipe—close to 200 feet tall and six feet in diameter.

Toward the end of the nineteenth century, the city fathers decided to camouflage all three standpipes by erecting exotic structures around them. On the north side, the results are the tallest freestanding Corinthian column in the world—nicknamed Old White—and an even taller Victorian version of a Moorish minaret, complete with projecting gargoyles, and balustraded balconies—nicknamed New Red.

But my favorite is the Compton Hill Water Tower. The main portion is a huge tower built of buff-colored brick and terra cotta decorated with carvings of mythical animals and leaf patterns, all capped by a bell-shaped roof. Attached to the main structure is a slightly taller asymmetrical turret of rusticated limestone that reminds me of a minaret from Disney's *Aladdin*. Just beneath the bell-shaped roof of the main tower is an observation deck with a 360-degree vista. Since this was the first Saturday of the month, the water tower was open to the public—which is why I chose it as our picnic spot. A panoramic view of the city awaited anyone with the desire and the energy to climb the 198 steps that spiraled up that standpipe. I definitely had two kids with the desire and the energy.

When we finished our lunch, I gathered up the picnic leftovers, folded up the blanket, and put them into the car with Yadi. I vented the windows and promised Yadi that I'd be back soon. Then the kids and I headed up the stairs to the observation deck. The views were amazing in every direction, although Sam seemed more wowed by the sight of the playground on the far side of the park below the tower than the Arch and the Mississippi River in the distance.

When we got back down, Sarah agreed to take Sam over to the playground for thirty minutes and then meet Yadi and me back at the Naked Truth statue near the water tower for a game of Frisbee. I got Yadi out of the car and walked back over to the statue, which was a larger-than-life bronze figure of a naked woman seated on a stone bench with arms outstretched and holding torches. It caused quite a scandal a century ago when it was, literally, unveiled.

There was a bench nearby facing the statue. I settled down, opened my purse, and pulled out my copy of Willa Cather's *Death Comes for the Archbishop*. I'd been on a Willa Cather kick the past month, having read *My Antonia*, *O Pioneers* and *Song of the Lark*. I'd started *Death* the night before and couldn't wait to get back to it. Yadi lay down in the grass at my feet.

I'd no sooner opened the book and removed the bookmark when someone in my peripheral vision approached the bench.

"Rachel Gold."

I turned to see Ken Rubenstein. He was dressed more for a day at the office than at the park in a brown v-neck cashmere sweater over a blue-and-brown tattersall dress shirt, gray pleated-front wool slacks, and cordovan loafers.

He gestured toward the bench.

"May I?"

I shrugged. "There's plenty of room."

He took a seat.

After a moment, he said, "Amazing structure, eh?"

I looked up from my book at the water tower, nodded, and returned to my book.

"Did you know it was a big attraction during the 1904 World's Fair? Thousands of people went up it."

"I didn't know that," I said, without looking up.

"Hasn't been in service as a water tower since 1929."

"Okay."

"They took it out of service when Stacy Park Reservoir went into service. Not far from where you live."

I turned to him. "What's not far?"

"Stacy Park. In Olivette. Not far from your home."

"How do you know where my home is?"

He smiled and shrugged. "Phone book?"

"I'm not listed."

He raised his eyebrows. "How about that."

I stared down at my book, no longer able to read the words.

"Were those your kids?"

I looked at him. "What kids?"

"The ones you took up the tower? Sam and Sarah, right?"

I said nothing.

He smiled and gestured toward the sky. "Beautiful day, eh?"

"Are you stalking me?"

"Stalking? Good Lord. That sounds—well, downright unsavory."

I closed the book and turned to him.

"What do you want?"

He smiled. There was not a trace of warmth in it.

He said, "You have a reputation as someone whose word is good. I wanted to remind you to keep your word."

"About what?"

"Your certification. The one attached to our settlement agreement. Where you stated that you weren't representing any parties who were challenging one of my company's projects."

"So?"

"Exactly."

"I'm not following you," I said.

"You would appear to be in violation of that statement."

"Oh, really? How so?"

"I don't know which of my projects you're planning to challenge. At least not yet. But if you persist in your efforts, Counselor, I will have no choice but to turn this over to my lawyer. That is no idle threat. Rob was disappointed, to say the least, that he never got to square off against you in court last time. Apparently, you two have a history. I'm quite sure he'd jump at the chance to do it now, especially if you're the defendant."

"Hold on. Let's back up. Who do you think I'm representing?"

"I don't know yet."

"Would you like me to tell you?"

"Please do."

"No one."

"Come on, Rachel. I hardly think you're off on some lark on your own."

"What are you talking about?"

"I'm talking about Corundum Construction."

"What about it?"

"What business is it of yours?"

"Actually, Ken, that's a good question for you."

"Pardon?"

"What is your relationship with Corundum Construction?"

"What makes you think I know anything about Corundum Construction?"

I gazed at him. "Talk to your lawyer."

"Why should I talk to him?"

"He represents Corundum."

"So? He represents lots of other clients."

I shook my head and stood up. "We're done here. I am not representing any party that is seeking to challenge any project of Ruby Productions. Period."

Yadi scrambled to his feet.

I stared down at Rubenstein. "Have your lawyer call me if you have any further questions. And be sure to tell him that if he tries to sue me over some trumped-up claim of breach of contract, I will haul him in front of the disciplinary commission and I'll seek sanctions against you as well."

"Whoa. Time out, lady. We got off on the wrong foot today. I didn't come down here to pick a fight with you."

"I didn't come down here to talk to you. This is Saturday. I'm here with my family. You and I are done. Please get away from me."

"Come on, Rachel."

"Get away from me."

He stood, his face flushed.

"You listen to me," he said. "This is my livelihood we're talking about."

"Mine, too."

"Don't try to fuck with me."

I stared at him. "And don't try to fuck with me."

From a distance, Sarah called, "Rachel."

I turned to see her and Sam approaching.

"Rachel."

I turned to look at Rubenstein. His face was flushed.

"You have no idea who you're messing with," he said.

"Neither do you."

And I walked away.

My Tough Gal façade disappeared almost as soon as Ken Rubenstein did. I was so rattled by our encounter that I gathered the kids and Yadi and drove straight home, glancing in the rear view mirror most of the way. I decided that we would all stay in that night. My mom and I cooked up a feast, we played some games of Uno and Scattergories, popped some popcorn, and watched *The Princess Bride*. I made sure the burglar alarm was set before going to bed.

I woke up Sunday feeling a little better. By Monday morning, my paranoia level had dropped back to normal, and on Tuesday I had turned my focus to drafting a complaint in a brand new copyright infringement lawsuit that had absolutely nothing to do with Nick Moran, Ruby Productions, Corundum Construction Company, or my late and unlamented Frankenstein case.

Gene Chase was the furthest thing from my mind that afternoon when my secretary buzzed to tell me that Detective Roberto Tomaso was on Line 2.

"We got the results," he said.

"From the autopsy?"

"I promised to call you when they came in."

"And?"

"Interesting."

"Interesting?"

"Interesting."

"Meaning what?"

"Meaning maybe you ought to drop by."

"I'm heading over now."

# Chapter Forty-one

"Dr. Phil says drownings are tricky," Bertie Tomaso said.

Dr. Phil was Philip Edison, the chief medical examiner for St. Louis.

I said, "What's so tricky?"

"Everything—including whether the corpse you fished out of the water actually drowned."

We were seated in Bertie Tomaso's office. He had Gene Chase's autopsy folder on the desk in front of him.

He looked up at me. "Can you handle morgue shots?"

"Sure."

"Check this one out."

He slid an 8 x 10 color photo across the desk top. It was a head shot of Gene Chase.

"My God," I said.

The face had extensive lacerations and bruises. There was an open wound along one cheekbone and what appeared to be a dent high up on his forehead. The dead man looked as if he'd been attacked by someone wearing brass knuckles or wielding a club.

"What's your conclusion?" he asked.

"Beaten to death."

"Sure looks that way, eh?"

"He wasn't?"

"Probably not."

"Look at his head."

"Exactly. That's one of the tricky aspects of drownings, especially in a moving body of water. Corpses in water lie face down. Always. And always with the head hanging down. Bodies tend to move downstream head first. That means the head becomes a battering ram. And with the head hanging down, the blood congests there, which means you can even have post-mortem bleeding if the head bangs into something sharp enough to break the skin. So it's *possible* someone beat the crap out of him, but it's more likely that he got banged up like that after he was dead."

I leaned back in my chair. "Or maybe before he was dead."

"Explain."

"If his killers knew that a coroner would have a hard time figuring out the timing of those injuries, they could have killed him and tossed him into the water."

He held up his hands, palms toward me. "Be patient, gorgeous. We're getting there."

"Proceed."

"The blood tests confirm he was drunk. The blood alcohol content was almost point two."

"How drunk is that?"

"Shit-faced, falling-down drunk. And, again, not unusual."

"What do you mean?"

"A significant portion of male drowning victims are drunk."

"There must be a good punch line there."

"Probably. But here's where it starts to get weird. With your typical drowning victim, you expect to find white foam in the nostrils and in the mouth. None here. With your typical drowning victim, you expect to find a significant quantity of water in the lungs. Not so here."

"No water?"

"Not much, and certainly not as much as you'd expect to see if the victim died in a typical drowning."

"So you're saying he didn't drown?"

"No. Dr. Phil still thinks he drowned."

"So where's the water?"

"In his stomach."

"He drowned by drinking water?"

"Sort of. It's called dry drowning. It's a less common way to drown, but it still happens."

"What is it?"

"Dry drowning involves something called—let me see, where is it—" He skimmed down a page of autopsy notes. "Here we go. It's called a laryngospasm. It's a reflex action in your throat when water enters the windpipe. Your vocal chords clench up and seal off the wind pipe. That prevents water from entering the lungs. We've all experienced it to a certain degree. It can happen to you if you're drinking something and it goes down the wrong tube—or you're in the ocean and get blindsided by a wave. You start coughing like crazy and for a moment you can't breathe. It's pure reflex. It'll even happen if you're unconscious. Anyway, because of laryngospasm, in the initial stage of every drowning the first bit of water goes down the other tube and into the stomach. No water and no air enter the lungs in that first stage because the wind pipe is sealed off. In most victims, the laryngospasm relaxes after the victim loses consciousness. When that happens, the water flows into the lungs and causes a wet drowning."

"But if it doesn't relax?"

"Then the victim essentially suffocates. A dry drowning. Happens about ten percent of all drownings. The seal to the lungs stays shut until after cardiac arrest."

"And that's what happened here?"

"According to Dr. Phil."

I studied Bertie. "But there's more, right?"

He smiled. "Correct."

"What?"

"Dr. Phil had them analyze the contents of his stomach."

"I thought you said it was water."

"For the most part. There was a little undigested food."

"What did the analysis show?"

"The water in his stomach was mostly tap water."

I frowned. "Tap water?"

"The stuff that comes out of your faucets and garden hose. That same stuff that's in your toilets and your sinks and your bathtubs."

"I don't understand what that—oh." I leaned forward. "So he *was* murdered."

"That's the way it appears."

"In his house?"

"Don't know that yet. We have a forensic team over there now. We'll see what they come up with."

I shook my head. "I don't understand, Bertie."

"Understand what?"

"If they're so smart, why did they drown him in tap water?"

"First of all, because it's a helluva lot easier than dragging him down to the stormwater ditch in the middle of a thunderstorm and trying to shove his head under water. But assuming they're smart, they could still drown him in a tub or sink because the majority of the time it won't matter. In a typical wet drowning case, most of the aspirated water gets absorbed into the blood stream before the victim dies. In fact, according to Dr. Phil, that's part of what kills you. You get some sort of circulatory overload with all that water, and then your blood pressure nosedives and you go into cardiac arrest. Any remaining tap water that's still in your lungs would get diluted by the ordinary water currents in the River Des Peres. It's only in a dry drowning that none of the tap water gets absorbed because it's all sitting down there in your stomach."

"Wow."

"Yeah, wow."

"So what's next?"

"We'll see what the forensic team turns up in his house. We'll see if we have any witnesses in his neighborhood. Did he work at that Corundum Construction outfit?"

"No. He told me he worked at a warehouse on North Broadway. I can check my notes and call you."

"Great. We'll talk to folks there, too. Try to identify co-workers and friends, start to fill in the picture of who this guy was and who might want him dead. You get any Corundum names from him?"

"Just one. Rudy Hickman."

Bertie repeated the name aloud as he wrote into his notebook. He looked up.

"What was Hickman's involvement?"

"He was the guy I talked to on the jobsite. From what Chase told us, it sounded like Hickman was the go-between with Corundum. He gave Chase the release and he gave Chase the cash."

"You have anything more beside his name?"

"No."

"We'll locate him and see what he says."

"Do me a favor, Bertie. Have someone—preferably you—take another look at Nick Moran's file. I know we don't know the full story of the connection between Nick and Chase, but we now know that someone killed Chase and tried to make it look like a routine drowning. Maybe someone killed Nick, too. Maybe there's something in his file that doesn't jibe with a routine overdose."

Bertie sighed. "Yes, ma'am. Meanwhile, what else can you tell me about this Corundum outfit?"

"I tried to track them down through their building permits. I came up with a bunch of circumstantial evidence out in the suburbs that seemed to indicate they were involved in a scheme to corrupt city officials."

"Out in the county?"

"Outside your jurisdiction."

"At least for a corruption claim. Out of curiosity, what kind of circumstantial evidence?"

"Do you know what tax increment financing is?"

"Sure. TIFs. Corporate welfare. Subsidizing your local Walmart through sales taxes. Classic zero-sum gain."

"Exactly."

"So?"

I explained what I'd found, namely, the pattern of rehab and renovation jobs on the homes of suburban city officials that seemed to correlate with their votes in favor of TIFs involving Ruby Productions.

"Ruby. That's that Rubenstein guy?"

"Right. I think there may be a connection between Ruby and Corundum."

Bertie laughed. "What an arrogant son of a bitch."

I gave him a curious look. "Who?"

"Rubenstein. He's a crossword puzzle nut, right?"

"Big time. He enters those national competitions. Why?"

"Corundum. It's a Friday *New York Times* crossword puzzle clue."

"What is a Friday clue?"

"The *New York Times* crossword puzzle gets harder each day of the week. Monday's a breeze, Thursday's pretty tough, Friday's a bitch, Saturday's almost impossible. Assuming Rubenstein is the guy behind Corundum, it's a Friday clue."

"A clue for what?"

Bertie gave me a wink and shook his head. "I don't want to spoil the fun."

# Chapter Forty-two

I rolled my eyes.

"What?" Benny said

"They actually let you wear that on campus?"

Benny glanced down. He had on a t-shirt that read: *Attention Ladies: I Enjoy Grey's Anatomy.* He looked up with feigned innocence.

"What? A man can't express an opinion?"

"Have you actually watched the show?"

"I tried once."

"And?"

"I got as far as the second commercial break."

"You should be ashamed."

"Hey, there was a Knicks game on. I'm supposed to pass that up for this chick-flick dreck?"

"That's my point."

He gestured at his t-shirt. "This is just my attempt to assure the distaff side that I'm a sensitive, caring New Age guy."

"Which you aren't."

"Now just hold on, woman. I have actually cried while watching television. On more than one occasion, too."

"Other than while watching a sporting event?"

He paused. "Probably not. But cut me a little slack here. You think the networks are ever going to air a show with anything as heartbreaking as the Giants losing to the Ravens in Super Bowl Thirty-Five? Certainly not on *Grey's Anatomy*, for chrissake."

"So does it work?"

He winked. "Girls like guys who like *Grey's Anatomy.*"

"You are a total pig."

"But I'm your pig."

"If you were my pig, Benny, first thing I'd do is call the vet and get you fixed. By the way, did I hear you correctly? 'Distaff'?"

He smiled. "To paraphrase the deathless lyrics of the Pussycat Dolls, 'Don't cha wish your boyfriend had words like me? Don't cha?'"

"Distaff sounds like vintage *Playboy Advisor* to me, Hef."

"I confess I never read the *Playboy Advisor* in my youth. I was too busy studying the interviews. But back to business. Is this creep really going to show up?"

"He said he would. I offered to meet him at my office but he preferred yours. He thinks a professor's office is a more neutral site. Thanks, by the way."

"Like I'd let you meet him on your own?"

"I don't think he's dangerous."

"You don't know that. According to you, at least two people's deaths might be connected to that Corundum outfit. That means it's time to play it safe. To quote Auric Goldfinger: 'Once is happenstance. Twice is coincidence. Three times is enemy action.'"

"Auric Goldfinger?"

"The bad guy in the James Bond movie. So give me some context here. What's the purpose of meeting with—what's his name?"

"Milton Bornstein. He's one of the Cloverdale City Councilmen who voted in favor of the TIF."

"What do you want from him?"

"The name of someone at Corundum Construction. Someone higher up."

"Why?"

"To see if we can interest the St. Louis County Prosecutor's Office. Bertie's a city cop. All this suburban stuff is outside his jurisdiction—and his department is focused on Gene Chase anyway. Unless they get lucky, they'll be plodding along for weeks—or even months. And even if they solve that crime, they may not find any connection between that murder and Nick's."

"Assuming Nick was murdered."

"Right."

"A big assumption."

"Fair enough. But let's assume he was. The next question is, 'why'? Given what we've found so far, it's probably because of something he knew about Corundum. If so, that means it probably has some connection to this pattern with the TIFs. If we can tie a big name or two with that pattern, we might be able to interest a prosecutor."

"In Nick's death?"

"Not initially. The hook for the prosecutor is the corruption angle. But if Nick's death is connected to that, then maybe—just maybe—they'll turn up that link."

Benny scratched his neck as he thought it over. "It's a long shot."

"It's the only shot I can think of."

He grinned. "As Immanuel Kant once said, 'What the fuck?'"

He checked his watch.

"If this turkey of yours actually shows up," he said, "let me do the talking. I got an idea how to reach this guy."

Ten minutes later, as Benny was filling me in on an antitrust paper he was presenting at an upcoming conference, there was a knock on the door.

"It's open," Benny hollered.

Milt Bornstein peered in. He was wearing aviator sunglasses, a khaki trench coat, and a gray herringbone beret pulled low over his eyes. If this was his idea of a disguise, it failed. With his sharp nose, long ears, and high bald forehead, he looked unmistakably like Milt Bornstein in aviator sunglasses, trench coat, and herringbone beret.

"Come on in," I said.

He glanced from me to Benny and back to me. "Who is this gentleman?"

Benny snorted. "Look at the nameplate on the door, douche bag. This is my office."

Bornstein looked at me. "I didn't realize Professor Goldberg would be joining us. I thought we would just be using his office."

"Hey, pal," Benny said, "when you're in my office you address your remarks to me. Now close the fucking door and sit your ass down."

*Oh, boy.* Benny was on a roll. Nothing to do but sit back and watch.

Bornstein hesitated a moment and then entered the office. He closed the door and took the seat next to me facing Benny's desk.

"Take off those ridiculous shades," Benny said.

Bornstein removed them and placed them in the inside pocket of his trench coat.

Benny stared at him.

"You disappoint me, Milt."

Bornstein frowned. "What do you mean?"

"Ms. Gold asked you for a name and gave you a deadline. What did you do? Jackshit. You let that deadline pass. Even worse, you apparently tipped someone off about your meeting with Ms. Gold. What in the hell were you thinking?"

Bornstein sat motionless.

Benny shook his head. "Here's the deal, Numb Nuts. You either make amends right here and right now, or you can bend over and kiss you sorry ass goodbye."

Bornstein's eyes started blinking.

Benny put his hands together, fingers interlaced, and placed them on the desk in front of him. He leaned forward, eyebrows slightly raised.

"Well?" he said.

"What—" Bornstein stammered "—what are you trying to suggest?"

"I'm not trying to *suggest* anything, Miltie. You know and I know that you have been a bad boy. A very bad boy. You sold your vote on that TIF. You took a bribe in the form of a swimming pool to be built in your own backyard."

"But there's no pool there."

"Not yet."

"There will be no pool." He crossed his arms over his chest and tried to look smug. "You have nothing."

"Of course we do, you putz. We have the fucking building permit. And we have your vote in favor of that TIF."

"That's not enough."

"Miltie, Miltie, Miltie." Benny shook his head sadly. "It's way more than enough because you're not the only one. We've got Corundum Construction projects for city officials in several other suburbs where TIFs got approved. And each of those Corundum Construction projects involved corrupt little weasels just like you. And that's your only hope, my friend. Because those projects have already been built. And that makes those aldermen and council members even more attractive targets than you."

"Targets?"

"For the grand jury and the prosecutor, Milt. That's why we invited you here today. There's going to be an investigation and a grand jury and a blizzard of felony indictments and a big sensational trial with a bunch of nervous city officials sitting in the dock. But first we have to talk with the prosecutor. And that's your chance, Milt—and your choice. Your only chance and your only choice. You can give us your contact name and we can conveniently forget to include you in the list of corrupt city officials we turn over to the prosecutor. Or you can refuse to give us your contact, and we'll be sure to include *your* name at the top of our list. And trust me, pal, that list will be in the prosecutor's hands long before you can scurry back to your contact begging for help. You get my drift?"

Bornstein just sat there, eyes blinking.

Benny unclasped his hands and gestured with his thumb at the *Grey's Anatomy* slogan on his shirt. "You see this?"

Bornstein nodded.

"I happen to like the other *Gray's Anatomy*, too. The textbook by Henry Gray. You familiar with that one?"

Bornstein nodded.

"Fascinating stuff," Benny said. "Everything you need to know about the human anatomy. I took a look at it this morning, Miltie. With you in mind. And guess what I learned? If you get indicted, that prosecutor and judge are going to shove your bald head so far up your ass that when you fart your lips'll quiver."

Benny leaned back in his chair and crossed his arms over his chest. Bornstein's hands were clasped on his lap and he was staring at his knees.

"How's that diagnosis sound to you, Miltie? And that's only the beginning. Once you get to prison, you and your asshole are going to have even more adventures. So let's cut to the chase, eh? Either give me the name or get the fuck out of here."

Benny stood and leaned forward, his fists on the desktop. Bornstein flinched as he looked up at him.

"As you weigh your options, Milt, you need to factor in one more thing. Two men connected to Corundum have already died. You know what that means? If you walk out of here without telling us what you know, you can expect that before too long someone will come knocking on your front door. The dilemma for you is that you won't know who is doing the knocking. It could be an officer of the law standing there with your name on a grand jury subpoena or it could be a hit man standing there with your name on a bullet. So, at the risk of repeating myself, either give me that name or get the fuck out of here."

Bornstein lowered his head.

"You won't tell them about me?" he said in a hoarse whisper.

Benny gave him a benevolent smile. "Rest assured. Our lips will be sealed."

Bornstein looked down at his hands, which were now clenched beneath his knees.

Benny glanced over at me and winked.

In a barely audible whisper, Bornstein said, "The lawyer."

# Chapter Forty-three

Ironically enough, the lawyer called the next morning. He reached me on my cell phone as I was driving into the parking garage of the building in Webster Groves where Linda Dobbins now worked She had been Nick Moran's office manager.

"We need to meet," he said.

"About what?"

"You know what."

"No, I don't."

"Quit playing games. This is serious."

"What are you talking about?"

"My client is furious."

"Which client?"

"Come on, Rachel."

I pulled into a parking spot on the first level and turned off the engine.

I said, "What's your client upset about?"

"You."

"Tell him to chill."

"Cut it out, Rachel."

"What are you talking about?"

"This is serious—and it will get a lot more serious if we don't get this resolved as soon as possible. I booked a private dining room at the Noonday Club for lunch today. Just the two of us. I rescheduled two other meetings so that I'd be available. It's important. Can you meet me there?"

"I have some meetings out of the office this morning. I couldn't be there before one."

"One is fine."

I got out of the car and locked the door.

"You want to tell me what's so important, Rob?"

"Not over the phone. I'll see you at the club. One o'clock."

I rode the elevator up four floors to the offices of Salsich & Gerber, a small real estate firm where Linda now worked as a bookkeeper. The receptionist took my name, and a few minutes later Linda came out and took me to a small interior conference room near the back of the office. I'd called her at work yesterday and explained what I was looking for. She'd agreed to search through her records from Nick Moran's company, which consisted of a dozen file boxes and a set of CD-ROMs she kept stored in her basement.

"Any luck?" I asked.

"Not much. I looked through all twelve boxes. They were still pretty well organized. I'd already looked for Corundum for you last time, but I looked again just to be sure. Nothing. And no mention of Ruby Productions either. I checked that list of addresses you gave."

"And?"

I'd put together a list of addresses by going back through the Corundum building permits in the various cities with TIFs involving Ruby Productions and identifying the other aldermen or council members in each city who'd voted in favor of the TIFs—*i.e.,* the ones who'd had no work on their homes by Corundum. I'd thought that perhaps Nick Moran had done rehab work on one or more of their homes during the relevant time period.

She shook her head. "Nick never did any work at any of those houses. Same with the job files on the CD-ROMs. The only place I found any mention of Ruby Productions was in the email folders."

"What did you find there?"

"Just four emails. I printed them off for you."

She handed me a folder. "You know Nick. He just wasn't big on computers."

"I have to get back to my desk." She stood. "We're running last month's inventory numbers today. Just call me if you have any questions."

"Thanks, Linda."

"I hope you can find out what really happened that night. He was a good man. I miss him."

After she left, I opened the folder. Inside were four sheets of paper, each a printout of an email message with a header that showed the email had been sent or received from Nick's computer. The most recent of the four was a few weeks before Nick's death. The oldest was four years ago.

All four were from sub-contractors, each notifying Nick when they would be available to work a particular remodeling project. Linda's search had turned them up because each mentioned a prior commitment to a Ruby Productions project for certain dates. For example, one was from a guy named Billy at a company called Mound City Home Audio:

RE: In-Ceiling Speaker Install – 725 Davis Street

Hey, Nick, no can do next Thursday. Sorry, bud. Got a major install for Ruby Productions all week at their Balmoral Castles development in Wildwood. Does the following Monday work for you?

To which Nick had replied: "Monday works."

The other three emails—two from a glass company regarding a skylight and one from a company that installed outdoor fireplaces—were similar in content and tone.

I drove west to Fenton to see Nick's sister, Susannah Beale. We were meeting at her favorite spot, the local Krispy Kreme store, while her mother-in-law watched her kids. She was waiting when I arrived and gave me a big hug.

"Thank you so much, Rachel, and thank you for coming out here."

The last time we'd seen each other, she'd been almost six months pregnant with child number three and looked a little frazzled. Today she looked ready to go into labor. I went up to the counter, placed our order, and came back to the table with two glazed donuts and a cola for her, and a cinnamon twist and a coffee for me.

She said, "I know this has been a frustrating case for you."

I took a sip of coffee. "I've been able to find out a little more about that night, but there are still lots of holes."

I filled her in on what we'd learned from Gene Chase—namely, that Nick had died somewhere else and been dropped off in the park.

"Gene was connected to that Corundum company," I said, "and Corundum is connected to Ruby Productions. Ruby Productions might be connected to that list of names and addresses I gave you."

I'd given Susannah the same list I gave to Linda.

She sighed and shook her head. "I looked through all his papers. I couldn't find any of those names."

"What kind of papers?"

"Mostly bills, bank account statements, auto insurance policies—that sort of stuff."

"Anything personal? Letters? A diary?"

Her eyes reddened. "He wasn't that type. Nick had such a hard time reading and writing growing up. They finally tested him in high school and found he had dyslexia. He couldn't read a book—or even a newspaper—but he was amazing with machines and tools. Carpentry, electrical stuff, you name it. He could fix anything. He never had to read instructions, which he probably couldn't have anyway. All he had to do was study the machine, fiddle with it some, and next thing you know it was working again. But that's why there weren't many papers beyond bills and that sort of thing."

"That's okay. It means I can check that open item off my list. It helps me focus on where to look."

I took another sip of coffee and watched her eat her second glazed donut. She seemed a little more disheveled than last time, but with two little kids at home and the third about to arrive, she was entitled.

I said, "I located the three women whose names you gave me. I spoke with each."

"And?"

"You were right. Two of them had a fling with Nick."

Susannah smiled. "Good for him."

"The third one is Barbara Weiss. She was married. Still is, though she's separated from her husband. Your brother did work on their house. Think back. I know he mentioned Barbara to you. Did he ever mention her husband? Did he ever talk about the job?"

"Is the man a jerk?"

"Barb thinks so. Why?"

"Nick didn't talk much about his work with me, but he was over for dinner one Sunday night—oh, maybe three months before he died. I asked him how things were going. He said he'd learned a lesson: never do work for a builder. He told me he was doing a rehab at this guy's house and was going crazy. He thought he might actually lose money on the job because of all the re-dos the guy's inspector was demanding. 'Never again,' he told me."

"The timing's right. That's when he was working on that house. Do you remember anything else he said?"

She mulled it over. "No."

I made a note on my legal pad: *Barb Weiss—husband a builder—check out.*

"When you looked through Nick's bills," I said, "did you see anything from a dentist named Gutterman? Anything about a root canal?"

She gave me a puzzled look. "No. Why?"

"Just another loose end. One of the other women—Brenda—was married to a guy who did root canals."

"I don't think he had a root canal. If he did, I didn't see a bill for it."

I made another note: *No root canal—no tie to Gutterman besides rehab.*

I set down my pen and gave Susannah a smile. "Barbara Weiss was very fond of your brother."

"Everyone was."

Her eyes reddened again. She used the napkin to wipe her nose.

"Nick was wonderful, Rachel. My kids adored him. I brought some pictures today. So you could see that side of Nick."

She took an unsealed envelope out of her purse and opened it. She handed me a snapshot of a Nick holding a little blond girl in his arms. Nick was smiling toward the camera, and the little girl was smiling at him.

"That's Ashley. That was at her second birthday party. Nick made her a big dollhouse. Made it from scratch."

She showed me about a dozen photos of Nick, some with Ashley, some with her son Logan, and some with the whole family. It was clear from the faces in the photos that everyone in Susannah's family, including her husband Earl, adored Nick Moran.

I handed her back the pictures.

"I'm getting closer to an answer for you, Susannah. I promise. I'll call you as soon as I know something more."

"Thank you, Rachel. Thank you so much."

# Chapter Forty-four

The Noonday Club is on the top floor of the 40-story Metropolitan Square building downtown. As I got off the elevator and started toward the club entrance, my cell phone rang.

"Bertie?" I said.

"Whoa, you got ESP?"

"Caller ID. What's up?"

"Some intriguing new tidbits on your favorite case. You got time to drop by this afternoon?"

"I'm walking into a lunch meeting. How 'bout three?"

"See you then, gorgeous."

I put the phone back in my purse and walked over to the maitre d', who smiled and bowed slightly.

"Madame?"

"Rob Crane?"

"Ah, yes. Please follow me."

He led me back to a small private room with a large picture window that looked south past the Arch and down the broad waters of the Mississippi River. The dining table could have seated ten comfortably but was set for two, the place settings across from each other in the middle.

Rob Crane stood by the window, his back to the door, talking on his cell phone as he watched a tugboat pushing a string of eight barges upriver toward the Poplar Street Bridge. The barges were lashed in two rows of four and loaded with black coal. It was a sunny, clear day. From forty stories up, you could follow the river as it curled to the right just south of downtown and then swung back to the left off in the distance beyond the redbrick complex of buildings that comprised the brewery and headquarters of Anheuser-Busch.

Crane turned and nodded at me.

"Hey, Marty," he said into the phone, "I have to go."

He listened, nodding to what Marty was saying. Crane had on his standard power outfit: navy pinstriped suit, crisp white button-down shirt with gold cufflinks, navy-and-red striped tie, dark hair slicked back, strong cologne. He'd actually be sexy if he weren't such a testosteroned jerk.

"Sounds good, Marty. I'll take care of it."

He disconnected the call, slipped the cell phone inside his suit jacket, and held out his hand.

"Hello, Rachel."

We shook.

"I appreciate you joining me here today."

"You sounded distraught."

"Distraught?" He chuckled. "I hope not."

I shrugged but said nothing. This was his party.

He gestured toward the table. "Please sit down. I told Julius we'd need to be served promptly. I know you're a busy gal."

As if on cue, an elderly black man entered the room.

"Mr. Crane, sir?"

"Hello, Julius. This is Ms. Gold. If you can tell us about today's specials we'll place our orders now."

"Yes, sir, Mr. Crane."

He ran through them. I picked the Greek salad. Crane opted for the corned beef sandwich special, in defiance—or perhaps ignorance—of one of the fundamental teachings of our Talmud, which is never order a corned beef sandwich at a *goyishe* club.

Crane's phone rang again just as Julius left to put in our order. He checked the number and gave me an apologetic shrug as he answered. The call sounded personal. I strolled over to the window to watch the tug's progress upriver as Crane tried to end the call without being rude. He succeeded just as Julius entered with our iced teas. I returned to my seat.

Crane lifted his iced tea toward me with a forced smile. "Cheers."

I nodded, took a sip, and lowered my glass.

"Why am I here, Rob?"

"As you and I have discussed before, my client is—"

"—which client?"

"Which?" He gave me a look of puzzled irritation. "Ruby Productions, of course. What other client could I possibly be talking about?"

I shrugged. "Corundum Construction."

He paused, expression neutral. "Ruby Productions is my client. Of what possible relevance is that construction company?"

*Why* "What don't you tell me?"

"I don't represent—what's their name?—Corundum."

"Proceed."

"My client is convinced you are investigating the possibility of another lawsuit involving one of his TIFs."

"So what?"

"That would put you in violation of the signed representation of yours that we attached to the settlement agreement."

"Only if I had been representing another adverse party at the time of the settlement."

"My client believes you were."

"On what basis?"

"Among other things, based upon persons you contacted before the settlement."

"What persons?"

"In other cities where Ruby Productions was involved in projects."

"Your client is mistaken."

"Do you deny those contacts?"

"I don't admit or deny anything, Rob. It's none of your business—or your client's business. I stand by the truth of that statement I signed for the settlement. Period."

There was a knock on the door. Julius entered carrying a platter with our lunches. We waited until he had set them down. I noted that the corned beef special was served on white bread with two small condiment dishes, one with yellow mustard and the other with mayonnaise. Q.E.D.

Crane waited until Julius had refilled our iced teas and closed the door behind him.

"You claim your statement is true," he said. "Fine. I have a proposal for you that should be irresistible if you are in fact representing no party adverse to Ruby Productions."

I sighed. "Go ahead."

"Although my law firm is principal counsel to Ruby Productions, there are occasional situations where we are prevented from representing the company due to a conflict of interest with another client. Just last year, for example, Ruby Productions was in competition with a major local developer. Ruby Productions wanted the property for a gated community. The developer wanted the property for a shopping center anchored by a Wal-Mart. My firm represents Wal-Mart in certain matters, and as I result we were unable to represent Ruby Productions in that deal. My client wants to have a back-up attorney on retainer in the event that should happen again. My client would like you to be that attorney."

I laughed. "Me?"

He took a bite of his sandwich, nodded as he chewed, and took a sip of iced tea.

"To insure your availability," he said, "my client is prepared to pay you an annual retainer in an amount that would make it worth your while to avoid situations where you would represent clients adverse to him. A generous retainer."

"Define generous."

"Two-hundred and fifty thousand dollars per year. For ten years. Non-refundable. If he doesn't need your services in a particular year, you would still keep the entire retainer for that year. If he does need your services, you would keep track of your time at your normal hourly rate, and if your fee exceeded the retainer amount for that year, he would pay you the balance."

I nodded. "That is generous."

"It certainly is. Do we have a deal?"

"No."

"Why not?"

"I'm not interested."

He frowned. "You want a larger retainer?"

"I don't want any retainer, Rob. I don't want anything to do with your client."

His faced reddened slightly. He leaned back in his chair.

"So it's true," he said.

"What's true?"

"You are representing the homeowners."

"What I am doing and who I am representing has nothing to do with my rejection of your client's proposal. I am not interested in representing Ruby Productions."

"You are making a mistake, Rachel."

"It wouldn't be the first time."

"Perhaps, but this time it will cost you. Dearly. When I tell my client that you've turned down his offer, I am certain that he will instruct me to file suit against you personally for breach of the settlement agreement, and he will instruct me to prosecute it vigorously. He is my client. I will obey his request. I will prosecute his claim vigorously. Your clients will suffer, and so will you. There could be significant negative financial and professional consequences for you. You fought the Cloverdale TIF and you won. Why put all that at risk?"

"I'm getting tired of these threats, Rob. You guys need some new material."

He leaned forward.

"I urge you to reconsider, Rachel."

I set my fork down, tossed my napkin onto the table and stood. "We done here."

I paused at the door and looked back.

"See you in court."

# Chapter Forty-five

Jacki Brand shook her head when I finished. "That's outrageous."

Benny chuckled. "Old Ben Franklin's right on target."

Jacki turned to him. "Franklin?"

"Rachel's paying the price."

"For what?"

"For the way she chose not to end her high school date with Rob Crane."

Jacki turned to me. "What the hell is he talking about?"

"I'll fill you in later."

"Speaking of which, ladies, more salami?"

Benny was slicing slabs of Volpi's Italian salami at the side table in my office. I'd called him on my way back from my meeting with Detective Bertie Tomaso to see if he could meet with us. He came by at five o'clock, having stopped first at DiGregorio's on the Italian Hill to pick up a Volpi salami, a wedge of pecorino cheese, a crusty Italian bread, and two bottles of Chianti—proving again the good judgment of inviting Benny to your meetings.

"Two-hundred-and-fifty grand a year?" Jacki said. "Sounds more like a bribe than a retainer."

"That was my thought," I said.

Benny handed around another plate of salami, cheese, and bread.

"You think that jackass will really sue you?" he asked.

"Who knows. Ken Rubenstein makes lots of threats."

I took a bite of cheese and then a sip of wine. "This is delicious, Benny. You're in the wrong profession."

"I should be a waiter?"

"A wife." I checked my watch. "I could use one."

"Is your mom covering?" Jacki asked.

"Fortunately."

"So enough about Rob Crane," Benny said. "What's up with the cops?"

"A couple things."

"Such as?" Jacki asked.

"Such as Rudy Hickman has vanished."

"Which one is Hickman?" Benny asked.

Jacki said, "The Corundum foreman that Rachel talked to out at the job site that day. He was the go-between with Gene Chase."

She turned to me. "Vanished?"

"Apparently. Bertie sent a squad car to his apartment two nights ago. No one was home. The next morning they checked the job site where I'd last seen him. According to the work crew, he'd been gone both days. Back at the apartment complex no one knew where he was."

"Is he married?" Benny asked.

"Divorced. Five years ago. They talked to his ex-wife. She didn't know anything about his whereabouts, although they don't talk anymore."

"What are the cops doing?" Jacki asked.

"Nothing yet. According to his ex-wife, Hickman disappeared twice when they were married. Once for four days, once for two. Both times he went on a booze and gambling spree—once just across the river to Illinois, the other time all the way to Atlantic City. Just up and disappeared. So the cops are going to give him a little more time to show up. If he's still missing by the end of the week, they'll start looking."

"Did Bertie have anything else for you?" Benny asked.

"I'd asked him to take another look at the results of the tests they ran on Nick Moran's body fluids. He did."

"And?" Jacki said.

"You guys ever heard of a drug called Ketamine?"

Benny and Jacki looked at one another and turned back to me.

"It's a general anesthetic," I said. "Typically used on animals. But according to Bertie, it's become a popular recreational drug for humans, especially at club raves, where it's known as Special K. It comes in liquid, pill, or powder form. The powder form is the most popular. You can snort it or mix it in a drink or even smoke it."

"What's it do?" Jacki asked.

"In small doses, it makes you feel euphoric, which is why it's popular in nightclubs."

Jacki said, "And large doses?"

"Pretty much what you'd expect from an anesthetic. Medium doses distort your sense of balance and time, make you lethargic, incoherent. Large doses can cause disorientation, hallucinations, loss of consciousness. According to Bertie, that's why some creeps use it as a date-rape drug. Pour the right amount in your date's drink and she'll be zoned out in ten minutes."

"They found it in Moran's blood?" Benny said.

"Urine."

"How much did he take?"

"They don't know. The body metabolizes the drug pretty quickly. Usually in a couple hours. But traces of the drug can remain detectable for up to a week. That means all we know is that sometime before he died, Nick Moran ingested Ketamine."

"Didn't seem the club rave type," Benny said.

"You think he got date raped?" Jacki asked me.

"I think he got murdered. He didn't have any history of heroin use—or of any drugs. What I think is that someone mixed Ketamine into a drink, got him semi-paralyzed, and then shot him up with heroin."

"And decided to give him a blow job just for the hell of it?" Benny gave me a skeptical look. "What did Bertie say?"

"He says he's getting more suspicious."

"Enough to re-open the case?" Jacki asked.

I sighed. "Not yet."

"Why not?"

"He said it's not that unusual to find other drugs or alcohol in the bodily fluids of someone who overdoses—especially someone who doesn't appear to have a history of drug use. It happens in clubs, fraternity parties, elsewhere."

"This is really fucked up," Benny said. "You got a man who dies of a heroin overdose with a date-rape drug in his bloodstream and his shvantz hanging out of his pants. You got a key witness who ends up dead in a stormwater sewer with a belly full of tap water. You got another witness who conveniently disappears. And all three might be connected to a developer who's probably been bribing aldermen through a shell company. Top that off with the developer's lawyer, who's still peeved over that high school handshake and who's now threatening to sue you personally for breaching the settlement agreement. All that crazy shit—and meanwhile you got a bunch of law enforcement officials sitting along the sidelines with their thumbs up their asses."

"Don't forget about the judge," Jacki said.

Benny frowned. "What judge?"

"Howard Flinch. If Rubenstein actually sues Rachel for breach of the settlement agreement, the matter gets heard by Judge Flinch because it was his case."

"Jesus." Benny shook his head. "That'd be a three-ring circus from hell."

I started laughing and clapped my hands together.

Benny looked over at me. "What's so funny?"

"You're a genius, Benny. Judge Flinch. He's the answer."

"What's the question?"

"How to solve Nick's death."

"How the hell does Judge Flinch do that?"

"By being Judge Flinch. He's our wild card."

Jacki said, "I'm lost."

"You won't be by tomorrow morning at ten."

"What's happening then?"

"We're appearing before Judge Flinch on an emergency motion. You and me, Jacki. You'll be my lawyer."

"An emergency motion for what?" Benny asked.

I shrugged. "We'll need to figure that out pretty fast."

# Chapter Forty-six

Counting Judge Flinch, there were seven of us squeezed into his chambers that morning. I was there as attorney for the settling defendants in the Frankenstein case. Jacki was there as my attorney. Rob Crane was there on behalf of Ruby Productions, along with his posse, which today consisted of a junior partner, a senior associate, and a junior associate—all male, all dour. Rob, Jacki, and I were seated on the three chairs facing Judge Flinch's desk. Crane's posse stood behind him.

We were there on my emergency motion for a rule to show cause why Ruby Productions should not be held in contempt, etc., etc. The full title ran on for another three lines. The essence of the motion was that the court needed to step back into the case to (a) enjoin Ruby Productions and its attorney from making baseless threats against me and my clients, and (b) declare that there had been no breach of the settlement agreement. It was, to put it mildly, an unusual motion.

We'd finished it around ten-thirty last night. On her drive home, Jacki served a copy on Crane, along with a notice that we'd be appearing in court the next morning to seek a prompt hearing. He'd met her at the door in his bathrobe.

Judge Flinch was delighted to see us. As I had confirmed with his clerk, he had nothing on his docket the whole week. He was leaning back in his chair now and twisting the end of his mustache with his right hand as he appeared to ponder the situation. He was staring at Jacki.

"Tell me, Counsel," he said to her. "Is it Jacqueline or Jacki?"

"Jacki, Your Honor."

"Jacki, eh?"

He nodded and smiled, twisting the end of his mustache.

"You are a fine strapping young woman, Miss Jacki."

Jacki gave him a perfect Miss Manners smile. "Why thank you, Your Honor."

She looked elegant—and imposing—in a dark blue skirt suit and white blouse. In her blue pumps, she actually stood taller than Rob Crane. She'd towered over Judge Flinch when he stood to greet us as his clerk ushered us into his chambers.

That Judge Flinch was taken with Jacki only improved our chances. The motion was a long shot to begin with—a strategy worth trying only in front of someone like Judge Flinch. On our drive to the courthouse Jacki and I had gone over every scenario we could come up with, including various arguments Crane might try and various persona the judge might put on—but neither of us had imagined a Casanova in a black robe.

Crane cleared his throat. "To repeat, Your Honor, I can assure the Court that there is no need for a hearing over this purported settlement dispute. I can further assure Court that I will speak with my client today. I will advise him of Ms. Gold's position, as set forth in her motion papers, and I will discuss with him the possibility of a quiet resolution of this matter outside of Court."

Judge Flinch pursed his lips in what almost passed for a thoughtful expression and turned toward Jacki.

"'A quiet resolution,' sayeth he. What sayeth thee, Miss Jacki?"

*Oy*, I thought. *He's going Old Testament?*

Jacki shook her head. "I am afraid there can no longer be a quiet resolution, Your Honor."

"Really, Miss Jacki. What maketh ye say that?"

She gestured toward Crane. "Opposing counsel and his client have already broken the silence. They have rung the bell of breach. Frankly, Your Honor, as Judge Ito once said, 'You can't unring that bell.'"

I could have kissed her.

Flinch nodded gravely and sat back in his chair. "Excellent point, Miss Jacki. Excellent point. You maketh me seest the light."

I said, "If I may, Your Honor, let me also point out that the bell Mr. Crane and his client have rung is not some trivial sleigh bell. This Court fully grasps the significant public policy issues at stake in the underlying case. Indeed, I described to Ms. Brand this morning the Court's deep concern that the settlement of this matter would deprive the citizens of our community of the opportunity to observe a hearing on those crucial issues. So, no, Your Honor, the bell Mr. Crane and his client have rung is much closer in size and significance to the Liberty Bell."

Crane snorted. "Oh, for God's sake, Rachel, that is absolutely—"

"Mr. Crane!" Flinch leaned forward, his bald head flushed. "Do not argue with Counsel! Not in my Court and not in my chambers. Have you no shame, sir? Have you no sense of decorum? If you have a response to Opposing Counsel, you address that response to me."

"I apologize, Your Honor," Crane said in a clipped voice. He took a breath. "Contrary to Ms. Gold's ridiculous metaphor, no bell—sleigh or otherwise—has been rung by anyone. I had a private discussion with her about my client's concerns regarding her compliance with all terms in the settlement agreement. *Her* compliance, Your Honor, and not her clients'. That was a purely private and confidential conversation."

"Not anymore, eh?" Judge Flinch held up the motions papers, which included as Exhibit A my affidavit detailing Crane's threat and his client's offer of a multi-year $250,000 retainer. "This is public, Mr. Crane. Filed down there in clerk's office for the whole doggone world to see."

"Which brings me to *our* emergency motion," Crane said. "The one we filed this morning. My conversation with Ms. Gold was strictly confidential. She should never have revealed it in a public filing. That is why we are asking this Court to enter an order placing her motion under seal."

"That'll be granted…when hell freezes over." Flinch laughed. "Denied."

Crane nodded, expressionless. "We would also ask the Court to deny Ms. Gold's motion. We have filed no claim of breach of the settlement agreement, and we have no present plans to do so. We are investigating the matter and we will be happy to discuss it further with Ms. Gold and her Counsel. But at present there is no justiciable controversy, Your Honor. Nothing for this Court to consider or to rule upon."

Crane paused and gave the judge an exasperated man-to-man smile.

"Frankly, Your Honor," he said, "this whole proceeding today is based upon nothing more than idle—or more precisely—overheated speculation. If Ms. Gold really wants to play in the big leagues, I would suggest that she try to develop some thicker skin."

Jacki leaned forward and rested her imposing forearms on the desk. "Your Honor?" she asked in a sweet voice.

The judge almost blushed. "Yes, Miss Jacki."

"I realize the Court prefers that Counsel address all comments to the Court and not to one another."

"Ah, you are correct, Miss Jacki. Dost thou haveth something for thy Court?"

"I do, Your Honor. I wish to express my disappointment at hearing Opposing Counsel make that disparaging personal comment about my colleague. It is unseemly and unprofessional, Your Honor. I was wondering if perhaps you could advise Mr. Crane that if he ever says something like that again to Ms. Gold or about Ms. Gold, I will personally kick his ass."

"Ha!" Judge Flinch leaned back in his chair, eyes wide with delight. "What a gal!"

He turned to Crane. "Better watch your tongue, sir."

He looked back at Jacki and glanced at her arms, which still rested on his desk. "Do you lift weights, young lady?"

"I used to."

"How much could you bench press back then? Two hundred pounds?"

Jacki gave him a demure smile. "Actually, Your Honor, three hundred and twenty pounds."

"Whoa!" Flinch applauded. "What a gal. Well, Counsel, I am ready to rule."

"Your Honor," Crane said. "Opposing Counsel's motion has blown this matter way out of proportion. No matter how much they try to puff this up, this is a minor dispute."

"Minor?" Flinch said, eyebrows raised in disbelief. "If this is so minor, why did you bring all those lawyers with you. Hell, you outnumber the womenfolk here two to one. Four lawyers, and now you claim it's no big deal?"

He chuckled and turned to us. "You know why the lawyers in Mr. Crane's firm are like wolves? They travel in packs."

He looked up at the three lawyers standing behind Crane and gestured toward the door.

"Speaking of which, would one of you los lobos go out there and call in my clerk?"

The youngest of Crane's associates stepped outside and returned a moment later with the judge's docket clerk, a middle-aged black woman.

"Lucinda," Judge Flinch said. "Today is Tuesday. Block out this Thursday and Friday for a two-day evidentiary hearing on this emergency motion for—" he reached for the motion papers and frowned at them "—rule to show cause and so on and so forth. And notify the boys and girls down in the press room that it's open season for the media."

He turned back to us. "See you folks on Thursday at ten a.m. sharp. Be sure to dress pretty for the cameras."

# Chapter Forty-seven

I assumed Rob Crane and Ken Rubenstein would take the gamble, despite the considerable risks.

And they did.

I hoped they would lose.

And they did.

The official time of defeat—according to the time stamp on the two-sentence per curiam opinion faxed over from the Missouri Court of Appeals the following afternoon—was 1:37 p.m. The ruling denied Ruby Productions' emergency petition seeking a reversal of Judge Flinch's order granting a hearing on my motion or, in the alternative, seeking a reversal of Judge Flinch's order opening his courtroom to all media. In plain English, the Court of Appeals ruled that the hearing could proceed on Thursday with full media access.

What made the gamble so risky for Crane and Rubenstein is that any effort to gag the press not only heightens its interest in the dispute but elevates the story's significance in the reporters' minds. Nothing is more important to the press than a story about an attempt to muzzle the press—as evidenced by the flurry of media coverage generated in response to Crane's efforts. He had filed the emergency appeal Tuesday afternoon. We were the lead story on all local TV stations Tuesday night. By Wednesday morning, attorneys for two local TV stations had intervened in the appeal.

If Crane had won his gamble—*i.e.*, if he had prevailed in the court of appeals—the story would have faded quickly, along with whatever leverage I had. But the denial of his petition transformed the upcoming hearing, at least in the eyes off the press, into the biggest Missouri court battle since the Dred Scott case. It was, by any measure, a public relations catastrophe for Crane and his client. Indeed, Judge Flinch's docket clerk notified the parties Wednesday afternoon that she'd received inquires from representatives of the *Wall Street Journal*, the *New York Times*, CNN, MSNBC, Fox News and, of course, all of the local TV news shows.

I suspected that the publicity nightmare posed by the upcoming hearing would be the least of the concerns for Ruby Productions and its attorney. Although I still hadn't been able to fit all the pieces together, the pattern that had emerged from the connections among Ruby Productions, Corundum Construction, and the various city officials certainly resembled a criminal scheme. And if Milton Bornstein's experience was typical of the city officials, the list of co-conspirators included Rob Crane. And if that was so, then Rubenstein and his attorney had good reason to be flustered.

My first call from Crane came on Wednesday at eleven-thirty—almost two hours before the Court of Appeals ruled on his petition. The timing didn't surprise me. Crane's firm was wired into the system, which meant that someone at the Court had tipped him off. He said his client was prepared to settle the dispute by filing a stipulation in court that there had been no breach of the settlement agreement and, further, by agreeing to reimburse the plaintiffs for all legal fees and costs incurred in connection with the proceedings. I turned him down and replaced the receiver as he was trying to convince me to discuss the offer. He called back five minutes later. I had my secretary tell him I was busy.

And I was.

Jacki and I had been preparing for Thursday's hearing ever since returning from Judge Flinch's chambers on Tuesday.

Benny taught two classes on Wednesday morning but came by after lunch to help us out. By the time he arrived, we'd sent off the last of our process servers with subpoenas and were in the process of selecting which of the exhibits needed to be added to the big-screen presentation for the judge (and the TV cameras).

I'd placed a takeout lunch order with Adriana's on the Hill— an assortment of her Italian meatball and salsiccia sandwiches and a triple order of her homemade eggplant caponata. By the time Dorian returned with the order, we had received the fax from the Court of Appeals announcing the decision denying Crane's emergency petition. High fives all around.

Thirty minutes later we were in the conference room finishing our lunches and going over hearing strategies when my secretary cleared her throat. I looked up. She was standing in the conference room doorway.

"Rob Crane," she said.

"Again?"

She help up her hands. "He says it's urgent."

"Tell him I'm at lunch, Dorian."

"No," Benny said. "Take it."

"Why?"

"Think about it, Rachel. Tomorrow's hearing is *your* hearing. That means *you're* the only one with the power to stop it. No one knows that better than Crane. He and his client are strapped inside the Flinch Flyer, a/k/a the Roller Coaster from Hell. If they're starting to shit bricks over their predicament, then this just might be the right time to lay a real demand on those bastards."

I mulled it over and turned to Dorian. "Sometimes he's right."

She smiled. "Line two."

I used a napkin to wipe my hands and mouth, picked up the receiver, and pressed the Line 2 connection.

"Yes, Rob."

"My client wants to settle this dispute once and for all."

"That sounds familiar."

"I'm serious."

"I've heard that line, too."

"Jesus, Rachel."

"Go ahead. Make it fast."

"Number one: we will file a stipulation that there has been no breach of the settlement agreement. Number two: we will pay all fees and costs incurred in connection with this dispute. And number three: as a show of respect to your clients and a sign of our sincerity, we will make a payment of two-thousand dollars to each household in Brittany Woods."

He paused.

I said nothing.

He said, "I think even you would have to admit that my client has made an extraordinarily generous offer to your clients. It covers every possible concern of yours."

"Not quite."

"For chrissake, Rachel, what else could you possibly want from us?"

"The real story of Nick Moran's death."

"What?"

"You heard me."

"What are you talking about? Who is Nick Moran?"

"Ask your client."

"I'm serious."

"So am I, Rob."

I could hear him breathing on the other end.

"Nick Moran?" he said.

"Yes."

"He's dead?"

"Yes."

"You think his death has some connection to your case?"

"It doesn't matter what I think. You made me a settlement offer, Rob. I rejected it. You asked me what else I wanted. I just told you."

I paused and winked at Jacki.

"Rob," I said, "if you want to play in the big leagues, then listen carefully. You get me what I want, and we'll have a deal.

And just so we're clear, when I say I want the real story, that includes admissible evidence to verify it."

"Are you serious?"

"Dead serious."

I hung up.

Benny chuckled.

"What?" I said.

"You got some Kong-sized *beitzim*, woman."

I shook my head. "We don't have to go forward with the hearing tomorrow. This whole circus is for Nick and his sister. We're just trying to get the prosecutors interested in these TIF scams in the hope that maybe they'll stumble across Nick's killer in the process. If we can get to that same result quicker this way, if we can find out the real story behind Nick's death and turn it over to Bertie Tomaso without that hearing, that's fine with me."

"You think Crane knows anything about his death?" Jacki asked me.

"It didn't sound like it."

"So what do you expect him to do?" she said.

"I'm guessing he calls back in an hour to tell me that Nick Moran died of a drug overdose in Forest Park."

"What do you say then?" Jacki asked.

"I repeat my settlement demand: I tell him I want the real story—not the one that was faked up for the cops."

"Reality check," Benny said. "How's he going to get the real story?"

"If I'm right—if Corundum is somewhere in the background—then we get the answer by motivating the lawyer for Corundum."

"How?" Jacki asked.

"Fear. We need to be able to tie Crane directly into this kickback scheme, and then we need to make sure he understands his predicament."

"Can Bornstein do that?" Jacki said.

"In a heartbeat," Benny said.

"Yes and no," I said to Benny. "We promised him we wouldn't use his name."

"That's okay," Jacki said. "We'll have all those other dirty city officials under subpoena for tomorrow."

"Don't count on it," I said. "If those officials were really doing what we think they were doing, they're going to be lawyered up by the time they get on the witness stand tomorrow. I'm guessing most of them will take the Fifth, and the rest will lie. For our sake, I'm hoping for the Fifth."

"That'll still make them look guilty as hell," Jacki said.

"But not Crane," I said. "That's why we need to find an innocent city official. Someone who can tell the truth without fear of incriminating himself."

Jacki frowned. "An innocent city official? What does that get us?"

Benny laughed. "Rachel is a genius."

He turned to Jacki.

"You want to know what an innocent city official gets us? Rob Crane's balls in a vise, that's what, and Rob Crane's balls in a vise might just get us the name of the killer."

"Assuming he can find that out," Jacki said.

I poked my head out of the conference room. "Dorian?"

She came around the corner. "Yes?"

"How are you doing with the contacts information?"

"I have home addresses and phones for most of them."

"What about Cloverdale?"

She smiled. "All of them."

"You're awesome, Dorian. Bring in what you have and go home and get some rest. We're going to have a long day tomorrow."

I returned to the conference room.

I said, "Dorian found us home addresses and phone numbers for most of the aldermen and city council members who voted against these TIFs, including all of the Cloverdale no votes. We need to divide up the list and try to reach each of them tonight."

Jacki was frowning. "I'm still lost. You want us to talk to city officials who voted *against* the proposed TIF in their town? The good guys?"

"Right," I said.

"Why?"

"Remember Milt Bornstein's story. He told us that Rob Crane was the go-between. Crane was the one who proposed the deal with Corundum. Bornstein wanted an in-ground swimming pool. He'd already priced them out. It would have cost him at least thirty thousand dollars. Crane told him that if he voted in favor of the TIF, he could get that same pool built for five grand."

"Okay," Jacki said, uncertainly.

"Now we need to find someone who got the same offer from Crane but said no. Someone who listened to the proposal and rejected it."

Jacki frowned. "Crane wouldn't be crazy enough to make those kickback offers blind."

"I agree," I said. "I'm sure he was careful. I'm sure he and Rubenstein sized up each council member and only approached the ones who seemed susceptible. And I'm sure he was careful to raise the subject in a subtle way to gauge the other party's reaction before going any deeper. But no one is perfect. Maybe he misjudged one or two of them. If so, maybe we can find one who'd be willing to take the witness stand and describe the kickback offer. If we can do that, we'll put that person's name on our witness list and serve it on Crane. It'll be his very own Sword of Damocles."

Benny laughed. "I love it."

# Chapter Forty-eight

There were three television cameras in the crowded courtroom—one against the back wall and one along each side wall. I was at the counsel table to the left of the judicial bench with Jacki seated on my right, Benny on my left. At the other counsel table sat Rob Crane, Ken Rubenstein, and the three attorneys who had been in Judge Flinch's chambers with Crane on Tuesday.

The gallery behind us was almost full, although many of the seats were occupied by reporters or subpoenaed witnesses—mostly city officials, mostly accompanied by attorneys, which suggested this would be a big day for the Fifth Amendment. The entire Cloverdale neighborhood steering committee sat in the first row on our side of the center aisle, along with Nick's sister Susannah. The rows behind them on both sides of the aisle included a scattering of spectators mixed in with the press, witnesses, and lawyers.

Indeed, the only missing player in the courtroom was the judge himself. His order scheduling the hearing had stated "10 a.m. sharp," and thus we'd all been in our seats and ready to begin at ten that morning. At 10:10, I'd checked with his docket clerk, who assured me that there was nothing else on his docket. Nevertheless, it was now 10:20 and still no sign of the Honorable Howard Flinch.

We'd gotten to the courthouse around eight that morning to set up our equipment, which was all in place by the time Crane and his entourage arrived at quarter to ten. Our equipment included a large flat-screen LCD monitor on a stand against the wall above the empty jury box, which was to my right and the judge's left. The monitor was hooked up to a laptop computer on the table in front of Jacki.

I glanced over at the other table. Crane was jotting notes on his yellow legal pad. Ken Rubenstein was hunched over a crossword puzzle. The other three attorneys were seated motionless, each with a stack of papers in front of him on the table.

I studied Crane. Despite his macho façade, he had the slightly frayed look of someone who understands that he and his client were, in Benny's words, strapped inside the Flinch Flyer. His emergency appeal had failed, and now he was back in the clutches of Missouri's kookiest judge. Worse yet for Crane, the Court of Appeals' denial of his emergency petition had surely emboldened a judge who didn't need further emboldening.

As predicted, Crane had called me late yesterday afternoon to tell me that he'd done some investigation and had learned that Nick Moran died of a heroin overdose. I told him that anyone doing a name search on Google could have come up with the same answer. I wanted the *real* story.

"The *real* story," he'd repeated, exasperated. "That's not just what some newspaper said. It's what the police said."

"I told you my terms, Rob. The *real* story."

He didn't call back that day, and we hadn't spoken this morning.

I took out the typed list of names I'd prepared late last night. I showed it to Jacki and gestured toward Crane's table. She nodded. I walked over to Crane. He looked up from his notes. Rubenstein was still hard at work next to him, a stopwatch resting on the table near the half-completed puzzle.

I said, "Here's a list of the witnesses we may call. We aren't required to provide it to you, but I'm doing it as a professional courtesy."

Crane frowned as he took the document from me. Rubenstein clicked the stopwatch and peered over Crane's shoulder at the list.

I watched, trying to read Crane's reaction as he skimmed down the list. Most of the names should not have surprised him. They were the witnesses he would have expected I might call. He'd probably heard from all of their lawyers already.

One name on the list might have been unfamiliar to him; however, if he called around during a break he would discover that Robert Early was a frequent expert witness in lawsuits over construction costs.

But the last name on the list—placed last for a reason—was Abraham Lincoln Johnson. It was a name that would have special meaning to Crane. It was a name that should send a wave of unease down his spine.

He glanced up at me and then turned around to survey the gallery. I guessed—hoped—he was looking for Abraham Lincoln Johnson. He wouldn't find him. I'd told Abe not to come to Court until I telephoned.

"Do you have your witness list for me?" I asked, knowing Crane didn't and not really caring, since I assumed his sole witness was the man seated next to him.

Crane turned back from the crowd and looked down the table at the other three attorneys, who were looking back at him uncertainly.

"No," he said. "I don't anticipate calling many witnesses. This is your ridiculous motion, not mine. You're the one with the burden of proof."

Rubenstein stared up at me, anger his eyes.

I returned to our table. Benny stood and leaned in close.

"You're right about Rubenstein. I've seen him before, too."

"Where?" I whispered.

"Not sure." He leaned around me to have another look. "It'll come to me."

Just as we were taking our seats, the buzzer sounded and the bailiff announced, "All rise."

The side door opened and Judge Howard Flinch entered with a flourish and charged up the three stairs to his bench.

"What the fuck?" Benny whispered. "Is this Halloween?"

Instead of the standard black judicial robe, Judge Flinch was wearing a scarlet one with five gold-braided stripes on each sleeve. In his right hand he was holding a large silver gavel. I looked at him closer. He appeared to have used extra wax on the ends of his mustache, which were formed into large curlicues.

Flinch gave the courtroom audience a big smile, pausing to nod at each of the cameras along the side walls. With the scarlet robe and flamboyant mustachio, the effect was almost surreal, as if we were attending an avant-garde staging of a Gilbert and Sullivan operetta—a crack cocaine version of *Iolanthe*. I half expected him to burst into song. Instead, he plopped down behind the bench.

"Ladies and gentlemen," he announced, "please be seated."

As the crowd took its seats, he rapped the gavel three times. It sounded like three rifle shots.

"This Court will now come to order."

He turned to me with a big smile. "Ah, Miss Gold. How are we today?"

I stood. "Thank you, Your Honor. With me are my co-counsel, Jacki Brand and Professor Benjamin Goldberg."

"Professor, eh?" Flinch said, his eyebrows shooting up. "No pop quizzes today, sir."

The judge chuckled in appreciation of his remark. Benny forced a smile.

"And Mr. Crane," Flinch said, turning toward that table. "Here with your wolf pack, eh? Is that other gentlemen Mr. Rubenstein?"

Crane stood. "Yes, Your Honor. This is Kenneth Rubenstein, Chairman and CEO of Ruby Productions."

"No bike shorts today, eh, Mr. R?"

The judge chuckled again, clearly enjoying himself.

"Okay, Counsel, it's show time. Miss Gold, can you explain to the Court and to our viewers at home why we are gathered here today?"

That was the cue for Rob Crane to stand and again repeat his objection to the hearing, to repeat his contention that there was no issue in dispute because his client had never filed any court paper alleging a breach of the settlement agreement.

Judge Flinch rolled his eyes, mugging for the camera. "You need to get yourself some new material, Counsel. You made that same objection on Tuesday and I overruled it. Then you ran up to the Court of Appeals like a hysterical schoolgirl crying and wringing your hands and whimpering about that same objection and what did they do? Overruled it, too. I go turkey hunting each Spring down in the Bootheel, Mr. Crane. Over near Caruthersville. They got themselves a saying down there that fits your objection: That dog won't hunt. Overruled. Miss Gold, you may continue. And be sure to give us a little background on your lawsuit for our viewers at home."

I walked up to the podium and started by explaining the origins of the lawsuit, specifically, my clients' objections to the use of public financing and the powers of eminent domain for the benefit of private developers through TIFs in general—and in particular to the loss of their homes and neighborhood for a fancy new gated community. I explained that while I was aware that Ruby Productions had been the beneficiary of this sort of public financing in other communities, neither my clients nor I had any interest in challenging those other developments.

"The lawsuit that I filed, Your Honor, was all about, and *only* about, my clients' homes and my clients' neighborhood. Period."

I glanced back at Jacki, who nodded and pressed a button on the computer. The huge flat-screen monitor above the jury box flickered once and then displayed a black-and-white photo portrait of Nick Moran.

"As Mr. Crane can confirm," I said, "we lawyers represent more than one client at the same time. The gentlemen displayed on the screen is the late Nick Moran. Mr. Moran was a talented carpenter and craftsman whose business was home renovations. I knew him. He rehabbed my kitchen and did some beautiful renovations on the coach house behind my house where my mother lives. He was a true artist and a wonderful man. He died earlier this year. According to the police report" —and here the image switched to a display of the newspaper article on his death— "he died of a heroin overdose in his pickup truck, which was parked along a lane in Forest Park that is well known to the police as an after-hours meeting place for gay men seeking anonymous sex. Mr. Moran was partially undressed, which suggested to the police that he died of the overdose while attempting to engage in a sexual act."

I paused. The screen image switched back to the photograph of Nick Moran.

"A week or so after Nick's death, his sister Susannah came to visit me. Susannah Beale is here today, Your Honor. She is seated in the first row behind me."

I turned toward the gallery and nodded toward Susannah. She smiled and blushed slightly. I turned back to the judge.

"Susannah did not believe the police version of her brother's death. She didn't believe that her brother was a drug user. She didn't believe that he was the type who sought out anonymous sexual encounters with other men in a park. She asked me to look into his death. I was reluctant to get involved. Nick was her big brother. She loved him. She looked up to him. She believed he could do no wrong. Frankly, that was my biggest concern. I did not want to break Susannah's heart. How often these days have we learned dark and surprising secrets about people we know—especially, famous men, television preachers, U.S. Senators, governors—people who rail against homosexuality or adultery or prostitution but who turn out to be homosexuals or adulterers and johns themselves? Nevertheless, I agreed to investigate her brother's death—to determine whether he had died of an accidental drug overdose or whether he had been murdered."

The screen went blank.

"To borrow a line from the Grateful Dead, Your Honor, that investigation has been a long strange trip. As you will hear from the witnesses and see in the evidence, this long strange trip has taken me from that dark lane in Forest Park to what appears to be a massive criminal conspiracy involving the corruption of public officials throughout St. Louis County."

There was a low hum of surprised voices behind me.

"Your Honor," Crane demanded, getting to his feet, "I object. This is nothing but rank speculation and malicious character assassination."

"Those are strong words, Mr. Crane," the judge said. "But let's give Miss Gold a little more rope. She'll either hang herself or your client. Overruled. You may proceed, Miss Gold."

"Thank you, Your Honor."

The judge said, "I do hope we will soon be hearing from the lovely Miss Jacki."

He turned toward Jacki and gave her big smile. She smiled back at him.

"We will, Your Honor."

"Excellent." He twisted on one end of his mustache and turned back to me. "Proceed, Miss Gold."

I explained the initial stages of my investigation—of my source who witnessed the mysterious second pickup truck along Gay Way that night in Forest Park, of how I traced the license plate to the even more mysterious Corundum Construction Company, which appeared to exist nowhere outside the corporate records of the Missouri Secretary of State.

"But it *was* a construction company," I emphasized, "and that meant that if it actually constructed something it would leave a fingerprint in the form of a building permit. So I started searching through the building permit records in the city halls of every town and city in St. Louis County. And guess what? I started to find building permits. Like this one."

The monitor displayed a blow-up of one of the Asbury Groves permits, with the name Corundum Construction highlighted in yellow.

"And this one."

A blow-up of another permit.

"And this one."

Another one.

"I started dropping by these houses," I said, "hoping to find the pickup truck with that license plate number. Whoever was driving that pickup on the night Nick Moran died was probably the last person to see him alive. If I could just find that truck and talk to the driver, I might be able to tell my client how her brother died. So I kept looking and looking, and eventually—"

The monitor displayed the photograph I'd taken of the rear of the black Dodge Ram pickup parked in the driveway of 359 Dorantes Way in the town of Amity. The license plate was clearly visible.

"—I found it."

I paused. Judge Flinch was leaning forward, staring intently at the image. I could hear whispering in the gallery behind me.

I said, "But something interesting happened along the way."

A new image: a map of St. Louis County with five cities—Amity, Asbury Groves, Brookfield, Edgewood and Glenview Heights—highlighted in blue. Each of those towns had little yellow flags with the addresses of the homes with Corundum building permits.

Using a red laser pointer, I said, "This map shows the location of the Corundum Construction building permits. As you will hear today, there are four striking similarities about those permits."

"First, all of them were issued in towns where Ruby Productions was the developer of a project that would receive millions of dollars in city funds through a TIF."

"Second, each of the building permits was issued shortly after the city council voted to approve the TIF."

"Third, every single one of those building permits was issued to a city official. In fact, it appears that Corundum Construction only did work on houses owned by city officials in those towns."

"And fourth, each of those city officials voted in favor of the TIF."

That drew a reaction from the gallery.

"Your Honor," I said, "to give you a sense of the scale of what I am talking about, the TIFs in the five cities highlighted on the map total more than forty million dollars in subsidies given to Ruby Productions for its developments in those cities. That raised an obvious question: was there a relationship between Corundum Construction and Ruby Productions? And if so, was there any connection between that relationship and the death of Nick Moran?"

"Objection," Crane said. "This is a settlement hearing, not a death inquiry."

Flinch frowned and turned to me. "And your response?"

"That is my point, Your Honor. The efforts I am describing were part of a death inquiry that I was conducting on behalf of Nick Moran's sister. I saw absolutely no connection between that inquiry and the lawsuit against the Ruby Productions TIF. But when word got back to Ruby Productions, they treated my actions, my death inquiry, as a breach of the settlement agreement. The purpose of today's hearing is to prove that my investigation was focused on the death of Mr. Moran and not on any future possible lawsuit against Ruby Productions."

"We will stipulate to that fact," Crane said, "and this hearing can be terminated."

"Objection overruled, Mr. Crane. You may proceed, Miss Gold. And I do hope we will soon be hearing from the lovely Miss Jacki."

"Soon, Your Honor." I checked my watch. "May I call our first witness?"

But the Judge's docket clerk was standing. She handed him a note. He read it with a frown and then nodded at her.

"Something has come up, Miss Gold. It shouldn't take more than five minutes, but I need to address it now. Court will be in recess."

The bailiff called, "All rise!"

# Chapter Forty-nine

As soon as the door closed behind Judge Flinch, Benny grabbed my arm and leaned in close. "We need to talk."

I looked around. "Let's go back to the attorney conference room."

The three of us moved down the center aisle past the crowd, ignoring the questions shouted by the reporters, and ducked into the small conference room at the back of the courtroom. I closed the door and turned to Benny, who'd taken a seat at the table.

"Okay," I said.

"You told me that Rubenstein looked familiar. I had that same feeling when I saw him this morning. It was weird. I kept looking over, trying to make the connection. And then—" he snapped his fingers "—bingo. I recognized him."

"And?"

"Our T-ball team. He was that fucking asshole at the first game. The guy shouting at his kid and the other team and the umpire. The guy I wanted to kill but you told me to chill."

"My God." I said down, dazed. "You're right. That's him."

"Maybe he got the hint. I don't think he showed up after that first game."

I stared at Benny. "Did we really have his kid on our team?"

"I assume. Why else was he there? At least for that first game?"

"Rubenstein?" I said, trying to remember.

"Dorian?"

I looked up. Jacki was leaning against the wall, her cell phone to her ear.

"Do you know where Rachel's T-ball team roster is? The one from last summer…good…sure, I'll wait."

Jacki looked down at me. "She's getting it. It must have the parents' names."

"Okay," she said into the phone. "We're looking for someone named Rubenstein. The kids are listed by first name only? Okay, there should be a column with the parent…see it?…okay…and the other one?" Jacki's eyes widened. "Jeez. Thanks."

She disconnected the call and looked down at us. "There are two sets of parents where the moms and dads have different last names. One is Barrett's parents. His mother is Barbara Weiss. His father is Kenneth Rubenstein."

I looked at Benny, and then Jacki, and then back at Benny again, my mind racing.

"How did I miss this?" I said.

"Did Barbara ever mention his name?" Jacki asked.

I thought back to our meeting. "No. The only name she mentioned…oh, no. She told me that her husband had a contractor inspect Nick's work. The contractor's name was Rudy."

"Maybe the same Rudy who's gone AWOL," Benny said.

I leaned back in my chair. "That's what he was talking about that day."

"Who?" Benny said.

"Rubenstein. In the parking lot at the supermarket. When he accused me of being a hypocrite for refusing to talk to him without a lawyer but setting up a secret meeting with someone else without a lawyer. He was talking about Barbara."

"You think?"

I nodded. "He must have had her under surveillance."

"I know the type," Jacki said. "Jealous husband. Bet he knew about her meetings with Nick, too."

I ran my fingers through my hair, trying to make sense of this new piece of the puzzle, trying to figure out if and how it fit.

There was a knock. It was Judge Flinch's docket clerk.

"Hurry, Counsel. The Judge is coming back to the courtroom in one minute."

# Chapter Fifty

"Make it snappy," Judge Flinch said to me. "We'll break for lunch in forty minutes."

I turned to face the gallery. "Plaintiff calls Clyde Bennett."

Four rows back on the other side of the aisle, a man with a bushy white mustache and horn-rim glasses stood up. He was in his early sixties and had on a navy blazer open over a white dress shirt buttoned tight against his large belly. He had been seated next to a nattily-attired criminal defense lawyer named Clarence Rogers, who looked up at him and nodded slightly.

Bennett scooted down the row and then walked up the aisle toward the front of the court. He was slightly bowlegged, had leathery skin, and moved stiffly, wincing every few steps.

"Over here," the judge said, gesturing toward the witness box.

Bennett stepped into the box, raised his right hand for the clerk, and swore to tell the truth, the whole truth, and nothing but the truth so help him God.

"Mr. Bennet, my name is Rachel Gold. You are a member of the city council of Glenview Heights, correct?"

"Correct."

He had a deep, raspy voice.

I gestured toward the monitor screen, which displayed a color photograph of an English Tudor home.

"This is your home, correct?"

He squinted at the photograph. "Correct."

"Your home address is Twenty-Five Burwell Avenue in the city of Glenview Heights, correct?"

"Correct."

"Please look at screen, sir. You are looking at Plaintiffs' Exhibit Six. Is that the building permit issued by the City of Glenview Heights for the construction of an in-ground swimming pool and deck in the backyard of your home?"

"Appears to be."

"Is that a yes?"

"Yes."

"The building permit shows that the contractor is Corundum Construction Company, correct?"

"Correct."

"And Corundum Construction Company did indeed install an in-ground swimming pool and deck in the backyard of your home, correct?"

"Correct."

"That was about two years ago?"

"Correct."

"How did you select Corundum Construction Company to do that work?"

He frowned, as if he were trying to remember. "I don't recall."

"Did someone recommend the company to you?"

He was looking down. "I don't recall."

"How much did you pay Corundum Construction Company for their work?"

"I don't recall."

"You don't?"

"No."

"Just two years ago and you don't recall."

"I don't."

"Let's see if we can refresh your recollection, sir. We have a construction costs expert, Robert Early, who will testify later in this hearing that the average price range for the construction of your pool and deck is $30,000 to $35,000. Does that refresh your recollection?"

"No."

"Assuming our expert is correct, would you expect that you paid somewhere between thirty and thirty-five thousand for that pool and deck?"

"I don't know."

"Mr. Bennett, the subpoena asked you to bring to court today copies of your contract with Corundum and all payments under that contract. Have you brought them, sir?"

"No."

"Why not?"

He shrugged. "I guess I must have discarded them."

"What about the check register, sir? Did you bring that?"

"I guess I must have discarded that, too."

I turned toward Jacki and nodded. The monitor screen displayed a blow-up of a canceled check from Clyde and Elizabeth Bennett to Corundum Construction Company in the amount of four thousand dollars.

"Mr. Bennett, up on the screen is a copy of Plaintiffs' Exhibit Seven. We obtained it through a subpoena served on your bank. That, sir, is the only check from your account to Corundum Construction during the past five years. Do you recognize that check?"

Bennett stared at the check, his jaw slightly agape.

"Let me repeat, sir. Do you recognize that check?"

He turned toward the gallery. I followed his gaze.

I said, "Is that your attorney who just signaled you?"

"What?" Bennett said, flustered.

He pulled a slip of paper out of his shirt pocket and placed it on the ledge in front of him.

"Sir, directing your attention back to Exhibit Seven, is that your check?"

He read from the slip of paper, "On Counsel's advice, I invoke my right under the Fifth Amendment not to answer on the grounds that I may incriminate myself."

"Is that your signature on the check?"

"On Counsel's advice, I invoke my right under the Fifth Amendment not to answer on the grounds that I may incriminate myself."

"Is that check for four thousand dollars the entire amount you paid for the swimming pool and deck that Corundum Construction built for you?"

"On Counsel's advice, I invoke my right under the Fifth Amendment not to answer on the grounds that I may incriminate myself."

"Did you agree to vote in favor of the Ruby Productions TIF in exchange for that deal on your swimming pool and deck?"

He looked up with a dazed expression, hesitated, and looked down again. "On counsel's advice, I invoke my right under the Fifth Amendment not to answer on the grounds that I may incriminate myself."

"With whom did you discuss that deal?"

"On Counsel's advice, I invoke my right under the Fifth Amendment not to answer on the grounds that I may incriminate myself."

"Did you discuss that deal with a representative of Ruby Productions?"

"On Counsel's advice, I invoke my right under the Fifth Amendment not to answer on the grounds that I may incriminate myself."

"Let's cut to the chase, Mr. Bennett. Did you sell your vote on the TIF for a swimming pool and deck?"

He winced.

I waited.

"Well?" I said.

He looked into the courtroom crowd and then down at the slip of paper. "On Counsel's advice, I invoke my right under the Fifth Amendment not to answer on the grounds that I may incriminate myself."

"No further questions."

I turned toward Rob Crane. "Your witness."

Crane stared at Bennett as I returned to the table. Still up on the monitor was the blow-up of Clyde Bennett's $4,000 check to Corundum Construction Company with the notation *Pool/ Deck* on the memo line.

Judge Flinch was also staring at Bennett. He snorted and shook his head in disbelief.

"Well, well, well, Mr. Bennett. Good thing you had your cheat sheet up here. Otherwise you might have had to answer one of those questions."

The judge turned to Crane. "You got anything you want to ask this guy?"

Crane shook his head. "No questions, Your Honor."

"Mr. Bennett," the judge said, "I got one question for you."

Bennett looked at the judge, his eyes blinking.

"Sir," the judge said, "have you no shame?"

"Pardon?"

"That's my one question. Have you no shame?"

Bennett, clearly flustered, looked down at this slip of paper. "On Counsel's advice, I invoke my right under the Fifth Amendment not to answer on the grounds that I may incriminate myself."

Flinch laughed. "You're plenty incriminated already. You're dismissed."

He turned to the courtroom and raised his silver gavel. "Let's put on the feed bag, eh? Lunch recess. See you all back here at one-thirty."

He banged the gavel down.

"All rise!"

# Chapter Fifty-one

I was leafing through my folder of exhibits at counsel's table. Off to my left, a reporter from Channel 4 was doing a stand-up in *sotto voce*, summarizing the highlights of the morning's hearing. She and her cameraman had been waiting for me in the hallway after lunch, but I told them I couldn't comment.

Benny was at my side. Without looking up from my documents, I said quietly, "Some new faces in the crowd this afternoon."

"Yeah?" Benny turned around to look. "Such as?"

"Back row. Far left. Plaid jacket. That's Bertie Tomaso."

"Oh, right."

"Same row, near the aisle, woman in the grey suit. Sarah Polinsky."

"Who's she?"

"Assistant U.S. Attorney."

"Sweet."

"Row in front of her. Two guys from the county prosecutor's office."

"Even sweeter." He turned back to me. "This little hearing is turning into a major cluster fuck for Rubenstein."

"And Crane," I said.

I had two missed calls from him over lunch.

"Where's Jacki?" Benny asked.

"She's in the attorneys' break room going over her witness notes."

"Is she putting on all three?" Benny said.

I nodded. "The more the merrier. We want to keep our judge happy."

Benny chuckled. "Happy? He'll be pitching a tent under that robe before she has the first witness sworn in. What's the latest on Honest Abe?"

"He's a definite go. I told him to be here by three. I'm hoping the judge takes an afternoon break before I have to put him on. I want to talk to him again. Crane's freaking out."

"Oh?"

"According to Abe, Crane has called him three times. Abe's not taking his calls."

Benny chuckled. "This has to be a first."

"What?"

"Our best witness is a genuine used-car salesman."

"He'll be a star."

"I bet he's thinking the same thing. It'll be his first time on TV before midnight. Guy has the tackiest commercials in town."

"Rachel?"

Rob Crane stood alone by his table. His entourage was off to the side, all busily thumb-typing emails on their iPhones. Rubenstein stood over by the jury box talking to someone on his cell phone in hushed tones. He turned toward me and then turned away quickly. His demeanor had changed for the worse as the day wore on. He was clearly rattled by the proceedings.

Crane stepped over to our table. "Can we talk somewhere?"

I glanced over at the wall clock. It was 1:25. The lunch recess was supposed to end at 1:30.

"We don't have time. The judge could be out any second."

Benny stood. "I'll go get Jacki."

"We need to talk," Crane said.

"We can do it at the afternoon break."

He scanned the gallery and stepped closer in. "Who are you calling before the break?"

I knew what he wanted to know. I'd make him ask me specifically.

"More city officials," I said.

"Which ones?"

"Three or four. Depends how far we get before the next break."

He moved in so close that our faces were less than a foot apart. "What about Abe Johnson?"

"What about him?"

"When are you calling him?"

"Why do you ask?"

He stared at me. "Please don't call him before the break. We need to talk."

*Please?*

I studied his face. I could see the fault lines. Ever since discovering his client's connection to Barbara Weiss, I'd been mulling another approach to the hearing, a way to cut through the evidentiary underbrush to get where I wanted go. A lot riskier, yes, but maybe a lot more effective, too.

I shrugged. "We'll see what happens."

The buzzer sounded.

"All rise!"

# Chapter Fifty-two

Jacki put on the next three witnesses—all city officials. Given that we knew all three witnesses would refuse to answer the key questions on Fifth Amendment grounds, her challenge was twofold: to elicit certain basic admissions from each witness and then to use their Fifth Amendment refusals-to-answer as a way to "testify" through her questions. She achieved both objectives with each witness. Specifically:

From Elizabeth O'Shea, a member of the Glenview City Counsel, we learned that she paid only four thousand dollars for the opulent build-out of her basement, which included a movie theater, a rec room, an exercise room, a wet bar, sauna, and two bathrooms.

From Brett Annis, a member of the Edgewood City Counsel and a certified public accountant, we learned that he paid only six thousand dollars for a home addition that included a family room and new deck.

From Dr. Barry Haven, a Brookfield alderman, we learned that he paid the bargain price of two thousand dollars for an elaborate two-level cedar deck that included a hot tub and wet bar.

In each case, our own expert witness, Robert Early, would soon be testifying that these city officials—and the others on the witness list—had paid less than ten percent of the going rate for their home improvements.

And from each of her three witnesses Jacki elicited a Fifth Amendment non-answer to a series of the most incriminating possible questions, such as: "Did you enter into an agreement with your co-conspirator to sell your vote on the TIF in exchange for a cut-rate price on your home improvement?"

Rob Crane had no cross-examination for any of them.

As I hoped, after the third witness the judge announced that the court would take the afternoon recess.

Crane came over. "Can we talk?"

I scanned the gallery.

"Let me go out in the hall a moment," I said. "I want to see if my next witness is here."

"I'll be in the attorneys' break room. We need to talk."

"I'll be back in a few minutes."

I congratulated Jacki on her performance, and we walked out to the hall to see if we could find Abraham Lincoln Johnson. I couldn't be sure how Rob Crane would react to my "suggestion," and thus needed to be sure that Johnson was prepared to take the witness stand after the recess and deliver the knockout punch.

Although the hallway was crowded, Johnson was easy to spot. He was the only three-hundred-pound coal-black African-American man with wraparound sunglasses, a neatly trimmed goatee, and an outfit familiar to anyone who had watched one of his late-night TV commercials for Honest Abe's Pre-Owned Paradise, namely, an iridescent green sports jacket over a pale pastel silk shirt, red double-knit slacks, and a pair of shiny black alligator boots. He was surrounded by people, some of whom were asking for autographs. I assumed the autograph seekers were motivated more by his TV commercials than by his tenure as a member of the Cloverdale City Council, where he had voted against the Brittany Woods TIF.

"What's this week's Emancipation Proclamation?" an elderly man asked.

Johnson's TV spots—all shot with him standing on his used-car lot—included the Emancipation Proclamation of the Week, which was a special car deal that would "emancipate" his customers from their current plight.

Johnson looked up from the sheet of notebook paper he was signing for a young black courtroom bailiff and grinned.

"Oh, my friend," he said in his Sunday-morning-Baptist-preacher baritone, "this week is truly an Honest Abe week, praise God. Our emancipation proclamation covers none other than Honest Abe's namesake, the Lincoln. Yes, the noble Lincoln. We got ourselves vintage Lincolns, classic Lincolns and even a few barely-driven Lincolns, and all at prices that would make Mary Todd Lincoln herself drop to her knees and praise Jesus. So come on down, my friend, and Honest Abe will set your free."

"Mr. Johnson?" I said.

He turned toward me and smiled. "Yes, young lady. What can I do for you?"

"I'm Rachel Gold."

"Ah, the lovely lady lawyer." He bowed. "A pleasure, my dear."

"This is Jacki Brand. She's my co-counsel."

His eyes widened as he gazed up at her. "Greetings, Miss Brand. My, oh my, you are a fine specimen of a woman."

I said, "The Court is in recess for twenty minutes, sir. Perhaps you and Ms. Brand could talk in the witness room."

"Lead the way, Miss Brand."

I left Jacki with Abe Johnson and went across the hall to the attorneys' break room, pausing to peer through the glass panel in the door. Crane was inside, alone, pacing. I opened the door.

"Okay," I said. "What is it?"

"Are you telling the truth?"

"About what?"

"About this hearing? About your investigation?"

"What are you talking about, Rob?"

"This whole thing. Is this only about that Nick Moran?"

"Only? The man is dead, Rob. He was a good man. I'm convinced he was murdered. That's more than enough reason for me."

"But all the rest." He waved his hand. "Corundum, the kickbacks—that's not what this is about?"

"Not if I get my questions about Nick answered."

"Then why focus on this other stuff?"

"Because from what I've seen so far, his death is connected to that other stuff. So that's where I'm looking for my answer."

Crane stared at me. I stared back, trying to get a read.

*Now or never*, I told myself.

"I've been thinking, Rob."

"About what?"

"Changing the order of the witnesses."

"What do you mean?"

"The judge is getting sick of the Fifth Amendment. We're putting on our expert witness next. Benny will handle him. But after our expert I was planning to call Abe Johnson. Abe won't be taking the Fifth. He's prepared to testify. To tell the truth, the whole truth, and nothing but the truth."

I watched Crane struggle to hide his emotions.

"But I've been thinking about calling another witness before Abe."

"Who?"

"Your client."

Crane frowned. "Ken?"

"Yes, Ken."

"Why?"

"I know for sure that Abe has valuable information about Corundum, but I'm thinking Ken might have more valuable information about Nick Moran's death. If he does, I may not ever need to call Abe. But you know what my problem is?"

"What?"

"The Fifth Amendment. As I said, the judge is getting sick of it."

Crane said nothing.

I said, "I had assumed Nick's death had something to do with Corundum, but now I'm thinking it might be more personal than that. If so, and if I can make that connection through Ken, I won't need Abe. I can rest after Ken testifies."

I checked my watch and started for the door. As I turned the knob, I looked back toward Crane, who was staring down at the floor.

"Of course," I said, waiting until he looked up, "that assumes that Ken doesn't start taking the Fifth Amendment when my questions get personal. I'll let you know when I'm about to get personal. We'll see what happens. Either he'll answer those questions or, well, I'll move on to Abe."

I walked into the courtroom. Benny was up at counsel's table. Rubenstein was working on a crossword puzzle. Crane's entourage was seated and looking back toward the courtroom door, where Crane had just entered.

I leaned in close to Benny. "We're changing the order."

"How?"

"Your guy Early is ready to go, right?"

He nodded.

"Put him on next. When Jacki gets back, tell her we may need to move Abe to the morning. I'll be back."

"Where are you going?"

"Just out in the hall."

"Why?"

"I need to get my thoughts organized."

"Whose your next witness?"

I gestured toward the other table.

Benny raised his eyes, frowned, and then nodded.

"Go get ready, girl. We'll take care of things here."

"Thanks."

I started to leave but he grabbed my arm.

"What?" I whispered.

He gave me a wink. "Good luck."

# Chapter Fifty-three

"Next witness."

I stood. "Your Honor, we call Kenneth Rubenstein."

There was a murmur in the crowd. Rubenstein gave his attorney a baffled look and stood. He glanced at me, eyes wary, as he walked to the witness box.

The clerk swore him in and he took his seat and gazed at me.

"Mr. Rubenstein, you are the owner and president of Ruby Productions, correct?"

He gave me a sardonic smile. "I am indeed, Miss Gold."

"You've heard testimony today regarding Corundum Construction Company, correct?"

"I have."

"Ruby is Corundum, correct?"

He tried to chuckle. "Ruby is Ruby. Corundum is Corundum."

"What is corundum?"

"You mean the company or the mineral?"

"Start with the mineral."

"A form of aluminum oxide."

"You never took a course in geology, correct?"

"Correct."

"You know what corundum is because you are a crossword puzzle fan, correct?"

"I know what corundum is, and I am a crossword puzzle fan. I don't know that the two are connected."

"Actually, you are more than just a fan. You compete in national crossword puzzle tournaments, correct?"

"Correct."

"You have actually won a tournament or two, haven't you?"

"Four to be precise."

"At your deposition, when I mentioned corundum, you told me about a sapphire, correct?"

"I did. Sapphire is a corundum."

"But you only mentioned sapphire."

"I believe so."

"Back to my earlier question. Ruby is corundum, correct?"

"Back to my earlier answer. Ruby is ruby, corundum is corundum."

"Let's go back to crosswords. Please look over at the monitor, sir."

He did.

"You are looking at Plaintiffs' Exhibit Twenty-One. It is the upper left quadrant of the *New York Times* crossword puzzle from three years ago on Friday, April seventeen."

He studied the monitor. "If you say so."

"I understand that the Friday puzzles in the *Times* are some of the hardest to solve."

"That they are."

"Can you solve them?"

He smiled. "Absolutely."

"Every time?"

"Every time."

"Even in a crowded courtroom?"

He leaned back in his chair and crossed his arms over his chest. "Try me."

"I have the clues here, sir. My co-counsel has the answers. Let's see if you are good as you claim."

He gave me an amused look. "Fire away."

"Can I play, too?" the judge asked.

There was laughter in the gallery.

I smiled at the judge. "Certainly, Your Honor. But I warn you: Mr. Rubenstein claims to be quite good. Let's start with one across, gentlemen. Eight letters. The clue is: Painter of *The Snake Charmer.*"

"Rousseau," Rubenstein said.

"Whoa." The judge stared at the puzzle on the screen. "Is that right?"

I turned. "Jacki?"

She pushed a key on the computer and up on the monitor screen the letters R-O-U-S-S-E-A-U filled up the top row.

"Well done," I said. "Directly below that word is number four across. This one is also eight letters. The clue is: Sunblock."

"Coppertone," Judge Flinch called out.

"Too many letters," I said.

"Banana Boat," Judge Flinch said.

"Still too many letters, Your Honor. Mr. Rubenstein?"

He gave me a cocky grin. "Umbrella."

"Umbrella?" Judge Flinch said.

Rubenstein pantomimed opening an umbrella. "It blocks out the sun."

The impatience in his voice was evident.

"Jacki?" I said.

The second row filled up with the letters U-M-B-R-E-L-L-A.

"Below that is ten across," I said. "The clue is: Director abode."

"Boardroom," Rubenstein snapped.

Jackie pressed the key and the letters B-O-A-R-D-R-O-O-M filled the row.

"And below that. Fourteen across. Eight letters. The clue is: Tishri holy day."

"Whose holy day?" Judge Flinch asked.

"Tishri," I said, and then spelled it.

I turned to Rubenstein, who'd figured out what I was doing.

"The answer?" I asked.

He gazed at the screen and finally shrugged. "Yom Kippur."

Jacki hit the key and the letters filled the screen.

"Let's double-check our answers," I said. "One down is just four letters, and we already have all four filled in: R-U-B-Y. Guess what the clue is, Mr. Rubenstein?"

"I have no idea."

"The clue," I said, "is: Corundum. The answer is Ruby."

A murmur in the gallery.

"At least in the world of crossword puzzles, Mr. Rubenstein, can we agree that ruby is corundum."

Another shrug. "In the world of crossword puzzles, yes."

"As a champion crossword puzzle solver, you already knew that ruby is corundum."

"I knew sapphire and ruby are both corundum. Sapphire is the more common form."

"Can we also agree that the lawyer for Ruby Productions is the lawyer for Corundum Construction Company?"

His smile disappeared. "I'm not following you."

I turned to the court reporter. "Would you please read back the question to the witness.

She did.

"Which lawyer are you talking about?" he said.

"I ask the questions, sir. Let's make this easier. Take a look at the document on the monitor. That is Plaintiffs' Exhibit Thirty. It's a copy of a release agreement prepared by an attorney for Corundum Construction Company."

"Never seen that document before."

"We're going to zoom in on that little number in the lower left corner. That's a document identification number. Law firms use them."

"I'm supposed to know what that number means?"

"Let's look at Plaintiffs' Exhibit Thirty-One. That's a demand letter from your attorney, Mr. Crane, to me. Correct?"

"Appears to be."

"Let's zoom in on that document ID number. You see it?"

"Yes."

"Do you see it's in the same format?"

"But a different number."

"That's correct, Mr. Rubenstein. But the same format and typeface. And if we need to, we will put on the witness stand someone from Mr. Crane's law firm who can show us how to identify the attorney who created those two documents. But perhaps you can save us that trouble, Mr. Rubenstein. Did Mr. Crane create the release agreement for Corundum Construction Company marked as Exhibit Thirty?"

"I was not at that law firm at the time the document was created, so I do not have personal knowledge of who created it. I assume you don't want me to speculate, right?"

"That is correct, Mr. Rubenstein. So let's just cut to the chase. Did you instruct Mr. Crane to prepare the Corundum release agreement?"

"Objection," Crane said. "Attorney-client privilege. I instruct the witness not to answer."

"Hate to do it," the judge said to me, "but I got to sustain that one. Let's move on."

"Yes, Your Honor."

I turned toward Rubenstein, who had crossed his arms over his chest and was staring at me guardedly.

*Here we go*, I said to myself.

I looked back at Crane. Our eyes met. After a moment, he lowered his.

I turned back to the judge. "Your Honor, may I approach the witness?"

"You certainly may."

I moved from the podium toward Rubenstein, stopping when we were separated by just an arm's length. I needed our interaction to seem as intimate as possible. We studied one another.

In a softer voice, I said, "You knew Nick Moran, correct?"

"Not personally."

"Earlier this year he renovated the kitchen in your home?"

"He did."

"And the guest bathroom."

"Yes."

"That was his line of work. He did home renovations."

"So he claimed."

"The same line of work as Corundum Construction?"

"Seems similar, at least from what other witnesses have said about Corundum. I don't think he built pools, though."

"You've heard the testimony about Corundum Construction today."

"I certainly have."

"Have you heard any testimony that would link Corundum to Mr. Moran's death."

He smiled. "I certainly have not."

"Based on what you've heard today, Mr. Rubenstein, did Mr. Moran die because of what he knew about Corundum Construction?"

"Based on what I've heard, the answer to that is no."

"Leaving aside that testimony, Mr. Rubenstein, based on what you personally know, do you believe that Mr. Moran died because of what he knew about Corundum Construction?"

"Nope."

"What do you understand to be the cause of his death?"

"A drug overdose in Forest Park."

"What do you base that on?"

"That's what it said in the newspaper." He gave me a smug grin. "Sounded to me like he was a closet fag who got his rocks off with strange men in the park."

"Is that based on what you read in the newspaper?"

"I can put two and two together."

"Explain."

He chuckled. "Not rocket science, Counsel. The man is found in his pickup truck on that infamous lane in the park."

"You referred to him as a 'closet fag.' Did you base the closet part on what you read in the newspaper?"

"Again, I put two and two together."

"Explain."

"The man worked on my house. I didn't meet him personally, but I understand that he didn't seem like a queer. Thus, a closet fag."

"He actually seemed more like a ladies man, didn't he?"

He shrugged. "Just goes to show, eh?"

"To show what?"

"You never know."

"I was at his funeral," I said. "A lot of the women there were surprised."

He forced a laugh. "Like I said, it just goes to show."

There was a manic edge in his voice.

"Were you mad at him?" I asked.

"Was I what?"

"Were you mad at him?"

He stared at me, the vein in his temple pulsing. "Why would I be mad at him?"

"Were you?"

He seemed to think it over.

"I was not crazy about him."

"Were you jealous?"

He forced a laugh. "Jealous? Of what?"

I paused, letting his response hang out there. "You are many things, sir. Correct?"

He frowned. "Pardon?"

"You are a successful real estate developer, correct?"

"I am."

"And you are also an accomplished triathlete, correct?"

He smiled. "I am."

"And a crossword puzzle champ, and a father, and a husband, correct?"

He was staring at me. "I am."

"You are many things, sir, but you are not a cold-blooded murderer, correct?"

"Pardon?"

"You are not a cold-blooded murderer, correct?"

"Correct."

I paused again.

"In your business, sir," I said, "would it be fair to say that you set high standards for yourself?"

He leaned back, puzzled. "Could you repeat that?"

"Do you set high standards for yourself?"

"Yes."

"In everything you do, right?"

"Absolutely."

"What about the people who work for you? Do you set high standards for them, too?"

"You better believe it."

"I do believe it, sir." I gave him what I hoped would seem an admiring smile. "Do the people who work for you always live up to your standards?"

He shook his head. "Nope."

"Do they sometimes bungle your instructions, fail to properly execute the tasks you've given them?"

"That happens."

"That's what happened that night, didn't it."

"What night?"

"The night Nick Moran died."

"What are trying to say?"

I moved one step closer and lowered my voice. "He wasn't supposed to die, was he?"

"Supposed to die? You think I know the answer to that?"

"I do. He wasn't supposed to die, was he?"

"What kind of question is that?"

"They screwed up, didn't they?"

"Why would you ask me that?"

In a softer voice, I said, "You know why I'm asking."

His eyes darted around the courtroom. Eventually, they returned to mine, and then he looked down.

"I am asking you on behalf of his sister Susannah. I'm asking you on behalf of the others who knew him. And I'm asking because I don't think you're a murderer, Mr. Rubenstein."

I gazed at him, waiting until he raised his eyes to mine.

"Mr. Rubenstein, let me ask you again. Nick Moran wasn't supposed to die that night, was he? There was no intent to kill the man. This wasn't a premeditated murder. Your people failed you."

He was staring at me, a pained look in his eyes.

I said, "This is your chance to make that clear."

We stared into one another's eyes for what seemed an eternity.

"It's all going to come out anyway," I said. "Why wait? This is your moment. Tell me. More important, tell his sister. Help her understand her loss. Please."

He bowed his head and exhaled slowly.

In a quite voice, barely above a whisper, he said, "He wasn't supposed to die."

# Chapter Fifty-four

The ensuing media blizzard eclipsed all of the publicity Ken Rubenstein had chased for years through triathlons, crossword puzzle tournaments, and flashy residential real estate developments. Sound bites of his testimony made CNN and Fox News that night. The homicide charges landed the next day. Rubenstein's perp walk was the lead story on all four local TV stations, made the front page of the *Post-Dispatch*, and ran in the hourly news cycle on CNN for twenty-four hours. A week later, the issuance of nineteen federal indictments arising out of the corruption-of-public-officials scheme put him on the front page of the *New York Times*, and got him featured in an interactive chart on the *Wall Street Journal's* website which, if you clicked on it, generated a graphic showing him as a spider at the center of an elaborate web of venal public officials.

That press eruption had been preceded by a long moment of silence in the courtroom after Rubenstein's answer to my last question. Even Judge Flinch was speechless. I finally turned to the judge and told him that I had no further questions. Flinch twirled his mustache, frowned, and adjourned the hearing.

I had further questions, of course. Plenty. But I didn't want to ask them in front of a TV audience. Barbara Weiss deserved some modicum of privacy. Moreover, I knew that better qualified questioners were seated in the courtroom gallery, including Bertie Tomaso, who ushered Ken Rubenstein out of the courthouse two hours later in handcuffs.

Over a marathon police interview that began that evening and ended just before dawn, Rubenstein admitted what I had assumed, namely, that Nick Moran's death was an accident. According to his statement, the plan had been to incapacitate him, shoot him up with heroin, put him back in his pickup, park it along Gay Way, unzip his fly, pull out his penis, and call the cops. The motive was the oldest and pettiest one of all: jealous rage. Rubenstein's goal had been to humiliate the man who'd had the nerve to romance his wife—and to teach his wife a lesson, too.

Armed with a packet of Ketamine power, Gene Chase had met Nick for a drink, ostensibly to discuss some kitchen renovation work that Corundum Construction might be able to send his way. Whatever actually went wrong—too much Ketamine, too much heroin, or too much in combination—the resulting death had repercussions that eventually eliminated the two Rubenstein underlings who had participated in the scheme. Professionals handled their deaths, however. Rubenstein had seen what could go wrong when you relied on amateurs. Of course, so had the professionals, who made sure that all arrangements were conducted through double-blind communications. Thus Bertie was still trying to track down Gene Chase's killers and still trying to confirm that Rudy Hickman was in fact dead, since he had not been heard from since his disappearance.

Although Rob Crane had known nothing about Nick Moran, he knew too much about the rest. Whatever slim chance he had to avoid indictment ended with the performance of Abraham Lincoln Johnson. Honest Abe convened his own press conference on the courthouse steps after court adjourned. Standing before the cameras, he announced exactly what he had been prepared to testify to in court, namely, that Rob Crane had sought him out, arranged a meeting in a private room at his club, and suggested during that meeting that Johnson could parlay a vote in favor of the Brittany Woods TIF into a terrific deal on a backyard swimming pool and deck. Crane had, alas, misread the flamboyant used-car salesman. Honest Abe had been so outraged that he had threatened to go public right then and there. It took days of groveling for Crane to get him to agree to keep quiet—but only after promising that there would be no further tampering with the Cloverdale City Counsel. Johnson's discovery of Crane's breach of that promise made him willing—indeed, eager—to bear witness.

Crane's legal career was kaput. He'd have plenty of time to evaluate new job options during his years behind bars.

As for me, my job essentially ended with Ken Rubenstein's answer to my final question in court. Susannah was my client. She'd asked me to look into her brother's death—to see whether he'd died the way the police said he had. I'd proved he hadn't, and thus my representation was concluded.

Susannah invited me to a graveside memorial service for her brother, which was held earlier this Sunday afternoon. It was mostly a family affair. She delivered a short speech through tears, I said a few words, and then we drove back to her house for donuts and lemonade. After hugs all around, I said my good-byes and drove off.

Because the sky was blue and the air was warm and my mom had the kids for the afternoon, I decided to drop by the other cemetery, which is where I was now, seated on the memorial bench facing Jonathan's gravestone.

Some days I come here to talk to Jonathan, to share stories about his children. Some days I come here for advice—not actual words of wisdom from the great beyond, of course, but more a chance to voice my own fears and hopes. Today, though, I came for serenity—for a chance to share a few quiet moments away from clients and family and telephones and emails, to just, in my stepdaughter Sarah's words, chill.

But serenity eluded me. I thought of Nick Moran and the future that had been stolen from him. Though I'd helped solve the mystery of his death, I felt no sense of triumph or vengeance. He was, as Raymond Chandler wrote, sleeping the big sleep—and, like Jonathan, decades too soon. Some of the people who deserved to go to jail would go to jail, and in the process they would forfeit their careers and their reputations, but through it all Nick would continue to sleep the big sleep. There was no final retribution, no settling up in this lifetime—and hope of any such reckoning thereafter, of some final celestial accounting, offered me no comfort.

Thoughts of Nick and Jonathan triggered in my mind that haunting passages from *Ecclesiastes:*

> For the living know that they will die,
> but the dead know nothing;
> they have no further reward,
> and even the memory of them is forgotten.

"Never again," wrote the preacher, "will they have a part in anything that happens under the sun."

*Never again.*

I sighed.

Although I'd received praise in the aftermath of that televised hearing, my main reaction had been then, and was still, sadness. There was nothing to celebrate. Sometimes I wonder whether Nick's death would have been easier to accept if the original version—an accidental overdose—had turned out to be the correct one.

"Hey."

I looked up to see Benny standing there.

I forced a smile. "Hi."

"As the chicken said to the horse, 'Why the long face?'"

"What are you doing here?"

"Talked to your mom. She told me about the memorial service for Nick. I called your house a half hour ago. No one was home. Took a wild guess where you might be. I'm obviously the modern incarnation of Sherlock Holmes."

"Obviously."

"Scoot over."

I did.

He sat down next to me. "So?"

I shrugged.

"I knew it."

I turned to him. "What?"

"You're bummed."

"I'm just thinking."

"Oh, Jesus. Not that goddam Ecclesiastes again."

"What's wrong with him?"

"'Vanity of vanities, all is vanity.' Christ. Don't pay attention to that grim jackass."

"Oh?" I couldn't help but smile. "You have someone better for me?"

"Hell, yeah. Omar Khayyam. Dude had the right motto: shit happens, so lighten up and crack open another cold one."

"Was that line in the *Rubaiyat*?"

"Don't joke about my homey Omar. I actually took a course on him in college. Dude had the right philosophy. Take me, for example. I'm dating a waitress from Hooters, for god's sake. You think Ecclesiastes wouldn't be all over my ass? But Omar? He'd give me a high five. To quote the man: 'Drink! for you know not whence you came, nor why; Drink! for you know not why you go, nor where.'"

He gave me a wink. "And that's why I'm here."

"Oh?"

"I know why you go, and where."

"Where?"

He stood and faced me. "Your mom's taking the kids out to dinner, and I'm hauling your gorgeous tush down to the Broadway Oyster Bar. They got the Zydeco Crawdaddies playing there at five-thirty. I called Jacki after I spotted your car in the cemetery parking lot. She's going to meet us down there. We're going to get you some oysters on the half shell and a big plate of jambalaya and a bucket or two of Dixie beer and then we're gonna dance to *Laissez Les Bons Temps Rouler*. Let the good times roll, woman."

He reached out his hand. "Deal?"

My eyes watered. He pulled me to my feet.

I gave him a kiss on his cheek.

"Deal," I whispered.

To receive a free catalog of Poisoned Pen Press titles, please contact us in one of the following ways:

Phone: 1-800-421-3976
Facsimile: 1-480-949-1707
Email: info@poisonedpenpress.com
Website: www.poisonedpenpress.com

Poisoned Pen Press
6962 E. First Ave. Ste 103
Scottsdale, AZ 85251